Grindstone's Edge

The Road to Rocktoberfest 2024

Gabbi Grey

A xel

Last year, my band, Grindstone, hit the stage at Rocktoberfest, our big break at last. But in the middle of that triumph, my love life crashed into disaster. I've been in love with Hugo Threadgold for years, but he was once my high school music teacher, so I figured he was off-limits. Then, in Black Rock, I discovered he was aware of me too, and for a moment I thought I'd get it all. I came clean about my feelings, but my heart cracked when Hugo turned and walked away. I'm not giving up, though. I'm ready to lose my straight-guy image for him, if only I can make him believe in us.

Hugo

Ten years ago, Axel and his best friend, Ed, were my most promising students. I taught them everything I could about music, and watched them struggle to become the musicians they are today. But boys become men, and last October in Nevada, Axel told me he'd developed romantic feelings for me. I was rattled. I'd never let myself look at him that way. Now that he's put the idea in my head, I can't get him out of my mind. The man he's become is someone strong, talented, determined, and attractive. Someone I could fall for. But isn't it my duty to keep things professional and walk away from the man who tempts me as no one else ever has?

Grindstone's Edge is a book in the multi-author Road to Rocktoberfest 2024 series. Each book can be read as a standalone, but why not read them all and see what antics our bands get into next? Hot rock stars and the men who love them, what more could you ask for. Kick back, load up your e-reader, and enjoy the men of Rocktoberfest!

multimedia, audio, or other medium. We support the right of humans to control their artistic works.

No generative AI was used in the creation of this book.

Edits by ELF

Cover by Jo Clement

Dedication
William

Contents

Chapter One

Axel

Rocktoberfest.

2023.

"Axel." A voice I'd never thought to hear again rang in my ears.

I had been flying as high as a kite, looking around the concert venue. A natural high, of course. After eight years of hard-won sobriety, the joy I was feeling came from pure, natural endorphins.

I'd dreamed of this for a long time now. I was lead singer for the Canadian band, Grindstone, and we were performing at our first Rocktoberfest.

And absolutely not our last.

I was going to make damned sure we got invited back to Black Rock again and again. This year, we were performing early on Friday night. In my mind, I envisioned a year when we were a headliner show—Saturday night or Sunday afternoon. I could dream big while keeping my feet firmly planted on the ground. Just in case I started to get a swelled head, my bandmate—and best friend—Ed, would put me in my place. Would remind me every member of the band—from our manager to our roadies and our bus driver—was just as important as I was. Lead singers could be replaced. Strong women keeping us in line and getting us contracts with big record labels couldn't.

Which was the other hope for this show. Hopefully, our performance here would land us a contract with a big American record label. I just had to get through my interview this morning with an intrusive and very nosy documentary film producer, and then I could sit back and enjoy the rest of the week.

I spun to see the man I'd dreamt about so many nights of my life jogging over. He wore that smile I knew so well. The smile I held so dear. A smile I'd never thought to see again. I'd thought about that a lot, trying to let go of the regret only to have it boomerang back. I'd almost let it go, then it would come right back, slamming into my brain. "Uh, hey, Mr. Threadgold." I managed a lame wave.

He stopped just short of where I stood.

Wow, either he's shrunk or I've gotten much taller. Oh, wait. Growth spurt. Nineteen years old. Year after graduating.

"I think you can call me Hugo. We're, uh, both older."

True. He wasn't my teacher anymore. I wasn't his student. We no longer had that barrier between us. He looked older. Like life hadn't been kind to him. *Ten years is a long time.* What was our age gap? Fourteen years? Since I just hit twenty-eight last month, that made him around forty-two. "Hugo." I tried the name. The first two letters fell off my tongue in a whistle while the harsher final syllable caught my notice. *Go.* As in…should get out of there before I did something stupid. "Well, nice to see you…" I started to inch away.

He reached out a hand, nearly touched me, then pulled his hand back. "Sorry."

You're apologizing at the moment you almost touch me? After all these years? How often had I longed for that touch? In comfort. In support. And more. But teachers didn't touch students, and Mr. Threadgold, with his strict adherence to rules, never laid so much as a finger on me. "It's okay. We could, like, shake hands." Belatedly, I stuck out my hand.

After a long moment, he grasped it. His solid grip had breath squeezing from my lungs. He held my gaze until he finally released my hand. He ran his hand through his overly shaggy hair. Those red locks had been much shorter back when I'd first met him. When he'd been still fairly new at the teaching thing. The bright morning sun lit a few threads of silver at his temple.

He said, "I've followed your career."

"Yeah?" In a way, that warmed me. In another, it sort of irritated me. He could've said something before now. Let me know he was out there watching us. *To what end? So he'd come for you?*

"Yeah. You and Ed...you've really made something of yourselves, and I'm so damn proud of you."

His words should've encouraged me. Should've activated something warm in my chest. Instead, a hollowness followed. "Well, that's nice."

He glanced around. "I'm here with friends. Do you...do you think we could catch up? There's not much privacy..."

I was pretty certain there were places we could go...but that wasn't the point. Even as I had the thought, my phone buzzed in my pocket. I yanked it out.

Pauletta.

Reminding me of my interview. I was only supposed to be gone for a minute. "I, uh, have to go." I held up my phone, even though the screen had darkened. Our manager wouldn't have texted anyone else because none of them would've forgotten. I would've remembered too. If Hugo hadn't distracted me.

You're always distracted. That's why it's called attention deficit disorder.

Most of the time, I had coping mechanisms. Then something would derail me, and my bandmates would gently try to guide me back to the topic at hand.

"Right." He glanced behind him. "My friends are kind of in their own world. I'd have time to spend with you. If you wanted, of course."

My mind whirled. "Like, tomorrow afternoon? I have an interview for a documentary right now, a walk through the main stage tonight, and a group interview tomorrow morning, but then I'm free until rehearsal tomorrow night."

"That's...that's great. Where should we meet?"

I tried to think of somewhere inconspicuous. Until I figured out what he wanted, I didn't want Ed to know he was here. "Behind the hot dog stand? Say about two-thirty?"

I'd have to make sure I was finished with everything by then. Ed would switch with me if I needed to. He did so damn much to accommodate me—often without me even having to ask. Being best friends since we were in kindergarten cemented our relationship in a way that nothing else ever could have. Just two poor kids growing up in the rough Downtown Eastside of the richest city in Canada. What could possibly have gone wrong? Or maybe gone right.

"That's perfect. I'll be there." Unbidden, he grabbed my hand again. "It's great to see you. Until tomorrow afternoon."

He held on just a beat too long.

Is he going to pull me in for a kiss?

Absurd notion.

And he didn't. He released me, offered a little wave, and took off.

I didn't look at his ass as he went.

Well, maybe just a little.

And I most certainly didn't look at his back and muscular shoulders.

Just a peek.

He'd always been larger than life to me. Now...he wasn't as big. Not as intimidating. I'd remembered him as chiseled and, in my mind, ripped. Perhaps that had just been my imagination, as he always wore long-sleeved shirts. Although he rolled them up in the summer, seeing as our ancient high school didn't have air conditioning. I had a thing for forearms...

I jogged off in the direction of the tour bus.

Chapter Two

Hugo

I hadn't seen Renee or Copeland for hours. We'd driven down to Black Rock from Vancouver together in my SUV for Rocktober-fest. My best friend and her husband were good people. Really, when she started dating Cope, he'd become an unexpected best friend as well. He'd never resented Renee's closeness to me.

Renee and I had attended teacher's college at Simon Fraser University together. Then we'd started our teaching careers together at a failing school in an impoverished area of downtown Vancouver, bonding tighter over the challenges. We'd believed we could make a difference, but the lack of resources could grind anyone down. Renee lasted two years before she transferred to a high school in Shaunessy. Different problems for the mostly rich kids there. Certainly not the grinding poverty I saw daily.

I'd stuck it out.

Renee had stood by me during all those years.

Supported me.

Loved me.

Even through the disaster that was Gavin.

I shuddered.

And my thoughts looped back to my friends. They'd decided to drive to Reno in my SUV after we arrived, which was a long trip. We'd come early so we could secure a good spot for our tents. We'd opted for two small ones that fit perfectly under our canopy. I loved Renee, but her snoring was legendary. No medical intervention worked. She was otherwise healthy, so she was letting it ride.

Cope wore earplugs every night.

I planned to as well. Not just because of the proximity to my friend, but also the general noise of the entire environment. Not everyone went to bed well before midnight.

I wandered over to the main stage area and watched as technicians set everything up. I was familiar with sound equipment, of course, but this stuff was next level. I could never afford this for my kids. That thought brought a pang to my heart. Spending a chunk of my salary on instruments and gear the school desperately needed had been a point of contention between Gavin and me.

Well, no longer.

My mind flashed back to Axel as I watched a band wandering across the stage. I didn't recognize anyone, but that wasn't a complete surprise. I didn't bother trying to keep up with everyone. I had my kids to focus on.

Axel.

Ed.

Ed's hair was long dreadlocks these days while Axel's was shorter. The styles suited them. Generally I preferred long hair. For a Black man, though, that could be a challenge. My Anglo-Saxon heritage gave me sun-hating white skin, pale blue eyes, and flaming red hair. In teacher's college, and during my marriage, I'd kept my face smooth and my hair short. Manageable. Respectable. When I found myself divorced at age thirty-two, I rebelled. Grew my hair out. Stopped shaving.

As I scratched my chin, covered by my trim beard, I smiled a little. New flecks of gray appeared with increasing frequency, and I needed to consider whether to shave the damn thing off once and for all, or accept mortality and gray hairs.

My thoughts meandered back to the boys. To the men.

I'd spent a fair chunk of money securing them their first guitars. Acoustic in the ninth grade and electric the next year. Both boys worked part-time jobs, but much of that money went to support their families. Still, they saved enough to help pay for their guitars. They'd been exceptional students. In music, at least. Well, Ed did well in most classes. Axel struggled because of his attention issues. When he played, though, his focus was exceptional.

I turned and headed back to my camping area. A small gust of wind swept through, kicking up a bit of dust. In a previous iteration of my life, I might've cared about the grit. This Hugo Threadgold didn't. What was a little dirt? A little too much sun? Way too many people? When I'd heard Grindstone was performing at Rocktoberfest, I'd convinced Renee we just *had* to come. And so we had.

Back at our campsite, I eyed my cooler. Knowing hydration was important, I grabbed a bottle of water. I had my refillable one nearby and needed to start using that for the sake of the planet. I plopped into my camp chair under our canopy, and considered everything. I'd planned to skulk around the festival grounds until I *accidentally* found Axel.

Check.

I would convince him to meet up with me later, when he had a moment.

Check.

Now I had more convincing to do. I didn't like the idea of manipulating him, but a lot was riding on me coaxing into doing me this *one little favor*.

I snagged some crackers from our little pantry and a couple of slices of cheese. Hopefully when Axel said when we were meeting by the hot dog truck tomorrow, he meant we were getting hot dogs as well. I couldn't remember the last time I'd indulged in a hot dog. I glanced down at my middle section. Not as defined as it had once been. Gavin insisted I maintain an almost unachievable level of fitness. Between those gym sessions, my teaching classes, and Gavin's constant need to be out *in society*, I'd barely had time to breathe.

Ten years. Get over it.

Except I hadn't. As Renee reminded me every time I showed up solo at an event. After my marriage crashed and burned, I'd not tried to resurrect the single life. My ex had, with all due speed, married someone far more suitable. Someone who enjoyed the constant glad-handing. Someone with a respectable job who didn't spend his time in *that part* of Vancouver. Someone who didn't love kids and yearn for his own.

As Gavin's second marriage neared the ten-year mark, I could be vaguely happy he'd found someone *more suitable* while resenting the loss of my dreams. Sure, I could've tried again. But I hadn't wanted that pain. I'd redoubled my effort with the kids at school as well as volunteered at the cancer ward of the sick kids' hospital. Anything to fill my days and as many nights as I could. Anything to have excuses not to meet up with my family. The family who couldn't believe I'd let Gavin get away. The family who also insisted I needed to teach at a prestigious academy in Point Grey. I'd won several teaching awards in the past ten years—they thought I should parlay that into a well-paying job in the outrageously expensive west end of the city.

A wave of fatigue hit me. I hadn't slept well last night, and if I didn't get Axel to agree tomorrow, then the rest of the trip wasn't likely to be much better. This jittery feeling didn't sit right. Renee, Copeland, and I had brought a two-four of beer, but the twenty-four cans had to last the entire weekend. I didn't love beer, but didn't figure I'd enjoy wine in this heat. Renee was a huge brew fan, much to my and Cope's amusement, although she switched to alcohol-free every time she hoped she might be pregnant.

They'd been trying for several years, and after a couple of miscarriages, I'd stopped mentioning it. I had all my fingers crossed for a miracle, but also hoped maybe they'd consider adoption. They'd make such wonderful parents, and I saw foster kids in need all the time.

Of course, if I was going to have the kids I wanted, I needed to think about adoption too, even without a partner.

Age was catching up for me, much as it was for Renee. I didn't want to attend my kid's kindergarten graduation when I was in my sixties. If I didn't get up off my ass, that might happen. Hell, even that was too optimistic. If nothing changed, there wouldn't ever be kids.

I left the beer in the cooler. Axel was sober these days. Working hard at it, or so I'd heard. I could totally admit to following everything the band members did. And although I didn't intend to get close enough to him so he might smell my breath right now, I didn't want to chance it tomorrow. Just like I didn't need any more of a buzz today. I considered pulling my acoustic out of my tent, but that felt like too much effort. I checked my phone.

Ah. I only had to kill a couple of hours because Renee and Copeland would eventually return. After setting an alarm, I laid a cool cloth over my eyes and settled for a nap.

Chapter Three

Axel

H am sandwiches were my favorite, but mine turned to lead in my stomach as I waited for my turn for Thornton to interview me.

Songbird, our keyboard player, requested the first spot, claiming she'd be more nervous if she waited. I wasn't certain I believed her, but her little show of nerves earlier had me questioning my assumption she was cool about everything. We'd played biggish venues before—the Pacific National Exhibition in Vancouver, for one—but nothing like Black Rock. Nothing like Rocktoberfest.

She returned to the bus with a huge grin on her face, and she squeezed Big Mac's shoulder as our bassist headed out.

Meg, the drummer, continued to doodle in her notebook.

Ed, our lead guitarist, scrolled on his phone, and I sat with mine idle in my hands.

I should've been composing or going back over our set for Friday night or any of a dozen other things. Instead, my mind kept circling back to Hugo and what he was doing here. Well, obviously here for the music...because who would just choose to spend their time in the desert where the sun was hot during the day and the night was chilly? Especially given he should've been teaching now. He must've taken a whole week off work if he was already here. Of course, I hadn't asked him how he got here. Had he driven or flown?

Right, and that's what's really important?

Hmm. Maybe not. He was one of the first fans to arrive, though, as the show didn't start for another day. Was he with someone? That asshole ex-husband of his? Yeah, I knew about the divorce. Fucker didn't deserve a man like Hugo anyway. But I'd heard Hugo had been sad and that, in turn, made me feel sort of guilty over my glee at the dissolution of that union. Truly, that ex was a turd of the first order. I'd hated him the one and only time we'd met.

Big Mac returned from his interview, appearing slightly less queasy.

Meg smacked him on the arm as she headed toward the front of the bus. She nearly pranced as she made her way down the stairs.

"She's nervous." Big Mac pressed a hand to his belly. Then, after a moment, he went to the cupboard. He nabbed a large bag of malt-vinegar potato chips, ripped the bag open, and stuck his hand in, coming up with a mittful.

Only then did he look around. Clearly chagrinned, he offered the bag to Songbird.

With a smile, she declined.

Next, he presented it to Ed, who also declined. Ed's tight smile said more than anything he might've uttered. He wasn't onboard with this plan at all.

Finally, Big Mac offered me the bag. I snagged one chip, popped it into my mouth, then instantly regretted it as the tart taste hit my mouth. I loved salt and vinegar chips, but they didn't go well with...nerves? Pursing my lips, I pushed out of my seat and headed to the fridge.

Big Mac dropped onto the bench seat and started nosing at Meg's sketchpad.

Ed smacked his hand. "Don't. Doesn't matter how you feel about her. That's her private journal, and you're not entitled to look." He turned his fiery gaze to me. "Don't even think about grabbing a soda. You'll burp on camera. Juice or, better yet, water."

"Hey." I didn't like it when he bossed me around.

Especially when he was right.

I sighed dramatically and pulled an apple juice from the fridge. Before I could contemplate mixing the flavors of malt vinegar and apple juice, I popped the lid and downed half the bottle.

Okay...gross.

Big Mac laughed at my obvious wince.

I might've exaggerated it just for him.

Songbird rose, stretched, and pointed to the back.

We all waved, and she headed back to her bunk.

Meg trudged up the steps to the bus. "Axel, you're next."

I wanted to comment about the pep in her step that appeared missing, but I wasn't certain I needed to know the reason. This was Meg. While Songbird might have some secrets, Meg always laid everything on the table. She took no prisoners. I hoped Thronton was too cool to have made a mess of talking about Meg's Indigenous heritage, but something had her down. Probably not that. Didn't make my nerves better.

Ed waved me toward the door. "Go."

"Yeah." So I wasn't wasting the apple juice, I downed the rest of it. For good measure, I let out a beautiful belch.

Big Mac guffawed, Meg grinned, and Ed rolled his eyes.

Yep, all was right in the world.

I headed out into the brilliant sunshine, putting on my shades. I wouldn't be able to wear them for the interview, I didn't figure. Apparently, Mickey, the director of the documentary, had scouted out the perfect location for filming the discussion. They had a good eye, so I trusted them.

Thornton, I was less comfortable with.

Pauletta, our manager, swore the guy was on the up-and-up.

Ed warned all of us at every turn to be careful. Somewhere in between there, I figured the truth lay.

Pauletta greeted me as I stepped off the bus. "This won't take too long. We're hoping to do it in just a couple of takes."

"Hopefully less."

She snickered. "If you behave, focus, and give your best shot, then yes, we might be able to do it in less."

I pressed a hand to my chest and offered a wounded expression. "When am I ever not well-behaved?"

Another snicker. "Don't lay it on too thick, Axel. Just be yourself."

Knowing what she meant also involved acknowledging I didn't always take everything as seriously as maybe I should. Just... Ed and Pauletta took control of things. My job was to show up, sing my heart out, and go home. When I wasn't singing, I was supposed to stay out of trouble.

We came to an area with a bit of shade.

Mickey greeted us first, sticking out their hand. Their red, curly hair blew in the soft breeze. "I know you know me, but I want to formally thank you for doing this. Nothing to be afraid of."

"I wasn't until you just said that." I shook their hand, oddly touched by the formality.

Lydia, with her camera, and Kato, with his sound equipment, stood off to the side. He had a small mic attached to a power box.

Knowing this was for me, I headed his way. Within moments, he had me hooked up. When he gave me the thumbs-up, I pivoted to Thornton.

Ah, I saw why Ed was so taken with the man. Not just looks—although they played a big part. The man was downright edible. That wasn't all Ed saw in him, though. In odd moments of silence, Thornton appeared...almost wounded. Like he had something deep inside him that caused him great pain. He might hide it from the rest of the world, but I spotted it.

Sometimes it took one wounded soul to recognize another.

Was that who Ed saw? Someone in pain? Someone in need of comfort?

"Are you ready?" Thornton's smile lit his face, but didn't reach his eyes.

"Yeah."

He pointed to a little rocky area.

I grinned. "That's not going to be comfortable."

"We can—"

"No, I like it." I met his gaze. "We'll both be in a hurry to finish."

He cocked his head. "You wanting to rush through this?"

"Nah." I shrugged. "I just know you want to get to Ed. He's the real catch for you."

"You're the lead singer." Thornton gestured toward the rocks.

We sat next to each other, but cheating a bit toward the middle so it would look more like a natural conversation on camera.

"You're the lead singer." He repeated his comment, but clearly this time the camera was rolling.

Deftly, Kato stepped into range with his boom mic and Lydia had her camera trained on us.

"I am." I continued grinning. "As the *face* of Grindstone, I have a lot of responsibility." I used air quotes for *face*.

Thornton nodded slowly. "Responsibility. Yes, a lot of fans look up to you."

"Well...I'm not the only one. Ed's got a whole fan club, and I suspect that when we break out, Songbird, Big Mac, and Meg will have a million people knowing their names as well."

"You've very confident."

I swept my arms expansively to encompass everything I could see. "We're here. At Rocktoberfest. And yes, we're playing early on Friday night. Yes, we're not a headlining band. But we're *here*." I had to make him understand. "I grew up...poor. Disadvantaged. In poverty. We struggled and—" I swallowed hard. "But I made it out of there. And yeah, the first couple of years beyond high school were rough." I quickly glanced toward Pauletta, who stood very close to Mickey. "Then Ed and I met someone who believed in our talent. She straightened us out, and we've been on a steady climb ever since. Five albums, and frankly, the best is yet to come."

Thornton smiled. "That's a lot of work. You graduated, what, ten years ago?"

"Yeah." My mind wandered to Mr. Threadgold on graduation day. The pride in those pale-blue eyes. The discomfort because of what I'd witnessed—whether his or mine, or both—I'd never been certain. "I try to forget about those days, but...if I hadn't struggled, then I think this moment wouldn't be as powerful as it is. Wouldn't have as much meaning."

"True. I feel an amount of gratitude for you from all your band-mates."

I snickered. "You weren't expecting that, were you? You thought we'd be a bunch of pampered musicians who expect everyone else to do the work."

His eyes narrowed. Just a fraction. Probably not enough for the camera to pick up...but I did. "I attempt to not have any preconceived notions before I meet someone."

"Sure. But you hear about things in the media or through the rumor mill. Whispers. We both know who the prima donnas are this weekend. The bands who will demand, expect, and possibly receive preferential treatment." I puffed out my chest a bit. "That's not me. If I ever get too big for my..." I struggled to remember the word my father used to use when he was putting me in my place. "...britches. Yeah, if I ever get an over-inflated ego, Pauletta will set me straight."

"And Ed?" Thornton blinked. "Or the other members of the band?"

Nice slip. God, you're head over heels for him.

"We're a team." I let the words sink in. "We take care of each other." Like intervening when my life was careening out of control and getting me the help I needed.

"Any regrets? Anything you wish you'd done differently?"

Yeah. Kyesha.

"Sure. How much time do you have?" I offered a cheeky grin, gently pushing my first love to the back of my mind. I'd made mistakes before her and more than a few after her...and I could bullshit my way through this easy question.

Or so you hope.

Chapter Four

Hugo

He's so gorgeous. With those tight pants, that sexy shirt, and that earring. The fucking earring.

I didn't want to think of Axel as attractive. Back when he'd been my student, he'd been awkward. Confident, but also a little goofy. Never arrogant, though. Ed ensured Axel took our rehearsals seriously. A few of the one-on-one lessons, though, I'd let him share his sense of humor. He'd been a kid, after all. Saddled with too many responsibilities at home for someone so young.

I saw it all the time with my students—they were often responsible for younger siblings, for working to bring in money, or even for taking care of parents with substance-abuse problems. Axel never shared specifics, but I suspected he fell into some—or all—of those categories. Certainly the working part. He'd busted his ass to earn enough to buy the electric guitar, even at the huge discount I quoted him.

I could still remember that smile when he gave me the money, and I handed him the guitar. I told him I'd gotten a deal.

One of the few times I'd lied to a student.

In truth, I'd ponied up a good chunk of the money myself. Had for Ed as well, but he'd seen through my lie. And had never, to the best of my knowledge, told Axel.

As I stood behind the food truck, waiting impatiently, questions swirled in my mind. What would we talk about? Would we have anything besides East Vancouver and music in common? Had he understood how badly I'd wanted him to succeed? Would he be creeped out if I told him how closely I'd followed his career?

I didn't have long to ponder those notions as he soon poked his head around the side. He waved.

After a fraction of a second, I waved back. This felt awkward as fuck—much as the handshake had.

"Are you hungry?" He grinned, white teeth gleaming.

"Yeah." Better not tell him I'd pretty much skipped lunch and was feeling a little light-headed. At least I'd remembered to refill my reusable water bottle and had been drinking plenty.

"Do you like hot dogs? Or would you like something else? Ed's gone vegetarian, and I've tried, but..." He shrugged. "Just not my jam."

I grinned. "I am *not* a vegetarian. Nor do I have any food allergies."

He grinned back. "Greek? I'm hankering for a lamb gyro."

"Sounds brilliant." *Okay, not sounding too eager. Maybe I'll make it through this after all.* Because even though I'd always had the upper hand in our dynamic, I felt like his adult fame was subtly shifting the power. Like he had all the say in what was happening. And given how much he had going on this weekend and how few commitments I had, that sort of made sense.

But that small change was causing the world to feel off-kilter.

Or maybe it was the lack of solid food.

We moved to the Greek truck. Before I could ground myself, Axel handed me a gyro and a diet cola. Did he remember I drank diet cola or was he merely guessing? Still, I didn't even have time to grab my wallet before he'd paid and he was beckoning me around to the back of the truck. He pointed to the shade, then dropped onto the dusty ground, a little billow of grit surrounding him.

When in Rome. I liked the idea of being out of the sun as well. This small slice of heaven came with lower temperatures and the tantalizing smell of fried onions and roasted meat. My stomach growled.

"Eat." Axel pointed to my food. Then he cracked open his can of cola and took several long pulls. When he'd consumed what I judged to be half the can, he belched, looked vaguely chagrined, and again pointed to my food.

Obediently, I took a bite. The flavor hit my tongue in just the right way as the meat dribbled juice. I moaned.

Axel grinned. "You're so easy to please." He took a nibble of his food.

"Look, there's something I want to—"

He pointed to my food. "First we eat, then we talk. I don't want to be rude. Big Mac always talks with food in his mouth. It's gross."

I didn't know Big Mac's habits, of course. The slender man was on the short side and played bass like no one's business, but I'd never met him. "Dude absolutely shreds."

Axel cocked his head. "Okay, so you've followed the band. Eat now, talk later." With that, he took a huge bite of his food. And after a few mouthfuls, had consumed the entire meal while I still took small bites and chewed carefully.

My stomach preferred a slower consumption of food.

After scrunching his food wrapper into a little ball, Axel took another long drink of soda. He let out a contented sigh as he leaned back against the truck. "That was amazing."

"Mmm." My mouth was full, of course, so that was the best I could manage.

"So, I want to apologize."

"Hmm?" Damn not being able to speak.

He met my gaze. *Ah, so this was always his plan. Little shit.*

"I feel like I need to apologize. That last time we saw each other... Well, aside from graduation. I don't know if you remember—"

"I remember." I managed to swallow. "And you don't—"

"Yeah, I really do." He fingered the wrapping. "I lost my temper. Believe it or not, I don't do that often."

I *did* know that. In the four years I'd worked with him, he'd never lost his temper. Never shown any sign of anger, even at the dire circumstances he lived in. Never had a nasty word with Ed or any of the other kids. And I'd never heard of an incident since he'd started to be in the public eye more. If he felt rage, I'd assumed he kept it inside. I worried he might implode if it got to be too much—but also knew he never lost it. "Yeah."

"But..." He winced. "That guy—"

"Gavin."

"Yeah."

"My husband."

"Yeah."

"Now my ex-husband."

Another wince. "Yeah, that sucks."

"You knew?" I eyed the last few bites. *I need to eat that, but I'm not certain my stomach will allow it.* "I mean, he's pretty public, so I guess you might've pieced things together. But no one at the school knew I was gay—"

"*Was* gay?"

"Am gay." I quickly clarified in case my words left any lingering doubt. Always had been and always would be. I could adore women, but I'd never be attracted to them. Never want them sexually. Not like men. *Not like him.* "People in my social circle knew. My parents knew, obviously."

He laughed. Not an entirely pleasant sound. "Yeah, well we certainly weren't part of your social circle. So I hadn't known you were married to a dude."

"Gavin and I divorced, and my family acted like I'd never been married. Although they were part of the same crowd as Gavin, that was never my scene. I disappeared, and no one in the snooty stratosphere asked any questions. Or if they did, my mother never said. And she loved to gossip. Had no problem telling me Gavin remarried pretty much the day after our divorce became final."

Axel sucked in a sharp breath.

"I wish him well." I poked an onion. "I didn't then...but I do now."

"He's an asshole."

"I'm not going to dispute that."

He let go a long sigh. "I'm sorry I yelled. Just...I didn't know you were gay. That was shock. Not a good shock or a bad shock...just a surprise I didn't see coming. Then, on top of that, meeting your butthole husband. And the things he said—"

"I'm so sorry for that." Acid churned in my gut, mixing with the food and threatening to bring it all back up.

"What are you apologizing for?" Axel furrowed his brow. "Like, you did nothing wrong."

"Well...I'm sorry I didn't tell you. Did you really hate me after that?"

"Hate you? What do you mean?"

"You were really angry at me."

He shrugged. "Yeah, 'coz I thought we were friends, and you didn't even tell me you were gay. And maybe, as your student, I didn't have the right to know. But Ed admitted to me he had feelings for both guy and girls. I worried he might like me *in that way*. He swore he didn't, and I believed him. But it would've been nice to talk to someone who understood that I could like guys but just want Ed as a friend."

Axel likes guys. I pushed that thought down to focus on the past. "You could've come to me."

"I didn't know you were gay." He gazed out over the sea of tents—more being erected as time moved on. People wanting the best spots.

"Oh. I suppose...So you didn't think that I was trying to...well...you know? I thought you were angry because you were uncomfortable around me."

"Uncomfortable?"

"Like you thought I was going to try something." *Like Gavin accused me of doing, even though I never had those thoughts.*

"Hell no. Fuck, I'm sorry you thought that."

"So you didn't think I had been inappropriate at all?"

"Fuck no! Who was the motherfucker who said that to you? You were the best teacher. I never felt anything like that around you. Like I said, I didn't even know you were gay. You were never inappropriate with any of your students. You were always so careful."

"Oh. Good." His words left me nearly speechless. Of course, Gavin had been the *motherfucker*. The man I'd loved, who'd undermined me in that nasty, painful way. The doubt had lingered all these years. Until now.

Chapter Five

Axel

I couldn't believe Hugo had spent the past ten years worrying that I'd somehow thought he'd been coming on to me. The truth was as far from that as another galaxy. Slowly, I pushed up from the ground and dusted my hands off. I downed the rest of my cola and headed over to the garbage and recycling bins. Glancing over my shoulder, I found Hugo following me. To my dismay, he poured his soda onto the dusty ground and tossed the rest of his food into the compost container. "You could've finished that."

He met my gaze. "I think I've had enough." He rubbed his belly.

I winced. "Sorry. Maybe I shouldn't have brought that day up."

"I'm..." He scratched his beard. The beard he hadn't had ten years ago. His longer hair was new as well. "I probably should've found a way to get in touch before now."

"You've been following my career?"

"Yeah."

"And I'm the reason you're here?"

"Well, the band." He looked away.

A warning pinged in my mind. He wasn't telling the truth. Correction—he wasn't telling the entire truth.

I stepped away from the trash and toward a post.

Hugo followed.

We stood mere inches apart.

Because of the height difference, I needed to tip my face down.

He tipped his gaze up to meet mine.

I was so damn glad neither of us wore sunglasses. His rested on the top of his head while mine were tucked into the neck of my T-shirt. We'd need to put them back on soon but for the moment, in the brilliant sunshine, his blue eyes sparkled.

I touched his cheek.

He stepped back, pulling away from my caress. Putting distance between us.

I advanced. In my gut, I knew he wanted this. *This* was the reason he'd come. And *this* was the reason I'd pined over him for years and years. Even when I hadn't known he was gay, I'd felt an attraction to him. And while Ed was sharing how he felt about boys, I'd never said anything. Knowing what my father's reaction would be kept me firmly away from ever speaking about my curiosity. About the inappropriate attraction I felt toward my music teacher.

And about the dozens of men I'd met in the intervening ten years who I would've hit on...if not for my hangups about being gay. Ed might not be out publicly, but he did have guys he dated.

I had no men. Just a string of nice women whose company I enjoyed.

Hugo took another step back, and his back pressed against the food truck.

Having the advantage, I advanced again.

He held up his hands.

I grasped them, reveling in the strength, in the softness of the skin mixed with the calluses on his fingers from hours of playing guitar.

Hugo broke eye contact, ducking his head.

Waiting patiently wasn't my strong suit, but I wanted to give him a chance to come to me.

He didn't.

So I placed my index finger under his chin and tipped his face up toward me. *I could get lost in those eyes. And hear me...there's nothing wrong with this. Back then, of course. But not now.*

Even as he held my gaze, he blinked rapidly.

Does he have something in his eyes? Is the sun too bright? I angled myself so I blocked out the sun. That didn't ease the shimmering in his stunning eyes. *Am I reading true desire or am I imposing my wishes on him? Ten years of yearning's clouding my judgement.*

Yet he didn't pull back.

I grasped his cheeks, caressing them then cupping him under his jaw.

He still didn't withdraw.

My grasp was gentle. If he wanted to escape, he certainly could.

But he didn't.

"I think you came here for me," I told him. "I'm going to kiss you. If I'm wrong, if you don't want this, say no."

His lips parted but he said nothing, his gaze fixed on mine.

So I leaned toward him and pressed our lips together. Just the lightest brushing of lips. Once. Twice.

Then, at once, he opened his mouth and wound his arms around my neck, dragging me closer.

Taking this as both permission and an invitation, I thrust my tongue into his mouth. I tasted onions and—more important-ly—something unique to Hugo. I'd kissed plenty of women in my life, but none ever tasted like this. *Would all men taste like this or just him?* Didn't really matter as the headiness of actually kissing Hugo went straight to my head.

And, naturally, to my cock.

I went from vaguely interested to fully erect in a short span of time. My body ached for him in a way I never had for anyone. Like if I didn't have him in this exact moment then I'd die. Need clawed at me as I continued to plunder his mouth—searching the recesses with my tongue. Trying to command the kiss—to take charge—even as I felt control slipping through my fingers like grains of sand.

I eased my hands down his flank, then eased them around to grasp his ass. Again, with no resistance, just a gasp and the tightening of his hands on my shoulders. I grabbed his oh-so-perfect ass and yanked him toward me.

My cock brushed against his very-interested one.

He moaned into my mouth, thrusting against me again and again. His desperation seemed to match my own.

I wasn't going to spend a lot of time thinking about this. Ex-cept...not only was I finally kissing a guy, I was finally kissing Mr. Threadgold. And my high school crush on a generous and kind teacher was now playing out in real time. He'd insisted he hadn't seen me *that* way back in high school. Which came as a relief. Clearly, though, he saw me *that* way now.

I thrust against him over and over—searching for desperately need-ed friction. This was so different from rubbing against a woman. I'd always believed the women I was with enjoyed themselves. But with Hugo, I didn't need to wonder. And if we kept this up, I was certain I was going to explode, and I was pretty certain he would as well.

"Did you hear Hellsbane is back this year?" A deep male voice spoke with reverence.

"And they're back with Blade. And the hologram," a higher voice added with clear enthusiasm.

Hugo pulled back, essentially ripping himself out of my arms.

A group of four goths passed by us. They didn't appear to notice us. Or were too kind to say anything.

I kept my head turned away. I wasn't well-known by any stretch of the imagination, but I didn't need to out myself just one day before the biggest night of my life. *Out myself. Come out of the closet. Holy shit, what are you thinking?* Obviously I wasn't. And my erection wasn't waning, even as Hugo pressed fingers to his lips. Were they tingling like mine? Did he feel this undeniable connection? Would he be willing to do that again? To pick up where we left off? I advanced.

He held up his hand.

This time, I halted. Even I, not the shiniest penny in the jar as my mother would say, could read a hard *stop*. My ragged breaths matched his, and my erection continued to strain against my leather pants. "Hugo—"

"No." He gulped in air. "This is wrong—"

"No, it's not." I sliced my hand through the air. "It would've been wrong ten years—"

He spun and took off.

I stood, stunned. Thirty seconds ago, he'd been pliant in my arms, and if I'd suggested we go behind the food truck so we could fuck, I wouldn't have been surprised if he'd said yes. Which was nuts. To jump so far so fast. Yet with my cock this hard and condoms in my wallet? Things could've ended very different.

Would've ended very differently. Hell, if the bus was empty, I would've risked it and taken him back there. Having sex in a bunk wasn't easy...but it was totally possible. I should know. Had done it more often than my bandmates knew.

Or...at least I was pretty sure they didn't know.

You're getting off topic.

What topic? He's gone. You'll probably never see him again.

My phone rang. I yanked it from my back pocket and swiped. "What?"

"Dude, chill." Big Mac laughed. "I'm just letting you know we're heading to the main stage for our rehearsal. You're on your way too, right?"

"Yes." I might've snapped that. Big Mac didn't deserve my ire, but the object of my annoyance...of my affection...was nowhere to be found.

"Right. See you in ten." The call disconnected.

I stood, rooted to the spot, for another good half minute. Follow Hugo? Walk away? What the fuck had just happened? I'd finally kissed a guy...and that guy had bolted? Somehow, I didn't think my inexperience in the *kissing a guy* department was the issue.

Again, I slashed my hand through the air. Then I spun and stalked off in the opposite direction.

Chapter Six

Hugo

"You look like your puppy just died." Renee eyed me.

I tried to glare. "I don't have a puppy." Hadn't been allowed one as a child. I'd thought maybe when I married, but Gavin had an allergy to every animal known to man. Even hypoallergenic ones. Then I was single—working and volunteering all the time. Puppies just weren't possible.

Grouch had been the one companion in my life. The old cat showed up at my door one day, let himself in when I opened said door, and had made himself at home. I fashioned a litter box, bought food, and put fliers up around the neighborhood. Even posted on social media.

A neighbor let me know Grouch was a feral cat who'd lived in the neighborhood for years. She didn't believe he had an actual owner.

I took him to a wonderful vet—whom Grouch determinedly didn't like. I got him fixed and cared for him. He was pretty old, and the vet was surprised he'd survived so long on the streets. In the end, he didn't last two years.

As much as I wanted to get a kitten, or even an older rescue cat, to replace him, I still worked tons of hours. Grouch hadn't cared. He'd asked very little of me—just shelter, food, and petting. I'd given all that freely. But love couldn't keep him going forever.

Cope nudged me. "Okay, now you've got me worried too."

Right. Because spacing out thinking about a long-dead feral cat I once housed is totally normal behavior for a functioning adult.

Except I didn't feel like I was functioning. My circuits were completely fried. Axel had done this. Specifically, kissing Axel Townsend had completely derailed me in every possible way. I wasn't certain coherent words were even possible. "I'm fine."

Renee laughed. "Oh, Hugo, you're anything but *fine*. You're the opposite of fine. We leave you alone for just a day and we come back to find you completely..." She scrunched her nose.

"Decompensating." Cope with his cute psychological terms.

"Oh, good one." Renee slapped my thigh. "Honestly, Hugo, what's up?"

"Hey, isn't Grindstone rehearsing now?" Cope checked his watch. "Right now."

Renee leapt from her chair, then reached to grab my arm.

"I think they're already done." They were. I knew this because I'd watched, hidden behind some sound equipment. Well, peeked. And listened. As they'd run through their entire playlist.

"How did we miss that?" Renee punched me in the biceps.

Hard.

I shrugged. "You were late coming back from Reno. I knew they'd already performed, so I didn't say anything. We'll see them tomorrow night."

"How were they?" Renee dropped back into her camping chair.

Cope, who hadn't actually risen with his enthusiastic wife, settled back more comfortably. "Yes, why didn't you say anything?"

"They were amazing. They're always amazing. But I didn't want you to feel bad for missing the rehearsal. I'm certain they'll be even better tomorrow." Not that they'd been perfect tonight. A little...I sought the right word. Harried? Rushed? Possibly. But given how many bands had to get in a rehearsal, their speed was hardly surprising.

No way Axel could've seen me, though. *Did he know I was there? That I heard every note? That I regretted walking away from the most passionate kiss of my life?*

Way to end a dry spell.

Over and over, I told myself I was too busy for a relationship. That although I wasn't in the closet, I also wasn't out. School administrators knew. I didn't hide my sexuality—I just didn't advertise it either. And possibly to the detriment of kids like Ed and Axel who could've used a safe teacher to share their confusion with. I'd never sensed either was bi. And maybe...no, Axel made it clear Ed was. Right? And he'd not come out and said it, but I worked with the assumption he wouldn't have kissed me that passionately if he was straight.

"I think you're reliving the show." Cope grinned.

"Or his misbegotten youth." Renee grinned. "He once wanted to be a rock star."

Cope and I both groaned. We'd heard her retelling of this story so often. I'd been part of a Nirvana cover band one summer in the late nineties. We'd barely been teenagers. My parents, upon securing a promise of good grades in exchange for high-end music equipment, allowed me and my friends to set up a mini-studio in our massive basement. Nothing had come from it—we'd been a pretty talentless bunch—but my love of music was cemented.

After that, I'd applied myself diligently to learning as much as humanly possible about music, music theory, and bands. Only not rock bands. No, I saw my strength would be in nurturing talent. Completing my musicology studies at the University of British Columbia led to obtaining a teaching degree then heading with my lofty ideals to the roughest part of Vancouver, intending to make a difference. Not look back at my ridiculously brief performing days. "We agreed to never speak of this again."

Renee fluttered her eyelashes. "Speak of what?"

"Of me getting wasted one night and letting you listen to the recordings." The tapes of my Nirvana cover songs. I should've thrown them out years ago. Part of me, though, longed to relive those days. When life had been simpler. When all I'd had to do was promise my parents good grades and I'd gotten a summer free of responsibilities. Kids in my neighborhood hadn't needed to get part-time jobs. We could fuck around all we wanted, with mommy and daddy's money supporting us. Given the few horror stories we'd heard about drug addiction, it didn't surprise me that my parents chose to keep me close at hand. Plus, the basement had been soundproofed.

"I think we should make Copeland listen to the recordings." Renee's grin widened.

My stomach sank. Letting her listen to them while I'd been drowning in alcohol after the dissolution of my marriage was one thing. Listening to them sober to someone whose opinion I respected was something else entirely. I'd tried that—with Gavin. He'd ridiculed me. From that moment on, I'd sworn no one would ever hear them again.

Should've destroyed them.

Except I would've missed out on that maudlin night with my best friend as I drunkenly railed against my asshole ex-husband for abandoning me and stealing all my hopes and dreams of having a family of my own.

"I think that's a brilliant idea." Copeland gently nudged my knee with his.

I both loved and hated how comfortable my friends were. They were secure enough in their relationship that they didn't always need to sit next to each other. To fawn over each other. To hold hands. Not to say they didn't do plenty of that—they did. But I enjoyed they didn't rub their couplehood in my face.

What that also meant, however, is they felt comfortable boxing me in on both sides and having way too much fun getting handsy with me. Nudges, smacks on the arm, kisses on the cheek.

You love the affection and attention.

Okay, so yeah. Given that was all I got, I did enjoy the closeness we all shared. When I first met Cope, and saw how taken he was with Renee, and she with him, I'd assumed I'd lose my best friend. The opposite happened. Now, in all practical senses, I had two best friends.

"Sheesh, Hugo." Renee angled herself so she was no longer watching concertgoers wander by as the sun crested the horizon. "You're all up in yourself today. You keep wandering off."

"I haven't moved a muscle." Yet her meaning was clear. And I couldn't dispute it. "I think I'm going to bed." I'd have a piss, brush my teeth, and call it a night.

"Your tent will still be hot." Renee glared.

"I opened the flaps hours ago, and there's a nice breeze. I'm going to be fine." Personally, I would've been happy to nearly suffocate in a blazing-hot enclosed space if it got me away from the scrutiny she aimed in my direction.

Cope rose. "I enjoyed that beer a little too much. I'm coming with you."

Renee rose as well. "I'm wandering over to the main stage to see what's going on."

"I'll join you in a bit." Cope looped his arm around her, tugged her in for a kiss, then gently let her go.

The casual affection tightened my chest. I wanted that with someone. And, if I was honest, had never had it. Gavin hadn't been affectionate. Aggressive in bed? Certainly. Gently and caring out of it? No. Especially not with other people around. He had a reputation as a hard-nosed businessman to maintain.

Or so he'd claimed.

The grapevine informed me, on occasion, how he made a show of affection with his second husband. How happy he looked. Implicit was the criticism that not only had he not been happy with me—but that somehow I was to blame. That I was at fault for not being a good enough husband. That I hadn't initiated mushiness and therefore Gavin had been forced to seek it elsewhere. The exact opposite was true...but I never bothered to argue my side. People saw what they wanted to see.

And I tried not to become embittered as I heard how happy Gavin was. When I saw how happy my best friends were.

I snagged my toothbrush. "Let's go, Cope."

Renee headed off toward the distant music while Cope and I trudged to the washrooms. He didn't push me to talk, and I was grateful.

After I'd done everything I needed to do, I headed back to our tents. Renee had secured our set-up, and all I needed to do was crawl into my tent. I didn't feel claustrophobic, even though the fit was tight. I was slightly chilled, though, as the sun had set and a light breeze had picked up. This late in October, some nights could be cool this high in the mountains, even if we were still in a desert. As some residual heat lasted from the day, I opted to lie on a blanket draped over my air mattress with my sleeping bag loosely over me.

I fingered my ear plugs as I killed the battery-powered lantern. I hated wearing them, but I was also a pretty light sleeper. Every recommendation website I'd checked said they were a must.

Huh.

As I replayed my day, they slipped from my fingers onto the mattress. Easily within reach if I needed them.

Axel.

Okay. I'd known he'd be here, so seeing him hadn't been unexpected. He'd invited me for a catch-up, so I couldn't claim surprise at that. Him baring his soul to be hadn't been expected.

Had he really, though? We'd spent time talking about my ex, about that final confrontation, and about how my withholding something very personal from my students hurt. I honestly had never thought my coming out might make things easier for my kids.

Or so you tell yourself. You're just a coward.

Well, that wasn't a lie. I was afraid students and parents would see me differently because they would. Obviously the bigots and homophobes would have one perspective. Allies could be just as unwavering—and expecting me to represent. I just wanted to focus on teaching and music. And teaching music. Who I dated, and might even take to bed, wasn't anyone's business.

Which looped me back to Axel.

You're thinking too much.

Maybe I was. Maybe I wasn't seeing what lay before me. Maybe I was replaying that kiss over and over and over again. His soft lips pliant against mine. His hard cock rubbing against me. The desperation I'd felt. The obvious need he'd felt. Those formed a heady combination I couldn't get out of my mind.

Unbidden, my hand slithered down my body, tucking itself under my waistband until it surrounded my erection. The erection I shouldn't have.

Axel needed to remain untouchable. Until I'd seen him yesterday, he had been. Honest to Christ, I'd never looked at him *that* way. I could admit he'd grown into an attractive man and he was often accompanied in photos and stories I'd seen by women who met society's high—and stupid—perception of beauty. As a teacher, I spent my time trying to raise the self-esteem of kids who weren't viewed as good-looking. Like that mattered. A guy could be devastatingly handsome and still be, as Axel had less than tactfully put it, a motherfucker.

Still, when character and looks came together, that was heady stuff. Like Axel. Need snaked within me, heating me. Almost to the point where I could push off the sleeping bag. But then I'd get cold. Somehow, staying hot reminded me of the afternoon sun. Of Axel's dark-brown skin. Of the steamy look in his eyes when he'd leaned down to kiss me.

Fucking hell, I was going to do it. I was going to masturbate in a tent two feet away from my best friends.

They're not there.

But they could come back.

Good thing you didn't put in your earplugs.

Not only did I hate hearing my breathing with plugged ears—I didn't want to be caught unaware. I couldn't imagine Renee poking her head in my tent. But that lack of imagination had bitten me on the butt more than once in our many years of friendship.

I tugged on my cock.

Need thrummed in my blood.

Normally, things took time. I was older.

I imagined him. Remembered him. His skin. His taste. How I'd wanted his tongue swirling around my cock instead of inside my mouth. How I'd damn nearly come in my jeans in a semi-public place. How, if I could've made it work, I would've dragged him back behind the truck and we would've fucked. Me in jeans and him in leather pants would've made life interesting—but we would've figured it out. He'd always been creative. I'd always been clever.

Cum erupted from me and spurted over my hand. Belatedly, I realized I should've used a tissue or something to try to cope with the sticky mess.

I let out a long sigh, trying to school my harsh breathing.

God, I hope no one can hear me.

Ah well, this was Rocktoberfest. People everywhere in the area were getting lucky. Getting laid.

Hell, Axel was probably getting lucky.

Getting laid.

Yeah, but with a man or a woman? *And you could've been that man... If you hadn't run away like a frightened child.*

Yet another regret I'd have to live with.

Chapter Seven

Axel

As I sat at the table in our bus sipping a cola, I eyed the two ginger ales next to me.

One for Ed.

One for Thornton.

Because I was under no illusions that Ed would confront me without his new sidekick. Which bugged the shit out of me because this wasn't Thornton's business. Hell, it wasn't even Ed's business. Except Ed had a funny way of determining what was his business and what wasn't. He frequently ventured into territory that should've been private.

And I let him.

Because he'd been right once. Eight years ago. About us needing to get clean.

He's been right about a shit ton more than that, and you know it.

Resentfully, I took another sip.

Ed and Thornton boarded the bus, and both approached me, each looking so very serious. I wanted to make a joke but now didn't feel like the right moment for that.

My best friend handed his new *boyfriend* a ginger ale. Then he snagged his and plopped down next to me.

Thornton sat next to him. He pulled out his phone, swiped a couple of times, then placed it before me.

Orienting myself took about five seconds. "You son of a bitch. You had no right—"

"Probably not—" Thornton the asshole cut me off.

Which only made me madder.

"Doesn't matter." Ed sighed. "We can leave the ethical and moral debate for another day." He hit pause of the video. The video of me and Mr. Threadgold. Talking and, if memory served, mere moments before we were about to kiss. And as much as I wanted to watch that kiss—to try to put it in perspective by being the observer—I just couldn't.

Ed just had to keep going. "He's our teacher, Axel. This is all kinds of wrong." He took a long breath. "Was this going on in high school?"

"What?" I needed to clean my ears out because clearly Ed wouldn't be suggesting I'd kissed our high school music teacher. While back in fucking high school. I gaped at him, truly horrified.

After a long moment, Ed let out another breath. "Well, thank fuck."

"I can't believe you thought—"

"The man's almost twenty years older than you, Axel. And, try to deny it all you want, you were a vulnerable kid. Hurting. In a lot of pain—physical and emotional."

Oh you did not just fucking go there. You did not *just say that in front of a stranger. In front of a man here to dig up my deepest and darkest secrets.* Our *deepest and darkest secrets.*

Completely and utterly uncowed, Ed continued. "And it would've been very easy for someone to take advantage of you."

"Well, you too." First, because that was the truth. Secondly, because I so badly needed to deflect this off me. Throwing the steaming pile of shit back in his lap felt vaguely fair. If a little offside.

He merely raised an eyebrow.

"And anyway..." I tapped my finger on the table. "He's only four-teen years older. I'm an adult. He's...a slightly older adult."

"How long has this been going on?"

"What?" *Fuck. He doesn't get it. I have to make him understand.* "There isn't a *this*." I scratched my scalp. "Like he saw me and called me over." *No sense mentioning we'd arranged to meet. Or that I'd poured my soul out to him.*

"What is he doing here?"

"I honestly don't know." *Another lie. Jesus, you're going to self-com-bust, you've told so many of them.*

He rolled his hand. Like he wanted me to continue. To keep digging this hole he intended to push me in.

"And, like, we got to talking. Just talking." I emphasized each word. "And I thought about how great having him here was. And how we'd just been talking about him this morning and, voilà, here he is. I mean, that's great, right?"

Ed's stony expression remained.

So I kept going. At this rate, I was going to dig a hole to China. "And, like, we got to talking. To reminiscing."

"Like about when you were his student?"

Ouch. That tone could've cut glass. "Sure." Inwardly, I winced. "But like more about our career. He's followed us closely. And even seen a couple of concerts. He was at the PNE last week. Isn't that cool?" Because if I made it about *us* and not about *me* then maybe Ed would back the fuck off.

Or not.

He pursed his lips. "No, not really cool. More like stalking."

"It's not like that, Ed. I swear."

"You don't know what it's like, Axel. You had your tongue down his throat within five seconds of seeing him again. Hell, not that it fucking matters, but I didn't even know he was gay." He arched an eyebrow. "Or that you were."

Oh crap. Maybe that was the real source of the pain. That he'd always been so honest with me about his bisexuality and I'd done nothing but lie to him all these years. In my wildest imagination, I'd never imagined I might wind up with a guy. Those urges...well, if I could be satisfied with a woman and not face all the rampant homophobia, then why bother.

Maybe because you've never met the right man?

Oh, shut up.

My inner voice was really pissing me off tonight.

Ed waited.

So I turned the table. I glared at Thornton. "You shouldn't have taped me. You had no right."

Bastard shrugged. "Maybe. Maybe not. Regardless, you're going to be onstage at one of the biggest music festivals in the States. Hellsbane was barely known last year. Look at them now. If you nail your performance tomorrow night, you might just hit that level of stardom." He held up his hand. "Now, I don't care about your sexuality. You might've noticed I'm not exactly out—I don't want it to be the focus of my work. I don't want to be the *gay* documentary filmmaker."

If he was trying to appease me, it wouldn't work. He might also be trying to appease his own guilt...but I wasn't letting him off the hook so easily. I didn't care that he was right. That people would perceive him—and his work—differently.

People suck.

Then his words struck me. "What are you trying to say?" I tried to glare. "I'm not gay."

Ed stared at me, blinked a couple of times, then continue to regard me. "But—"

"That was...just a kiss. You know, like..."

"You seem to be saying *like* quite a bit during this conversation. Being articulate has never been a problem with you, Axel, so I'm worried." He tried to grab my hand.

I yanked mine back. "I have to go."

"Go where?" Ed glanced around.

"Somewhere other than here." I rose, then met his gaze. "You just don't get it." I pounded my fist on the table, nearly knocking over the soda cans. "You're both so far out of line. Filming me." I pointed to Thornton. "And confronting me." I jabbed a finger at Ed. "Fuck you both."

I stomped to the front of the bus, down the stairs, and right out the door.

That righteous anger carried me all the way back to the main stage. One of the bigger named groups was performing their rehearsal. *What are their names? Oh my God, I can't believe you forgot.* I wanted to argue I was entitled to forget at this point.

How fucking dare they? First Thornton with his fucking camera. Then Ed for feeling he had the right to confront me. Fuck them both.

I want Hugo. I need Hugo. To warn him. To have him comfort me. To have him either share my righteous fury or to tell me I was overreacting and blowing things out of proportion—both of which were entirely possible. Even I could admit I was too close to the situation to see it rationally. Surely Thornton wasn't going to include the footage in his documentary. Everyone would see what a sleazeball he was. And surely Ed wasn't going to tell everyone else.

As far as they all knew...I was straight. And yeah, Ed coming out as bisexual today was a big deal. Just like if Pauletta ever found the courage, that would be a big deal too. Maybe, with the way she kept looking at Mickey, she might come out as pan? Or was that potential relationship just a flash in the pan, much like Ed and Thornton's was? Because *no way* were those two going to last. Fucking like rabbits was one thing.

They thought I didn't know.

But I totally did.

Was I going to wander all night? I didn't know where Hugo actually was, so that didn't help. I made my way back to the food truck, but he wasn't there. And why would he be? I'd kissed him. He'd panicked. I hadn't gone after him. Then I'd been almost late for rehearsal. Not actually late...but Pauletta drilled into us from the beginning that better ten minutes early than two minutes late. So we were always early. To do anything less was to disrespect the woman who'd brought us this success.

Fuck this shit.

I'd sneak back into the bus and head to bed.

Sneak? Who are you kidding?

Okay, especially if Songbird and Big Mac were playing cards, entering unnoticed would be a challenge. But I could claim a headache—which I was totally starting to get—and head to the back.

Maybe a quick shower and then early to bed. Tomorrow night was going to be the biggest night of our careers. More sleep rather than less would help with the nerves. Performance nerves.

Or so I told myself.

Because in no way was the churning in my gut due to the best kiss I'd had in my life.

One that might've just cost me everything.

Chapter Eight

Hugo

S tanding amid a huge, rocking, headbanging crowd, I watched Grindstone own the stage. Until they changed the tone, and the fans quieted to listen.

Cause we've got nothing but time to our name
Oh, no money, glory, or fame
But I don't need those to love you
All I want is to hold your hand
So, take me to our promise land
That's all I need to love you

My breath caught. I hadn't heard this song before. As Axel softly, but surely, sang, each note resonated within me. This was...fucking brilliant. *Did he write it? Did Ed? Did they cowrite?* I'd heard they often did, although Ed was usually the driving force behind the songs. The way Axel sang this, though...

Moving fast
Though I want this night to last
So, I'm taking a deep breath
Let my worries go to rest
As I take your hands
"Do you think this night will end?
Or will the sun leave us alone?
And the night become our home"
As I share this thought with you
The sun rises, and damn, what a beautiful view

Renee gripped my hand, and I was certain she held Cope's with her other. I was grateful—not just for the unspoken support—but for the knowledge she was as enthralled as I was. That she saw what I saw. Felt what I felt.

The final notes carried across the hushed crowd.

And then the place erupted with noise, whistles, and general pandemonium. This wasn't a song I'd ever heard—and I'd heard everything commercially available and everything they'd played at the concerts I'd attended. But this one hadn't ever been played before in front of an audience. At least that I knew. To perform something so intimate, for the first time, in front of such a huge crowd? On the biggest night of their careers? That took fucking guts.

Renee wrapped her arms around my waist and pulled me in for an awkward side hug.

Cope still gripped her on the other side.

Once the crowd simmered down a bit, the band broke into a song I recognized.

"Oh, Hugo, I'm so glad we came." Renee rested her head against my chest as I settled my newly liberated hand around her. "You have the best ideas."

Kissing Axel flashed into my mind. That definitely had *not* been the best idea ever. Nor had running away instead of staying around to have an earnest conversation about what had happened.

I kissed Axel Fucking Townsend. The unreality of it sank in slowly as Grindstone finished off their set. The crowd roared their appreciation—and demanded more—but the other bands waited to appear, so the group took one final bow and disappeared as the roadies came onto the stage to clear out Grindstone's equipment and to move in the next band's.

Renee glanced up at me. "That was intense."

"Yeah."

"You ever heard that song? Was it "Sunrise"?"

"Yeah, "Sunrise"." I repeated the word even as some of the lyrics floated back. There'd been both elements of melancholy and parts that were hope-filled. Again, I was dying to know who'd written the words. "We sticking around? I hear this next band is quite creative..."

And we stayed. I would've loved to track Axel down, but I suspected he'd be off with his bandmates celebrating. And so he should. That performance had been epic. One for the ages.

Or so it seemed to me. Maybe it'd just been another day for Axel and Ed. Or maybe the crowd hadn't been as electrified as I was. Yet, as I had the thought, I caught several people discussing Grindstone even as this new band began. Even though, true to the rumor, their songs were unique. And a hit with the crowd, which relieved me. Nothing worse than being in an audience who didn't appreciate the effort and hard work being put forth by the performers.

We stayed for three more bands before I was ready to call it a night.

Renee and Cope were, according to them *just getting into it*, and eager to hear the headliners.

Not wanting to rain on their parade, I slipped away. I took my turn in the john, then meandered between the food vendors. A soft ice cream cone appeared to be the perfect choice as far as I was concerned. The noise from the bands wasn't as intense here—more like an echo.

In my mind, as I licked my cone, I kept replaying "Sunrise".

Will they release that song on their next album? Will I ever get to hear it again? Obviously it wasn't written about me...but those words sure spoke to me—

Someone bumped into me and muttered. "Behind the truck. Now."

The one where Axel and I had met earlier.

I nearly dropped my ice cream. Fortunately, I had mad balance skills, and I managed to stay on my feet and not wind up with ice cream on my shirt. "Damn, Axel."

Even in the dark secluded area where we'd landed, I caught his devilish grin.

He licked my cone.

I groaned.

"Even better than the one I just had." He licked his lips.

"The one you just..."

"With the band. We always have ice cream after the show. Back in the tour bus."

"Ah."

"Of course that was after I caught Ed and Thornton fucking in the shower."

My mind stuttered on that.

Axel licked again, grinned, then—very slowly—that grin dropped. "The fucker filmed us. The kiss."

"Ed?" I couldn't fathom why he'd want to, but—

"Nah, the *other* fucker. Thornton Graves."

"The documentary filmmaker." I winced. "Oh shit."

"Yeah." He snagged the entire cone and, proceeded to demolish it.

"What does this mean?"

Axel wiped his hands on the napkin, then tossed it in a garbage can. "I honestly don't know. The video quality wasn't great but…"

"But clearly we were identifiable."

"Yeah."

"Ah. I see." Except I didn't.

"Look, he didn't have a right to tape me. There's, like, an expectation of privacy—"

"Except we were in public."

He winced. "Yeah, I thought of that. I suppose if he wanted to out me—to out you—then he could release it. Or, like, for maximum impact, release it within the documentary."

"Do you think he will?"

Axel scratched his stubble-laden jaw. "A couple of days ago, I would've been certain about the answer. Now, I'm not so sure. If Ed asks him not to, then maybe he won't. Or if our manager asks the director not to, they might agree. I just…" He winced. "I don't know." He arched an eyebrow. "Okay, now I've told you. And consumed all your ice cream. We need to talk."

Ah…the four words one never wanted to hear.

"Can we walk?"

"Of course." Only as we headed out, though, did I realize his intention. We couldn't see each other's faces. I couldn't read his expressions. See the depth of passion, or of pity, in his eyes. I was pathetic.

"What did you say?" Axel turned as I did and our gazes clashed.

I pressed a hand to my chest. "Me? I didn't say anything."

"Ah, but you were thinking something."

"Uh, Axel?"

"Yep?"

"I think it's safe to say that a person is thinking something at any given moment. Unless they're asleep."

"Huh."

We resumed walking. "What?"

"I can think of a couple of times when I was on dates when my mind went completely blank."

"I'd say..." Hmm. "That sounds definitively unchivalrous."

He guffawed. "Only you would use that word. And only you would think that. I'm quite certain there've been women dating me who'd felt I wasn't worthy of their attention."

"Why would they say that?"

"Because I'm vacuous. Just a vessel to sing and without any true substance."

Okay, this had to stop. Again, I halted.

After a step, he did as well. He turned back to face me. "What?"

"You're not *vacuous*." I almost asked him if he knew what the word meant, but that would've been just about the most condescending thing I could've said.

"I lack depth."

I glared. "I heard you sing tonight. That performance didn't come from someone who lacked depth." Again, I placed a hand against my chest. "That came from someone who feels things deeply."

""Sunrise"?"

"Yes."

"That was mostly Ed."

Mostly...but not all. "He had a reason to write the song."

"Yeah."

"And you had a reason to sing that song."

"Well..." He scratched his scalp. "Yeah. To be truthful, I did."

"Will you share?" *Am I prepared for the consequences if he does?*

"Nah. Not today, anyway."

Which implied there might be a tomorrow. "Why are you here?"

He grinned. "Because I want a repeat."

"Another gyro? I believe we need to head back—"

He snagged the hand I'd pointed back the way we'd come.

"That's not what I mean."

"Ah." Which was what I'd assumed, but better to be innocuous and right than wicked and wrong. "The kiss."

"The kiss, yeah." He slowly drew my hand to his lips. And, to my utter shock, he kissed my knuckles.

"Uh...there's more?" I cleared my throat. "Because kissing, at least to me, seemed like a really bad idea."

"You don't have any idea what you're talking about. Kissing is never a bad idea. Not with the right person."

The implication being, of course, that I was the *right* person. So what type of people were the *wrong* person? The women he'd dated? The kisses he'd never partaken in? "Why me, Axel? I'm your teacher—"

"Was."

"Was." I repeated his word. "But that's not just semantics. There's a major power imbalance here."

He rolled his eyes. "Sure. I'm the rock'n'roll frontman. You're *just* the teacher."

You knew he'd turn this on you...which is why you'd walked away.

"Look—"

"I'm twenty-eight fucking years old. If I want to kiss my former teacher, I will. Former by *ten fucking years*. Jesus, have you listened to yourself? Or is that douchebag ex-husband of yours still occupying real estate in your magnificent brain?"

Was I supposed to take issue with the douchebag, real estate, or magnificent?

I didn't know where to start. "Axel—"

"I'm a virgin."

Okay, that I didn't see coming.

Chapter Nine

Axel

J esus Fucking Christ. Did you seriously just blurt that out? Blame it on the ADHD or some shit. At least take it back, and—

"Axel?"

Hugo's gentle voice soothed me. And pulled me back.

"That's...quite a revelation."

Oh shit. I laughed. "I didn't mean, like, with women. Or anything like that."

Hugo let out a quick laugh. "Okay. Not that it matters to me either way, but I figured you making it this far, that you must've..." He gestured.

"Fucked?"

His brow knit. "That wasn't what I was going to say. Just..."

"That because I'm a rock'n'roll dude that I might've been having lots of sex with lots of different people?"

"Uh..." He frowned. "I'm pretty sure that wasn't what I meant."

"Oh? What did you mean?" I should've cut him a break, but I was having a good time. Even relaxing after that fairly heavy revelation. *At least he didn't laugh at me.*

Yet.

He cleared his throat. "Just that I was aware of several encounters in your past. If they didn't happen, then perhaps I was misinformed—"

I swatted away his thought as if taking issue with a mosquito. "You weren't *misinformed*. I had a couple of girlfriends in high school that I got to third base with and more than a few women over the past few years that I was carnally intimate with." *Don't think about Kyesha.*

And yet I did.

"Ah." He scratched his cheek, scraping his beard in the process.

A beard I very much wanted to touch again. I remembered its softness, and that kicked my libido into gear. At a rather inopportune moment. "Look—"

"Why are you telling me this?"

"Because I figure if you have some aversion to virgins that it's better we get that out of the way."

He choked out a laugh. "You're being awfully presumptuous."

Yeah, I was. I could also remember with vivid clarity *that* kiss. The one that changed everything for me. And yeah, it'd been over a day ago. Maybe it should've faded a bit from my memory. "Look, Hugo..." I drew in a deep breath. "I performed tonight knowing you were in the audience. I felt it—" I pounded my chest. "—deep in my bones. I would've rocked it anyway...but knowing you were watching? That you felt that too?"

"Axel—"

"No." I said the word sharply. "Let me get this out. If you want to walk away after this, then that's totally fine. But I need you to know what's in my heart." *Okay, don't overplay your hand. You have his attention. Don't blow it.* "Tonight was my best performance ever—and I've had some good ones. But…knowing you were out there lit a flame in me that hasn't died. And maybe those embers have been dormant for ten years. I don't know. Because, rightly, we didn't do anything ten years ago. You wouldn't have, because I was your student, and I didn't say anything because I was so hurt at you keeping such a huge secret from me."

"Axel—"

"Not yet." I drew in a lungful of air. "But I moved on. And have put a lot of miles on this body. Some good…some not so good."

"The drinking? The drugs?"

Our battle for sobriety wasn't a secret, so I didn't begrudge him the interruption.

"Yes and…" I winced. "I didn't always take as much care of the women I dated than I should have, if you know what I mean?"

"You got them pregnant? Gave them diseases? I don't know what you're trying to say, Axel."

Horrified, I held up my hands. "No, none of that shit. Seriously. That's not…" Damn, what was I trying to say? "I haven't been a good person as often as I might've liked. I've tried to honor…"

Shit.

"Honor." He prompted me. Even in the dark, his blue eyes shone. He was trying to understand, and I was being as absolutely as inarticulate as possible in the moment when clarity was most required.

"I'm trying to make up for mistakes of my past. And not being truthful was one of them. I didn't care for the women. I didn't lead them on…but I maybe wasn't as honest as I could have been."

"You let them think you might be seriously interested in them?" His eyebrows rose. "Is that what you're trying to say?"

"Well...yeah, I guess so. Aside from..." *Her.* "Yeah, there hasn't been anyone serious. At least on my end. And I feel like I should've done better. But if I had—"

"You wouldn't be standing here with me telling me that you're a *virgin*." He used air quotes.

I laughed. "Well, yeah."

"Are you asking me to change that circumstance? Is that what this conversation is about?" He blinked. "Because I don't make a habit of deflowering virgins."

That made me chuckle. "No wilting boys swooning at your feet?"

He cast me a sharp look.

I shrugged. "You know what I mean."

"Don't say *boys*. That word has implications I don't want to contemplate. My students are firmly in the *never fucking ever* category."

"I know." *Jesus you're fucking this up badly.* "I like you."

"As I do you."

I sighed.

He shook his head. "If you can't come out and ask, I don't see how we can possibly—"

"Will you give me a fucking blow job?" I whispered the words urgently. "Or, I don't know, let me give you a blow job." I glanced around. "Just...maybe not here?"

"Axel...you don't know what you're asking."

"Sure I do. I know what a blow job is. Have received..." I stopped for a moment.

"Too much information."

"Like, hundreds. Oh." His words penetrated my brain just a moment too late. "Sorry."

"Propositioning someone like this can be dangerous. You, of all people, should know that."

"*Of all people?*"

"Yes. Like famous."

"More like infamous."

He slashed his hand in the air.

I stilled.

"We haven't even discussed the kiss." Hugo arched an eyebrow.

"You mean why you ran away? I don't see you running right now."

He let out a long breath of air. "I can't get you to take this seriously, can I? Is everything a joke to you?"

"Well, if you ask Ed, the answer would be a firm *yes*."

"And if I asked you?"

"Take me back to your tent, and I'll tell you the truth."

"Uh…" His mouth opened and closed several times as he clearly sought the right words. "What if I said I had a bunkmate?"

"Do you?"

"Well, not exactly."

"Is there someone sharing your tent? Your bed?" *Jesus, have I completely misread this situation?* I'd kissed him, believing he was single. And maybe that'd been way too presumptuous of me.

"I'm single. I've been single since…well, pretty much since Gavin left me."

I gaped. "That was how many years ago?" I knew, but I needed it confirmed.

"Ten years." His tone had a warning edge to it. "Which you know. I'll repeat, you weren't the reason my marriage disintegrated." He sighed. "But my students were the catalyst. Gavin's accusations nearly broke me, and I had to get out."

"Douchebag."

"Yeah, you can say that again."

"Douchebag."

He sighed. "I get it. Point made. I've had a few, uh, encounters—"

I snorted.

"Right. You're the guy who doesn't take anything seriously."

"I do. I apologize. You haven't been with many people in the last ten years. So you're alone in your tent. Or at least you're not sharing a sleeping bag."

He let out a breath. "Yes."

"Okay...so why are we not in your tent exchanging blow jobs?"

"God, Axel."

For the first time, I advanced on him, coming up to him so our chests nearly touched. "I know what I want. You know what you want. You don't have company. I want to be your company. Let's just do it. That's the slogan, right?"

"Something like." He cleared his throat. "My friends are in a tent less than two feet away."

I laughed. "*That's* what you're worried about? I can be as silent as..." I floundered.

"A church mouse?" He supplied that with a remarkably dry tone.

"Well, sure. I have to say I've never thought of church mice. Are they quieter than normal mice? Do they get sacramental wine with their cheese?"

He gazed up at me. I read exasperation and amusement. He really wanted to be annoyed with me...but I also made him smile—something he clearly didn't expect.

In that moment of indecision, I made my move. Whether he saw it coming or not, I wasn't certain, but when I grasped his cheeks and lowered my head, he didn't resist. I would've stopped, of course. If he'd given me any indication he wanted me not to press my lips to his. To nibble his lower lip. To thrust my tongue inside his mouth when he opened. When he wrapped his arms around my neck and pulled himself flush against me, I tasted victory.

"Whoa...uh, shit." A woman's voice pulled us from the kiss.

Hugo turned toward the voice while indelicately shoving me behind him. "So sorry, ladies, we were just leaving. You have a nice evening." He snagged my arm and dragged me farther into the darkness.

At least three distinct giggles followed us as we ducked behind another truck.

"Hugo—"

"That was way too close. You need to be more careful."

"Hugo—"

"We need to get you back to my tent. Do you need to go to the bathroom? I did just before I saw you, and—"

"Hugo."

"What?" He might've snapped that.

"Just lead me to your humble abode."

He met my gaze. "Yeah. I can do that."

Chapter Ten

Hugo

A xel Freaking Townsend was sitting in my tent next to me. In the top ten of *never going to happen in my life*, this would've been the number one. Actually, meeting Beyoncé would've been at the very top. Being alone with Axel was pretty high on my hypothetical list.

Until tonight. Well, if I was honest, yesterday while we'd talked, I'd imagined more time alone with him. When we'd kissed, I'd imagined more...of everything.

Renee's snores carried into our tent.

Axel met my gaze.

"She'll go like that all night. Both of them wear industrial earplugs."

"I can see why. You must as well. I mean, I get you were worried...but I think there's very little chance we're going to wake your friends." He leaned toward me. "I can be very quiet. Like a church mouse."

That made me smile. Only the lantern illuminated the tent. Axel sat across from me, hunched and adorably too big and lanky for the space. But he was clearly trying to be natural. Which also made me grin.

"Okay...do we just..." He indicated my crotch.

I handed him one of the two bottles of water I'd snagged from the cooler before we'd come in here.

"But if I drink, I might have to piss, and that would be..."

"Unfortunate?"

He glared.

I laughed. "A sip, Axel, to relax."

"This isn't booze."

"No, it most definitely isn't. I'd never offer you any alcohol we have with us. I take your sobriety as seriously as you do." I took a sip of water.

He followed suit.

"You know..." I played with the neck of the bottle.

"Yes..." He cocked his head. "You want to ask me something."

"Well... You don't happen to remember those songs you used to write."

"Songs that I used to..." The moment he remembered was very clear. "You recall that? After all this time?"

"You were one of my most talented students, Axel. Of course I remember."

"But why bring it up now?"

Hugo considered. "Because, I suppose, it's a way of showing you that I never forgot you—in a student/teacher way. Those songs had an impact on me."

"Okay, that's been a nice reminiscence down memory lane. Let's forget this entire conversation." He scooted closer to me. "Because there are definitely other things I'd rather be doing."

For just an instant, I wished I'd brushed my teeth. Except I hadn't known I was going to see Axel. Like, at all. He'd just had the biggest night of his career…how was I supposed to know he'd come and haunt the food trucks? "Did you seek me out tonight?"

He laughed. "Did I hang around great-smelling delicacies in the hopes of being fed? You better believe it."

"Are you hungry?"

"Hell no. I ate my ice cream before and then I ate your ice cream just now. So I'm not hungry. For food." He scooted even closer.

Okay, no mistaking what he meant. *Shelve the discussion—you always did have a lousy sense of timing.*

Arguing with that would've been pointless because the words were the absolute truth.

Axel drew his fingers along my forehead, down my cheek—taking time to run his nails through my beard—and then he cupped my jaw. He drew me forward, so I leaned toward him.

Our lips touched. Very gentle. Just a light brushing. No pressure. No angst. No needing to violently come together. *Shouldn't there be? Shouldn't we be ripping our clothes off?* Except he'd had years to consider this possibility, if his words were to be believed. I'd had just over twenty-four hours.

He snagged the hem of my T-shirt. We broke apart long enough for him to yank it over my head.

Figuring reciprocity was in order, I did the same for him. In the lamplight, his chest shone. He had only a smattering of chest hair. I had a bit more, but I wasn't as hairy as, for example, Copeland. The guy gave Bigfoot a run for his money.

Axel tentatively reached out to place his hand over my heart. "It's racing."

"It's…been a long time."

Slowly, he traced his fingers down my chest, lower to my not-so-chiseled abs, and then over my jeans to cup my rather-interested cock. "You haven't forgotten everything."

"Uh...no." I could've argued that my erection was merely a physiological reaction to being touched, but that wasn't the case—and I knew it. This hardness was a reaction to being touched *by him*. Again...not something I'd contemplated, but something my body was completely onboard with. My mind struggled to catch up, though. This was Axel. My former student. Former being the operative word, but still a hurdle I struggled to climb over.

He held my gaze as he unbuttoned my jeans and slid the zipper down. Then he slid his hand under my briefs to grasp me intimately.

I nearly moaned in pleasure. Renee and Cope might be wearing industrial-grade earplugs, but that didn't mean people walking by wouldn't hear. *And why should you fucking care? No one knows it's Axel in here.*

"Can I blow you?" He licked his lips. "I've never..."

"I was pretty clear on your definition of *virgin*. I was planning to give you a blow job."

He closed one eye as if considering. "I would say learning technique is important, but this isn't my first rodeo. Dumb expression that. Anyway, I've had blow jobs before." He maneuvered so he was on his knees. "You lie down and I'll straddle you."

I hadn't thought I could get harder. I was wrong.

"Oh, and take your jeans off. I know you'll be cold—"

I grabbed his cheeks and yanked him toward me. I kissed him with all the pent-up passion and need that thrummed through my veins. "I'm already overheated."

He rocked back on his heels while I inelegantly shuffled out of my jeans and underwear. The cold air pebbled my nipples, but my erection never flagged. I wanted this. Needed this. Would take whatever I could get and, hopefully, return the favor.

By the time I was lying on my back, he had his jeans off as well. "So I don't scratch you." His explanation made sense as he straddled me.

In the dim light, the outline of his erection in his boxer briefs—with a telltale wet spot at the tip—excited me ever more. I could get over the former student thing. I could get over the rockstar thing. What I couldn't get over was Axel himself. So stunningly beautiful. And yet with depth I'd recognized the first day he walked into my music class.

First, he grasped me again. With just the right amount of pressure. Then, he ran his thumb around my tip, catching a drop of precum. He brought it to his mouth and sucked.

I grew even harder. "Axel."

He grinned. "Yeah, I get it." Then he positioned himself so he could take me in his mouth.

I wasn't a virgin in this department. Although Gavin hadn't enjoyed oral at all—too messy—he'd been willing to give on occasion. I'd exchanged a couple with guys after the end of my marriage. But all those memories faded as Axel swirled his tongue around my crown. He did very creative things that would've had me surging up if not for the last ounce of restraint I possessed. I wasn't going to choke a guy performing his first blow job. That...was a step too far.

As he drew me in deeper, I struggled with the need to touch him versus the unwavering desire to come. His talented mouth was truly spectacular, and as he sucked—I bucked.

I didn't mean to. But holding out was not going to be an option if he kept up his diligent work to bring me to a climax. "I'm coming, Axel. You should pull off, and—"

He sucked harder, scraping his teeth gently along my length.

In one epic moment, I moaned as my balls drew up and I emptied into his mouth. Pleasure crashed through me, seizing my body and overwhelming my senses. Time had no meaning as he continued to suck. I felt bruised and battered—but in a good way. In a way that only a truly awesome climax could make me feel. I pressed a hand over my mouth to stifle the harsh breaths.

He crawled up my body, removed my hand, and kissed me deeply.

I tasted myself on him, of course. But this was so much more. The carnality had me reaching my hand between our bodies, into his boxer briefs, and grabbing him.

He pulled back long enough to shove the briefs down before he guided my hand to his shaft. "Do it." He said the words through gritted teeth—encouraging me where no encouragement was necessary.

He wanted this.

I needed this.

To bring him as much ecstasy as he'd just given me. I swiped precum from his tip, but it wasn't enough.

"I'm going to hurt you."

"Friction is my friend." He snickered. "You think I haven't been jerked off dozens of times with no lube? I don't mind if it's rough." He grasped my hand and encouraged me to pick up the pace.

I replicated the motion—twisting, squeezing, and working to bring him to the brink as quickly as I could. Speed wasn't always a thing. Nothing wrong with savoring and enjoying the moment. Here, though, I knew what he needed.

"I need to—"

"I know."

"I'm going to…"

"Yes, please." I tugged harder—worried about hurting him, but also knowing how badly he needed this. In essence, how much I did as well.

Moments later, he erupted, spurting cum all over my hand. His labored breaths tickled my neck as he quietly groaned. "Jesus, Hugo, best orgasm ever."

Hearing my name on his lips did something to my insides. I'd only ever been Mr. Threadgold. Having something so intimate pass between us breached some kind of barrier. Knocked down a wall that had been erected fourteen years ago when he'd walked in...all gangly teenager with way too much angst and burden to be carried on his thin shoulders. The man he'd grown into was so very different. He tried to portray himself as not having a care in the world.

I knew differently. Probably always had.

After removing my hand, I drew it to my mouth and sucked.

"I'm going to get hard all over again." He rubbed his soft cock against mine.

"Speak for yourself. Refractory periods are a thing for us *old* people."

He smacked me—gently—upside the head. "You're not old."

"I'm older than you."

After holding my gaze for a long moment, he reached over to snag a couple of tissues. "Too bad you don't have the wet ones."

I did...but outside and no way was I going outside to get them. I wiped my hands and tossed the used tissue on the corner. Then I shivered. "Older, but clearly not wiser."

He chuckled. "You turn out the light, and I'll get the sleeping bag. I like how you set it up like a bed. Almost like you were expecting me."

This time, I chuckled. "Well, I don't like being confined. I'm a restless sleeper."

"Yeah. That reminds me..." He rifled through the clothes until he came up with his phone.

"What are you doing?" I wasn't worried...more curious.

"Setting an alarm. Thornton likes to get up early. I'm hoping he'll be exhausted after his extended sex session in the shower."

"Extended?"

"Well, he and Ed used up about all the hot water." He chuckled. "I had fun teasing them because that's what a best friend's for."

Which came as a bit of a relief. I hoped fervently that whatever fallout there had been from the video, they'd moved past it. I wanted to ask what that meant for his relationship with his best friend, but I also didn't want to open that wound if it was already healed.

He cuddled in against me. "Do we...you know...?"

"You know what?" I could play dense when I wanted to.

"Like...sleep...?"

"You set an alarm."

"For buttfuck early in the morning. Like crack-of-dawn shit."

"Because of Thornton."

"And sometimes Ed. I might be able to pass off that I went for an early morning walk or some shit...but I'd be wearing the same clothes. I'm far too clean-obsessed for that." He snorted.

"What?"

"Ed would laugh his ass off if he heard me say that. My room is always such a mess. But we have a cleaning service, right? Pauletta insists on that. Well, they should have something to clean..."

This time, I snorted. "That's one approach, for sure. So disorganized or dirty?" Right, because this was the most important part of our postcoital discussion.

"Disorganized. Messy. Ed says..."

"Says," I prompted.

"That I can't smell my own funk?"

No missing the wince in his voice.

"You smell just fine to me. And I'm not like that. Human smells don't bother me. Unless, like, you don't bathe for months on end. Remember, I teach high school. Some kids don't know to use deodorant. Some just can't afford it. I work with what they bring into the classroom." *Speaking of...*

"Tactful." He snuggled into me as I still lay on my back.

Speaking of...

"So..." I stretched then secured my arm around his shoulder.

"Yeah?" He tucked his head into the crook of my arm. With his hand, he started to play with my chest hair. He'd yet to see it in full light. The hair was much darker than on my head. Nearly light brown. When I was younger, I'd wished my hair was that color instead of the brilliant auburn. That might've also been because Gavin once made a comment about wishing I didn't stand out so much.

Douchebag.

I cleared my throat. "I wanted to talk to you about those songs you wrote."

"Seriously? I thought we went over this." He let out a breath of air that ghosted over my nipples.

I angled the open sleeping bag so it covered the shoulder he wasn't resting his head on. The night air had grown colder, especially against my rapidly cooling skin. "We did...just..." I swallowed. "They were really good songs. Do you remember how you used to bring lyrics, and we'd compose together? And how sometimes you'd bring a melody already in your mind?"

"Ed was there too."

"I know...but his stuff had a much harder edge. I'm talking about the ballads you used to bring." I shrugged. "A lot of teenage angst. So good."

"They were lovesick teenage garbage." He shivered.

Assuming he was getting cold, I pulled the sleeping bag over him. I couldn't tolerate having something over my face when I slept. Gavin preferred burrowing under the covers and not having any cold air touch his nose.

Seriously? That's what you're obsessing about? Get back on track! "I...still have all those songs."

His breath caught. "You're fucking kidding me. Tell me you're fucking kidding me. Fuck no, Hugo. Hell fucking no."

"Uh..." I was leaving many sentences unfinished tonight. I hadn't been certain how he'd react. If his newly rigid body posture was any indication, I'd have to say not happy.

"Well, burn them. Burn the whole lot of them. You have a house, right? With a fire pit? Or you can go out to Buntzen Lake and find a fire pit. Oh, or you could shred them. You're a teacher. You must have access to an industrial shredder. Down to confetti-sized pieces."

I waited patiently until he appeared to have run out of steam. "Axel, they're lovely songs. You were so talented—even back then. Why do you think I kept them?"

"Because you always were too sentimental for your own good."

That might've hurt...except those songs had been entirely senti-mental, so probably some of the insults were projection.

"You know..." He cleared his throat. "My rep would take a dive if people saw them and thought I wrote them."

"Pauletta?"

"Yeah."

"Well, she seems like a very practical woman. She must've seen your potential, even back almost ten years ago. Those songs were in you at the time—"

"Why'd you keep them? Seriously. You can't possibly have kept all the songs from all your kids. Your house would be full of paper. A fucking fire hazard.

He wasn't wrong. I hadn't kept ninety-nine percent of my students' work. Axel had been different. *If you'd only known how much.* "Because you were one of the most talented kids I ever taught. I kept them around to remind myself of what I could nurture. That I could bring that out of you." *And because my fucking ex thought they were trash. More fool him.* "I watched you rise—"

"Okay, now you're just embarrassing me. Please stop."

At his request, I did stop. If only to regroup and reconsider my words. "No. Don't be embarrassed. I love those songs. I mess with them sometimes. Writing more composition into them.

He groaned. "Oh God, I don't know how much more of this I can take."

"Do you remember "You Saved Me"?"

Chapter Eleven

Axel

*O**h Christ.*

I cleared my throat. "Not really."

His hand, wrapped around my shoulder, tightened. "I would never call you out for lying—"

"But I'm lying."

"Yeah, that's the vibe I'm getting. I just can't figure out why."

Because I wrote that song for you? About how you saved me? About how if I could just keep you in my life that everything would be okay?

He pressed a kiss to the top of my head. "Axel, that's one of the best songs any of my students have ever written. I'll be honest...I love it."

"Never tell anyone about it." *Please. Like fucking never, ever, ever.*

"I..." Another one of his infuriating pauses. "I want to know why you don't write more of the band's songs. I mean, Ed's fantastic, but

I can tell you're not the one coming up with them for the most part. Your style is more lyrical. More poetic."

"Hey, we do poetic." I scrambled for something to say in the face of something so deeply personal.

"Ed's style is hard-hitting lyrics with a solid beat. But "Sunrise"..." He stroked his hand up and down my biceps. "Was that you?"

"Both of us." *There, I admitted it.* But I wouldn't tell him the song was about Kyesha. I'd never share that part of the pain layered into lyrics that had come from my heart. From my soul. "Please stop, Hugo. This isn't helping."

"Oh." The words came out as surprised. "I just...wanted to talk to you about something, and this sort of...meanders into it."

I rolled my eyes, even though he couldn't see. "Okay, so what is it you want to talk about? My lyrical lyrics? The music I rarely compose these days because Ed's so freaking good at it? How I don't mind the harder-hitting sound because that's what sells?"

"Is that true?"

His question had me pausing. "Well, "Calling for Help" sold well. But the proceeds were all donated to a charity for kids needing help."

"I'd read that. Incredibly generous."

"A good tax write-off," I countered.

"Axel."

"Yes?"

"That flippant answer's not what I'd expect from you. I think you can do better than that."

I felt my cheeks heat. With my dark skin, others could rarely see me blush. As my chin rested against his shoulder, though, I worried at just how hot I was going to get. "Fine. Yes, we're good people. Responsible citizens. Worried about our younger fans and making sure help is there if they reach out for it."

"Was that so hard?"

"You have no idea." I might've mumbled that under my breath.

"Did you say something?"

Oh God, in that authoritative voice that I love so much. I liked being bossed around—as Ed figured out years ago. Only I rarely listened. My ADHD craved calm, chaos, and anarchy all at the same time and in equal measure. Possibly why the diagnosis had been so challenging. "I didn't say anything." See? I could be reasonable.

"That came across as somewhat disrespectful."

I pushed away from him a fraction. Looking toward his face didn't help because we were shrouded in virtual darkness. "Are you reprimanding me?"

"Ouch. Uh, no."

"Because that's kind of sexy—"

"Seriously?" He spat out the question. "Because authoritative has never been my style."

I laughed. "No, I remember you being quite egalitarian. Sometimes your students tried to walk all over you."

"But they didn't."

"Uh, okay, if you say so." I might've considered taking advantage of his kindness once or twice. But I never had. Because, deep down, I knew he had my best interests at heart. He earned my respect. And Ed's—which was even harder to secure. But now? In this moment? Pushing boundaries was proving fun. "You think you might want to be bossy?"

"Axel."

"What?" He wouldn't be able to see my attempt at innocence...but he'd likely get the gist of it.

"Can we be serious?"

"Of course." I attempted to put on my serious face. Knowing he couldn't see me, though, I broke into a broad grin. I was in Hugo Threadgold's arms. Only a dream of mine since I'd been a teenager. I'd known then it would've been wrong. But how could I have known it would turn out so right?

"I have a question."

"I kind of figured that." I chuckled. "I was trying to see how far I could get you off course before you gave up."

"Did it ever occur to you this might be important? Or at least to me?"

That thought had me sobering. No, it hadn't occurred to me. I thought we were playing games. Well, somewhat seriously. But if we got too intense, his chivalry—his need to do the right thing—might drive him to send me away forever. I'd only just found him. I wasn't willing to give him up. "Okay...this is me being serious. What is it that you want to ask?"

He took a deep breath, his chest expanding under my hand, which lay on his sternum. "Those songs—"

"The ones you kept."

"Yes."

"Okay..." In no way could this be going to a good place. But I'd wait to see where he was going.

"I'm wondering if I can publish them? You obviously hold the copyright—"

"Okay, first. No. Hell no. Absolutely not. Second, I'm not certain I would hold the copyright. Doesn't the school or something—"

"Even if they did, which I don't believe they do, I wouldn't consider publishing a student's work without them receiving whatever compensation might be available." He laid his hand over mine. "Hear me out."

"Ugh."

"Axel?"

"Yes." I let out the word on an exasperated sigh. "I said I'd listen. I'm listening."

"Okay." He shifted a bit.

"You all right?"

"Yes."

I decided not to argue. We were on a decent air mattress, but this was still camping pretty rough. I never camped. Not even glamping. We either took the tour bus or we didn't leave the city.

"My students would love those songs, Axel. They're softer than what you're known for, but they're no less powerful. And...I might even have a couple of students in mind to record them. The proceeds could be split with you. Or go to the school or another charity or whatever you want." He word vomited out everything in a torrent. Like if he said it all super quick, I might not blow a gasket.

Calm down. Just because you think it's the most stupid fucking idea ever, doesn't mean you don't owe him respect when you shut this down. "The answer's *no*, Hugo. I told you to burn them. I'd really appreciate if you did."

"Just like that?"

"Yeah, just like that."

"Oh."

Just how much disappointment can you put into that one word? He probably wasn't trying to make me feel guilty...but he was. *How do I get tonight back on track?*

The answer that presented itself was so simple and yet so complex at the same time.

Slowly, I eased my hand from his sternum to his abs and lower still. I liked that he wasn't ripped. That was Ed. And guys who felt looks were important. Hugo put his students first—that appealed far more. Even as I had the flitting thought, I continued my trajectory.

"Axel."

Which I read as part admonishment and part plea.

Down his happy trail I went, through his pubes, and to his soft cock.

The cock that leapt to life in my hand.

I chuckled. "Refractory period has passed."

"Oh, yeah." He thrust his shaft against my hand.

Encircling him was easy. Reveling as he grew in my hand was easy. Fighting my growing feelings from him wasn't so easy. "Can I blow you again?"

"I suppose." The grin in his voice rang through the small tent. "But I'd rather blow you."

I'd been the recipient of plenty of blow jobs in my time. Anticipation had never been so great as it was in that moment in a little tent in Black Rock at Rocktoberfest 2023. I wasn't Axel the rockstar. I wasn't Axel the band member. I was Axel the man. The man who very badly wanted to be blown by the person resting against me. I gave his cock an experimental tug. "I suppose."

He chuckled.

"But then I get to wank you off or something like that."

"Deal." He shuffled a bit. "You lie on your back.

"Okay...but I don't want to get cold." I might've whined that.

Slowly, he kissed his way down my body. He stopped only to whisper, "I'll keep you warm. I'll always keep you warm." Then he took my cock in his mouth. My mind, which had stuttered on the *always* fell into chaos as he sucked me deep, swirling his tongue around my shaft. "Oh man, that feels so good." I might've hissed the *so*.

"Mmm." He hummed around me as he continued to suck.

Electricity shot through my veins as I struggled to calm my racing thoughts. I'd thought blowing him was the best thing ever. That it'd drawn us closer together. Increased our intimacy. And that was true. So was the fact I was ready to come after just a few minutes of his intense ministrations.

When he cupped my balls, and slowly worked them in his dexterous fingers, my mind blanked out with white-hot pleasure.

"I'm coming."

"Hmm." He sucked harder, even using a bit of teeth.

I came. Hard. Fast. Spectacularly. Like I'd never come before. Which made no sense because a blow job was a blow job.

Right?

Except being blown by a guy who obviously knew what he was doing. Had experience. Knew what would make his partner feel good.

My harsh breathing filled the silence

Eventually, when he'd sucked every last ounce of cum out of me, Hugo pulled off with a little *pop*.

I couldn't help myself. I laughed.

"Don't know if it's a good thing that I'm being laughed at. First blow job I've given in a very long time. I'd like to think I'm still good at it."

I continued to laugh. "It was awesome. What about you?"

"What about me?"

Gently, I nudged my knee to rub up against his very interested cock.

"Oh."

"Yeah. Oh. So what're you going to do? Can I give you a hand job or...Oh."

"Oh what? I feel like we should pay a fine for every time we abuse that vowel."

It took me a good fifteen seconds to figure out what the fuck he was talking about. "Okay, that's cute. I meant…" I swallowed hard. "I've always wanted a guy to come on me. I mean, it would be better to see it but—"

The sound of flesh slapping flesh had my mind fixating on an image of him working his cock into a fury.

He moaned.

Moments later, hot cum hit my belly. My chest. Even a bit on my face.

Couldn't blame the guy—he didn't have a light.

This time, his harsh breaths filled the tent.

I laughed. "We definitely are going to need more tissues."

Slowly, he crawled up my body. Then he proceeded to lick as much cum as he could locate which led to some more epic kisses and more caresses, touches, and general getting into mischief.

Time spun out and had little meaning. Eventually he did clean us up—as best he could—and we crawled under the covers together. Even though I was the taller of the two of us, he spooned me.

I fell asleep with my mind alternating between reveling in the best night of my life and dreading what would come tomorrow.

My alarm woke me at the butt crack of dawn, but I discovered I was alone. I was expecting multiple texts from Ed, and maybe the others, but I found my phone blissfully clear of clutter. Well, except the notifications of all the positive reviews of our performance. Much to my irritation, Pauletta handled our social media. I was allowed to send her stuff I wanted to post, but she vetted and vetoed everything before sending it out. Probably for the best, given my lack of judgement and impulse control sometimes, but also fucking irritating. I wanted to be as close to my fans as possible.

She wanted to ensure proper space existed.

Fuck, where's Hugo?

I gotta piss.

Huh. At least I'd had those thoughts in the correct order. In the semi-darkness, I managed to locate my jeans, T-shirt, and shoes. Had I worn socks yesterday? I couldn't remember. *Doesn't fucking matter. Focus.* I snagged my phone, gave myself a quick pass to ensure I hadn't forgotten anything, then I headed out of the tent. I carefully secured it, then tried to orient myself as to where the johns were. Once I arrived, I was thrilled to find no line. I pissed, washed my hands, then stood for a moment.

Where the hell is Hugo? I guess I'd sort of figured I'd run into him at the johns. Was I supposed to go back to the tent and wait for him? Sneak back to my bus? Was this his way of kissing me off without actually having to do the dirty work?

Even as that thought invaded, I caught his voice coming from off to the side. I crept closer, super-curious who he was talking to at this unearthly hour of the morning.

"Fuck off, Merkerson."

Okay, shock enough Hugo was speaking to someone at this insane hour. But swearing? Telling someone off? Color me super surprised. My mind raced at the name. Hugo's ex was Gavin. Merkerson.... Merkerson... Mentally, I snapped my finger. He was the guy who'd recently been named principal of our old high school. Big fanfare because the guy used to head up some fancy prep school. Like, he should be lauded for taking a *demotion* to come work at an inner-city school. A school that was, admittedly, not doing great. But that, at least to me on the outside, seemed like a funding issue. Not a management issue. Ms. Kenall had been an amazing woman—principal there for my entire time as well as before and after. The school had a big celebration on her retirement. Ed and I would've gone, but we'd had a gig that night and that, as always, meant more.

"I said, fuck off." A big sigh.

Why was the principal talking to Hugo on a Saturday morning? Before dawn no less? Vancouver was the same time as us. If I could barely see the sliver of sun, it certainly wasn't cresting the sky back home either.

"I know you told me to track him down and get on my knees and blow him until he agrees, but I'm telling you now, Axel Townsend isn't going to do what you want. You need to find some other way to talk to him." He let out another exasperated sigh. "I'm telling you—it's not happening."

Finally, I understood what the expression *rooted to the spot* meant. I couldn't move. By all rights, I should've been able to. Just turn and head back to the bus. Climb into my bunk and pretend the last eight hours hadn't happened. Wake up with everyone else. Have coffee and breakfast and pretend like last night had been the best of my life.

Only they'd think I mean the show and I'd think of the stolen few hours in Hugo's tent. But all that was gone. The happiness. The warmth. Even the streaks of magenta and purple across the stunning sunrise—making the clouds turn a pink-silver—couldn't warm my insides. Didn't help I was only wearing a T-shirt, and we were nearing the end of October. Even in the desert, the nights could be frigid.

Still, I waited for his next words.

"Look, I know you suggested I get on my knees—"

Involuntarily, a gasp escaped me. I hadn't meant to. I'd just planned... To what? Run away? Pretend like none of this had ever happened? Block out the most amazing night of my life?

Hugo spun. "I have to go." He stabbed at his phone. Slowly, he advanced toward me. "I don't know what you think you heard—"

"What I think I heard?" I whispered that because not only were there tents nearby, but a couple of people milled about. Whether early risers to catch the now-stunning sunrise or stragglers who hadn't gone to bed yet, I wasn't certain. I slashed my hand through the air. "Well, you certainly performed well for your teaching position. Just imagine if you'd done it earlier?" I slashed my hand, trying to erase what I'd seen. What I'd heard. "I've heard enough. I'm outta here." I spun and headed back in the direction of the buses. Fortunately, I'd oriented myself on the way to the johns. I was able to stride back to safety quickly.

Hugo's heavy footsteps followed me. "Axel."

He might've hissed that. *At least he has the sense not to yell.* Right. Because causing a scene would be the worst part of this entire situation. I snorted. "Fuck off, Hugo." I made a beeline for the perimeter of the band buses.

"Axel." He seized me by the arm and spun me around. For an older—and shorter guy—he sure had strength. "We need to talk—"

I shook him off. "Yeah, like that's going to fix anything." I glared down at him. "I don't need to hear anymore."

"You don't understand—"

"Yeah, I always was the dumbest one in the class. So slow to figure everything out." I knew that wasn't true...but it'd felt true enough in school. Especially because I hadn't realized that not only was Mr. Threadgold gay, but that he'd been married.

To Douchebag.

"Is this man bothering you?" A security guard stepped out from between two buses. I'd waved to him when we'd arrived. Because that was the kind of guy I was. "Uh—"

The guy grabbed his radio.

Hugo backed away and held up his hands. "I'll go. No trouble here, okay. I'll go." He met my gaze. "One day, you'll let me explain. You'll listen."

"That sounds distinctly like a threat."

"No...just a promise." He blinked a couple of times. Then he turned and strode away, his red hair shining in the brilliant-pink light of the most-stunning sunrise I'd ever seen.

Even better than the song I'd written by the same name.

Chapter Twelve

Hugo

I knew I wasn't supposed to call myself stupid. That if my students did that, I'd gently explain that putting oneself—or one's classmate—down like that was bad for morale and for self-worth. Instead, one should strive to find the positive things and believe in oneself.

What a crock of shit.

I replayed the conversation with Principal Merkerson in my mind. The asshole. See? Sometimes saying something mean was completely legitimate. Like when Axel said Gavin was a douchebag.

"Have you talked to him yet?"

"No."

"I gave you the time off work, knowing you wanted to go to Rocktoberfest, so that you could talk to him."

"I didn't even know if he would recognize me."

"Bullshit."

"*Look, it's barely six-thirty. It's still dark here. This couldn't have waited?*"

"*Just do it! Just talk to him. You can be very persuasive.*"

Probably referring to the time I pled my case for more musical instruments. I shouldn't have had to beg. But I had. For my students. Now he thought I'd beg for Axel's help. "Look, this is a no. Even if I could ask him, which I can't, he's going to say no. He has...other obligations."

"*Go find him and convince him. You can be very convincing...*"

Oh, fuck off. *Well, apparently I had nothing to lose.* "Look, I know you want me to get on my knees—"

A gasp drew my attention away from Merkerson. "I have to go." *I stabbed at my phone. After putting it into my back pocket, I held up my hands and slowly made my way toward Axel.* "I don't know what you think you heard—"

"What I think I heard?" *He whispered the words, hurt writ large across his face.* "Well, you certainly performed well for your teaching position. Just imagine if you had done it earlier?" *He slashed his hand through the air.* "I've heard enough. I'm outta here." *He spun and stomped away.*

Of course, I chased after him.

As I headed back to my tent, I replayed the entire situation over and over again. Surely I could've done things differently. *Like maybe not taking my boss's call?*

Yeah.

That.

By the time I got back to my tent, I was done in. Ready to crawl back into bed and sleep for a month. Except... I groaned inwardly at the thought of all the tissues spread about the space. We'd...certainly made a mess. My sleeping bag and blankets were also likely covered in dried spunk. I considered being clean important, but I wasn't the fastidious neat-freak Gavin had been. Huh. Probably still was.

I'd slept in cum-covered sheets before. Gross, sure. But that's what showers and laundry machines were for—to clean up the mess afterward. Which made me realize I was probably still covered in dried jizz. I grabbed my toiletry kit and a towel and headed to the showers.

A brief and bracing shower later, and I was ready to face my tent.

Or so I told myself.

Until I found Renee and Cope sitting outside the tent, munching away on bagels with peanut butter—my favorite.

And almost enough to send my stomach into revolt.

Renee eyed me. "You look a little green. Too much partying last night?"

"Uh…"

She grinned. "I had to go to the bathroom in the middle of the night."

Oh shit. Oh shit. Oh shit. For reasons I couldn't fathom, that hadn't occurred to me.

"We're not going to ask you who your companion was." Cope eyed his bagel. "Oh, Renee woke me up so we could listen, briefly, to the fun you were having."

"That might've made me frisky." Renee grinned. "But I wanted my beauty sleep."

I winced. "Yeah, sorry about that."

"We're just thinking how awesome it is that you hooked up. Hell, did you bring condoms?"

"Uh…" *Crap. Think faster for fuck's sake.* "We didn't do anything that would've needed a condom." Not that I wouldn't have loved to make love to Axel—to go all the way. But we needed to work up to that. Slow and steady. *Right. He's not even fucking talking to you and you're thinking that one day you might...have sex? Jesus, that's bordering on delusional.* Another word I would never accept my kids using—even in jest.

"Oh ho." Renee giggled. "Well, TMI. Except I'm just so happy—"

"I want to go home." I winced inwardly, but maintained a stone façade. "Can you drive me to the airport in Reno? I can catch a flight back to Vancouver—"

"We'll all go together." Cope glanced at Renee. "We were really here to see Grindstone, and we did. Leaving a day early is no big—"

"I don't want to ruin—"

"What's going on, Hugo? Renee dropped her bagel onto her plate and looked like she was about to stand and, knowing Renee, get into my personal space.

"Never mind."

She handed her plate to Cope and somehow managed to get out of the low-to-the-ground chair gracefully. "Spill."

"I..." Words just wouldn't come. I couldn't share—even with my best friend and her awesome husband—how the best night of my life led to the worst morning ever.

And I'd seen the sunrise over the desert. Which had almost made it worse that I'd remembered Axel's song.

As I share this thought with you

The sun rises, and damn, what a beautiful view

Renee snagged my beard, trimmed though it was, and yanked my face—and therefore my attention—to her. "Hooking up with some rando isn't like you. Mooning over said rando afterward isn't you either."

That knocked me out of my funk. "How many rando hookups do you think I've had in the last ten years and, more importantly, how would you know if I did or did not moon over said mythical creatures?"

Cope snorted. "He's got you there, sweetheart."

"He tells me everything." She met my gaze.

I held it for a moment before looking away.

She let go of my cheeks and took a step back. "Well then."

"It's not..." I met her gaze again. "You don't tell me everything either. We still have some secrets—"

"I'm seven weeks' pregnant."

Cope sucked in a breath.

"What? How?" I wrinkled my nose. "Both dumb questions."

She offered a small smile. "Yeah, maybe. We weren't trying. I swear. We were focused on getting the money together for IVF. And then I peed on a stick."

Cope pushed out of his chair—far less gracefully than Renee—and snagged her around the waist and pulled her into a hug. He met my gaze. "We haven't told anyone. Not our parents or siblings. No one." He enunciated that clearly.

"I..." Again, I couldn't find the words. "Should you have told me?"

Renee kissed Cope's cheek before meeting my gaze. "If I'm going to lose this baby as well, it won't be because I did or did not tell you about the pregnancy. My doctor said everything looks good...but she said that the last two times as well. This is a wait-and-see pregnancy. IVF is off for now, obviously, but that might change if I lose—" Her breath hitched. "Or I might not have the strength to try again."

With all my heart, I wanted to tell her that of course this would be the pregnancy that would take. Of course this baby would be fine. Or course the fates would give her what she so desperately wanted.

But I couldn't do that. I couldn't give her hope when she had every reason to be pessimistic. Plus, she had a psychologist husband.

Doctor heal thyself might be the mantra, but it didn't mean he couldn't support his wife. Except he'd been just as gutted at both miscarriages.

Still, I put on my biggest smile and gently pulled her from Cope's grasp into my arms. "I love you."

"I know. And maybe someday you'll tell me what really happened."

That was a one-hundred percent *hell fucking no*, but she didn't need to know that.

After a long moment, she pulled away. "You know, I'm feeling really tired. If we get on the road within an hour, then we can be to Eugene by nightfall. We could do sightseeing in Portland tomorrow and Monday, and Seattle the next two days after that. We're not due back to school until Thursday."

Wednesday night, Grindstone was playing in Portland. Somehow I'd hoped we could catch the concert and drive all night to get back to Vancouver for school on Thursday. Like we were twenty-year-olds and not hitting our forties full force.

"Portland and Seattle sound amazing." Cope grabbed the plates and started to clear up.

"But Corvus Rising, Queen Anne's Revenge, Maiden Voyage, and Midnight Hunt are playing—we came here to party."

Renee placed a hand on my arm. "I had no idea I'd be pregnant when we booked this trip. I'm not going to pull the *sleeping on a bedroll is bad for my back—*"

"But it kind of is."

"Well, it's not helping my disposition. Anyway, I'm sure we can find a decent motel with two cheap rooms just outside Eugene."

I snagged my phone. "I think we can do better than that. My treat."

Both my friends appeared poised to argue, so I pivoted and headed away, going quite a clip. As soon as I knew I was safely out of grabbing range, I found a nice hotel in Eugene with a number of high ratings and good reviews. I booked two rooms. Even chose them next to each other. And prayed Renee's snoring wouldn't keep me awake through the wall.

Oh well...I brought earplugs.

Chapter Thirteen

Axel

When someone knocked at our door early on Halloween night, Ed's gaze shot to mine. We were nearly a week out from Rocktoberfest, but only a couple of days since his blowout with Thornton. I knew who was at the door—Ed didn't. *Have I done the right thing? For Ed? For Thornton? For me?* And, perhaps most importantly...for Kyesha. "Kids trick-or-treating?"

"They never have before." Ed frowned.

The knock came again.

I popped off the couch. "Cassie said she was working tonight. Maybe she changed her mind." But Cassie wasn't at the door. She'd come over the day we got back from our trip, had discovered I had no interest in having sex with her, and she'd walked out. Had told me to call her when I got my dick on straight.

Whether to my credit or detriment, I hadn't called.

Ed followed me to the door. "I'm not sure—"

I swung the door open and pasted on a smile. "About time, you fucker." I'd known he was coming. Had asked the concierge to let him up whenever he found the courage to show his face. Had I actually believed he'd get his head out of his ass and come?

No.

Had we talked about all the really deep unresolved shit between all of us?

No to that as well.

"May I come in?"

I held the door open and made a gesture welcoming him in. To his credit, Thornton entered tentatively. As if he wasn't certain how our reaction would be to him showing up. I knew how I felt—twisted up inside. I imagined Ed felt the same, but my friend could be unpredictable at times.

"Do you want something to drink, or are you here to dump and run?" Ed asked the question with just the right amount of bite.

I closed the door after Thornton came fully into the room.

"Ginger ale, if you have it."

I snickered. "I just figured you'd been trying to impress him that night." The night we'd all met. "Who the hell drinks that shit?"

"I do."

"Me."

I waved my hand in the air, indicating they both needed their heads examined. Then I snagged Thornton and dragged him into the living room.

Ed could handle pouring two drinks. When he came into the living room, however, he found me sitting on the chair.

Leaving the space on the couch next to Thornton open for him.

You're welcome. I'll be the bigger person here and admit you both need each other. That, despite everything, you should be together. Even if you getting together isn't the best thing for me. Not by a long shot.

Ed handed Thornton the drink...and their fingers touched.

Ha! Still there. No matter what Ed contends.

My friend sat on the couch. But as far away from Thornton as he could manage without it looking like he was avoiding the man he used to fuck.

Said man frowned for a moment, then smiled.

"Why are you here?" Ed again. Always abrupt when stressed.

Thornton tapped a flash drive I hadn't noticed with his index finger. "Rough cut."

Ed caught my gaze. *What the fuck?*

"That was...quick." I took a sip of my cola from the glass bottle.

Thornton gazed back and forth between the two of us. "We haven't got the sound fixed up, or the tracks overlaid. The narration is...rough."

"Yeah, you said." Ed cocked his head. "Do you really think we're buying what you're selling?"

I held up my hand. "Maybe the man deserves a chance? Maybe we should see what he has to say before we judge him?"

"Oh, like he gave us a chance? Like he didn't come into this whole clusterfuck with preconceived notions? About all of us, I might say. He doesn't care how he destroys, just as long as he gets—"

"Ed." I snapped my friend's name.

He shut his mouth.

"Why don't we watch the video and then hash things out?" Thornton's discomfort was so clear that I almost felt bad for the guy.

Almost.

"Fine. We'll watch your video." Oh yeah, Ed was *pissed*.

I leapt out of my chair, snagged the thumb drive, and set to work. Ed could barely figure out which remote to use. The electronics in the house were my domain. When I had everything set up, I returned to the couch. I nudged Thornton so I could sit next to him.

So those two idiots would have to sit closer together.

"Axel." Oh yeah, Ed was *pissed*.

"What?" I could play dumb. "I want to look straight ahead." Which I totally could've done if I swiveled the swiveling chair.

But Thornton might not know that.

And Ed was going to keep his mouth shut.

I pressed play, and the video began.

As the fifty-one-minute video scrolled across the screen, my mind spun. What I was watching was all about us. About Grindstone. Yeah, he touched on my early years with Ed—but the bulk of this was about our journey to Rocktoberfest. And the final shot was of the six of us when Pauletta told us about the contract.

No mention of Kyesha.

When the screen went dark, Thornton snagged the remote from my willing hand and shut the machine down.

None of us spoke.

None of us moved.

Ed cleared his throat.

I rose, snagged the remote back from Thornton, and headed to the entertainment system. I tried to retrieve the flash drive.

"I don't need it back. It's just a rough cut—"

"You didn't mention Kyesha." Which I'd thought was the whole point. Since Ed told me last week that Thornton was Kyesha's older brother, I'd expected vitriol. Okay, well after I got over my shock. Kyesha was Black. Thornton was...the opposite of Black. Turned out she'd been one of six children adopted by their parents—and he was their only natural child. Whatever that meant. Where I expected a confrontation here, though, I got...nothing.

Thorton glanced at Ed before returning his attention to me. "Yeah. I don't think it's finished." His hand rested on Ed's thigh.

I hadn't noticed it before.

Ed didn't remove it. He was as stiff as a board, but he didn't pull away.

"I'd like to do an interview." Thornton's gaze left mine and refocused on Ed. "Both of you." He let out a breath. "I know talking about her brings up bad memories—"

"You have no fucking idea what you're talking about." Ed's lower tone was almost a growl. In fact, I wasn't certain he meant for me to hear them. That was him—protecting me to the last.

"Ed—"

"No, Axel. This isn't up for debate." Again, low and growly.

Fuck this shit. I'd had enough of Ed protecting me. I could respect why he was doing it, but I needed to stand on my own two fucking feet. And take responsibility for my part in Kyesha's death. *Damn the consequences.* I stalked to my room. Then I reached under my mattress and pulled out the photo lab envelope full of pictures. Of Kyesha. My hand shook as I tried to take it in.

I'd known Kyesha died while I was in rehab. What I hadn't known—because I'd been too selfish to ask—was when. She was gone, and it hadn't mattered. Until last week when Ed and I finally—for the first time in almost ten years—actually talked about what happened. And the reason for his omission became clear. Back then, things had gotten bad. Really, really, really bad. I was doing drugs more than music. We all were. And Pauletta was threatening to quit and Ed finally—finally—got me to admit I had a problem. We left Kyesha in

Vancouver while Ed drove me up to Eternal Springs in Hope. Almost three hours away from the city of my birth.

What I hadn't known, because I'd never thought to ask, was what happened next. I checked into rehab and a few weeks later, when Ed could finally come to visit, he told me Kyesha died. Whether because I was so far down the rabbit hole already, or because my psyche couldn't cope, I just nodded and tried to move on with my life.

That critical lack of curiosity, though, came back to bite me last week.

Kyesha died while Ed was taking me to Eternal Springs. She took a pile of money off her credit card, bought drugs, then overdosed in our crappy basement apartment. While I was on my way to salvation, she'd died alone.

With shaky fingers, I thumbed through the photos. They told a story—from the healthy young woman who'd followed us from Portland after our first gig in the States to the drug-addicted thin and sickly woman who died. All there to be seen.

I'd never shown the collection to Ed. I'd simply hidden them away as if I could keep Kyesha's memories at bay as long as I didn't see these.

Steeling myself, I headed to my bedroom door. Ed and Thornton were on the other side—if Ed hadn't forced Thornton to leave. Part of me hoped he had and part of me hoped he hadn't.

In about equal measure.

I stepped into the living room, holding the envelope. "I keep meaning to put these in an album. But...that'd be like an irrevocable act, you know? Like admitting she's never coming back."

"Axel."

Ed's pain was clear—I wasn't the only one being hurt here. He'd loved Kyesha like a brother. He'd grieved her death as well. He and Pauletta had been left to pick up the pieces while I'd been off, ensconced in rehab—with all the time and space in the world to sort out my shit.

"No, Ed." I held out the well-worn envelope to Thornton. "He needs to see."

Thornton took it. His hands trembled. Then he dropped onto the couch.

Ed grabbed me by the arm and shoved me back toward my bedroom.

"You don't have to go." Thornton's voice shook almost as much as his hands.

"Just a few minutes." Ed sighed. "Maybe call us when you're, uh, done?" Then he pushed me into my bedroom and closed the door.

I dropped to my bed as I imagined Thornton looking over the photos. The snap of Kyesha and me together at the PNE. Smiling. Laughing. Happy without a care in the world. He'd find more of those. Some with Ed. Some with Pauletta. Some with different combinations. We photographed everything back then.

And, eventually, he'd come to the last picture. Kyesha in her favorite yellow dress. Only it hung loose. She appeared frail and thin. Hell, she'd *been* frail and thin. Painfully so. She'd smiled for me, that last time. But the spark in her eyes was gone. A few days later, so was she.

Fucking drugs.

She'd died of a meth overdose. Laced with some shit that had killed her. Tainted illegal drugs. That was the cause of death.

It didn't say *Axel Townsend as well*. She'd been doing drugs before she'd come north with us, but not to the same degree. She sank with us. Only we crawled out of that hole, and she never did.

"Are you okay?" Ed nudged me as we sat next to each other on my bed.

"What do you think?" I sighed at the end of the snap. "You were wrong not to tell me, and I was wrong not to ask, and it's wrong we're here and she's dead."

"And yet we can change none of those facts."

"You think I don't fucking know it?"

"Yeah..."

I thought he might reach out to touch me, and I also thought that might send me right over the edge. I'd enabled Thornton to show up. So he and Ed could sort out...whatever this was...before things became irreparable. Which, I guessed, meant I wanted them to work it out.

Huh.

I could've kept Thornton out of our lives—at least for a time—but I'd let him in. He wanted to do final interviews. Obviously to discuss Kyesha. Would he just want to talk to me or would he talk to Pauletta and Ed as well? If he hadn't known before, the photos would've confirmed that Kyesha had been my girlfriend. Ed cared about her, but he hadn't seen her as anything but a potential future sister-in-law.

Huh.

Maybe that was a step too far. We'd been so young. Just because I'd considered proposing, didn't mean Ed had thought that was in the cards. As close as we were, we didn't share all our secrets. I'd been under the distinct impression he thought Kyesha was a bad influence on me. He hadn't been wrong—doing the harder drugs had been her idea.

I startled at the knock on my door, but was up before Ed could move. I met his gaze, though, and received a nod from him before I opened the door.

"May I come in?"

Discomfort radiated off Thornton.

Ed pushed off the bed, turned me toward the door, and shoved me out.

"Hey."

"Right, like I'm going to let him hang around in your room." He winced.

The room *didn't* stink. Probably because Ed had opened the window for some fresh air. My dirty clothes sat everywhere, as the cleaning crew wasn't due for a day or two. I hesitated. Huh...I hadn't realized the room was cold. "Let me close the window."

Nope.

Ed propelled me into the living room. "Let the room breathe."

I huffed. Whatever that meant.

Thornton smiled. "God, you two really are like brothers."

I eyed Ed. Yeah, we fought—and loved—like siblings should. He was the brother I never had.

After a long moment, Thornton held out the envelope.

I took it.

"I'd love to get copies of those photos."

His words shouldn't have surprised me—but they did. I found comfort and pain in equal measures in these pictures...maybe it was the same for him?

"Yeah. I've got them on a CD. I can get it burned for you or—"

"Yeah, that'd be great." Thornton met my gaze. "Thank you." He scratched his chin. "I would still like to interview you." After holding my notice for a moment, he slid his attention to Ed. "Both of you."

"You might not like what we have to say."

Jesus, Ed, seriously? What're you doing? Poking the fucking bear? The man who holds our careers in his hands? Because if Thornton spun this the wrong way, it might be the end of our dreams.

The end of Grindstone.

"We can keep it light—" I had to try.

Thornton held up his hand to cut me off.

"I'm okay with the truth." He ran his hand through his hair. "You're going to tell me the hard truths. But..." He swallowed. "She was this vivacious person. Yet...she always felt a little sad. I wondered if she might have had undiagnosed mild depression. Looking at some of those photos...I just don't know. Was it all drugs and partying?"

Propelled by an impulse I didn't understand—but knew I had to follow—I dropped the envelope on the table and took Thornton's hands in mine. "I'm going to tell you a hard truth right now. Something Ed doesn't know. Something I think would hurt your parents...so I won't repeat it on camera."

Thornton blinked several times, but didn't let go of my hands.

I forged forward. "Your sister loved your family. She talked about them all the time. And she probably mentioned an older brother Thornton—and I probably should've remembered the name. But I've shoved those memories down, you know? As a way of coping.

"Yeah, she called me Tony." His laugh cut deep. "Used to drive me nuts." He cleared his throat. "You were saying...?"

"But she wasn't always happy." I glanced at Ed before returning my attention again to Thornton. We were the same height. "She didn't feel like she belonged anywhere, not in her adoptive family, not outside it. She wanted to know more about her roots. That's part of what she was trying to get from Ed and me."

"I don't—"

"Basically, she hadn't spent a great deal of time around Black people."

Thornton took a step back—undoubtedly from the painful, but necessary blow I'd just delivered. "She never..."

"No, she wouldn't."

This time, when he pulled his hands away, I let them go. Interestingly, we both gazed at Ed as if he could somehow magically fix this situation.

It's up to you. Ed can't bail you out of this mess. "She didn't love you any less."

Thornton's attention returned to me.

"But she needed more than just what she could get from your family. Our music..." I squinted for a moment, then continued. "She said it spoke to her. She leaned so hard into some of the lyrics, trying to hear who she was in the words we wrote. We hardly sing those songs anymore because we associate them with her."

"I wondered why she sometimes seemed so distant..." Thornton took a couple of steps toward the sliding glass door.

We were on the fifty-second floor. With the cold temperatures and the biting wind, it'd be cold enough to freeze my nuts. But I'd go with him...if he needed me to.

"It'll be cold," Ed warned Thornton.

He shrugged.

Ed threw me a look. One I recognized. Whatever happened next was just going to be between the two of them. Ed might or might not bring me up to speed later. But I'd come to the end of my usefulness. I snagged the photo envelope and was about to head back to my room. "I'm not sure what else to say."

Thornton met my gaze. "Sorry."

"Don't be. I'm here when you're ready to talk." I made my way to my space. Just before I closed my door, I heard the sliding glass door open.

In my bedroom, very alone, I headed over to the window and shut it. A nip still permeated the air, and I considered taking a hot shower.

I might've hit the treadmill, but that was in the living room, and I'd just made it clear I was going to give them space.

I snagged my phone out of my back pocket. I slid my clothes to the floor and laid on my bed. Against all rational thought, I scrolled to Hugo's number.

—*I need you.* —

My finger hovered over the send button.

Do it. Send it. You know you want to. You know you need to.

Hugo was a huge gaping gut wound. A simple bandage wasn't going to heal me. I needed stitches and antibiotics and the love I never got from my parents.

But I was going to get neither of those things tonight.

Tidy endings weren't my style anyway.

Or so I told myself as I put the phone on the nightstand. I yanked my comforter over me and went to sleep fully dressed.

Chapter Fourteen

Hugo

"Who shit in your Corn Flakes?"

I glanced down at the bowl of my favorite cereal.

Nope, even Renee's crappy comment wasn't going to deter me from my delicious treat. The one I indulged in when I was feeling sorry for myself.

Which my best friend knew.

"Never mind." I might've said that through a mouthful.

She tossed a piece of crust at me. She never ate her crust.

I snagged it midair, swallowed my mouthful, then popped the crust in as well. I was hungry. And not a good hungry. Not the *I've just run a marathon and lifted weights and swum the ocean* kind of hunger. No, the *I'm hurting emotionally and comfort food will make me feel better*.

Except Corn Flakes every day for two months hadn't moved the needle.

Nothing had.

Renee leaned back after having polished off eggs, toast, tomato slices, and turkey bacon. She placed her hands gently on her rounded abdomen. As if she could somehow keep her womb protected. Especially given what was inside.

Or who.

Or two someones.

Jesus.

Twins.

I still couldn't believe it. The couple who'd struggled with infertility and miscarriages for so long, took a break from everything and...boom!

Twins.

I'd been informed I would be the godfather-slash-honorary uncle, and I better have my diaper-changing skills ready to go.

As an older brother whose younger sister was raised by a nanny, I had no experience with infants. The kids I visited in the cancer unit at the hospital tended to be older. Lots of people visited to keep the young ones entertained. The older kids were sometimes neglected. Some wanted to be just left alone, but others craved intellectual stimulation. Me bringing a couple of guitars and giving impromptu lessons went over well. So when these nieces and/or nephews finally hit their early teens—or even a bit younger—then I was ready.

Diapers terrified me. Not because I couldn't learn, but because I worried I might, like, drop a baby or something. Or, almost worse, say something or do something that would scar them for life. I could handle teenagers for the most part, but fucking up some kid? That would gut me.

Like you did with Axel?

I'd hoped we could continue to talk through things. I'd scrutinized the media, and aside from the announcement of the deal with Grand

Central Records, there hadn't been much in the way of media coverage. Axel had appeared on the arm of an actress at a premiere a couple weeks ago, but either Ed hadn't shown up that night or he hadn't been photographed. If he'd gone with Thornton, I suspected that would've been the story. Were the two men still together? How was Axel coping? Had he shared his bisexuality with anyone? Thornton and Ed had obviously seen the video—which also hadn't surfaced—but had they had an honest conversation with Axel? Was he keeping things bottled up, or was he sharing what happened with people who could help him?

Too many questions, too few answers.

A cloth napkin hit me square on my face and landed in the leftover milk with a plop. "Hey."

"That's what your washing machine is for."

Still, even as Renee said the words, I tried to rescue the napkin before it got wetter. So much for environmentalism—I could've just tossed a paper napkin.

Of course, that was the point.

"Hugo."

At her command, I snapped my attention to her. "Yes?"

"Seriously. We're a week away from Christmas. We're two months past Rocktoberfest. You haven't been the same person since we got back. Hell, you weren't this mopey after your marriage ended."

"Really?" I squinted. "I seem to recall I was pretty bad."

"That's my point." She sighed.

A sigh I recognized well. I was about to be *schooled*. And because I loved her, I would listen.

I sipped my coffee, decided it needed to be reheated, and headed over to the microwave.

"Hugo." That might've come out with more force and a lot of exasperation.

"You know I don't drink cold coffee, and because you can't ingest caffeine, I didn't make a pot." I was so jumpy these days that I tried to limit my intake.

Another sigh. "I miss real coffee."

"Do you want more decaf?"

A third sigh. "I want you to tell me what happened two months ago. I want you to tell me why you're seriously contemplating going to your parents' house for Christmas when Cope and I have extended a perfectly reasonable invitation.

The microwave beeped, and I retrieved my coffee. "It's a generous invitation. But you're hosting your families—at the same time. Yes, this old house is big but..." With Cope working like a dog and Renee having some decent tenure in the school system, they'd managed to buy a ramshackle heritage house. I got the sense their families had kicked in a bit as well. That house screamed two things—children and renovations. My friends were on their way with one and struggling with the other.

Hence my showing up on a Saturday morning prepared to work. "We're ripping up the flooring in the second bathroom, right? Will we be able to get the new flooring in before the family descends?"

"They can use the en suite off the primary bedroom or the guest one down here. I don't imagine more than three people needing to go at once."

"And how many will be here?"

"Twenty-seven."

I winced. Visibly. "Well, that will keep you very busy."

"Cope's dad's running the kitchen and my mom's got the barbecue out back."

"It's supposed to be near freezing." I'd grown up in Vancouver—I had thin blood. I didn't tolerate cold.

Renee waved me off. "The colder the better. You forget Mom comes from Fort St. John. Anything above freezing is balmy to her."

Yeah, I remembered. I didn't understand the insanity of living in Canada's north. Or the north of any of the countries that buttressed the north pole. I didn't want Mexico's heat...but I didn't mind the occasional visit to Cancun.

But that had been during my marriage. These days I paid the mortgage, and that was about it. I didn't want—nor could I afford—big trips. I'd become a homebody.

Much to my parents' chagrin.

"So you're coming for Christmas?"

I blinked. "We were discussing ripping up warped vinyl floors."

She wagged her finger at me. "We were discussing why you're moping."

Fucking hell.

Suddenly, like a balloon whose air had just been released, I gave up the fight. I plopped down in my chair, pushed my cereal bowl back, placed the coffee on the table, and cupped it with my hands. Seeking warmth. Seeking strength. "I fucked up."

I expected a flippant response, but Renee held my gaze when I glanced up.

Then said nothing until I felt compelled to fill the silence.

A trick she undoubtedly learned from Cope.

"I met someone."

Her expression didn't change. Somewhere between neutral and *yeah, fuckwit, tell me something I didn't know.*

"And...he overheard something—"

She sat straighter.

I winced. "Merkerson called. At six-thirty in the fucking morning. I mean, I was on vacation—"

She held up her hand. "Why was Merkerson calling you while you were at Rocktoberfest?" Her eyes narrowed. "I can guess...but I'd prefer to hear from you."

Which I'd do...because I loved her. I sighed.

Her eyebrow shot up.

Yeah, I can sigh too. "So he called because he was checking up. He gave me the time off to see the concert because he assumed I would have an *in* with Ed and Axel. Former students and all that."

She rolled her hand, gesturing me to get to the good part.

"But I didn't have an *in*. I couldn't very well ask them to come back to the school to give a charity concert. Something that would undoubtedly elevate Merkerson."

"Undoubtedly." She might've groused that.

"And I know the school—and specifically the music program—really needs money. But Ed already volunteers with kids in the neighborhood. He must be aware more money's needed. The thing is, it's not up to him to fix our problems. Government needs to step up and do more. We pay taxes—more of that should go into the schools."

"Hugo." Said softly.

"I know." I sighed. "Opioid crisis. Homelessness crisis. Crime crisis. Crumbling infrastructure crisis. Climate change adaptation crisis." I pounded my fist on the table. "Yet, somehow, the kids always get left to the bottom of the heap. They don't vote, so they don't matter."

"That might be a touch cynical. Their parents vote."

"Their parents have a million other things to content with. You know this—if the kid's coming to my school, then the parents is likely working two or three jobs just to keep a crappy roof over their head. Or they're on social assistance. Or disability. The point is, very few people send their kids to a crumbling school on purpose. I mean, they retrofitted us for a possible earthquake but didn't fix the carpets, walls, or ceiling tiles. The school's falling apart, and we're not even on the plan to get a replacement." I wasn't telling Renee anything she didn't already know.

She worked for a prestigious private school on the west side.

I worked on the downtown eastside.

Two different worlds.

Which was why I couldn't just demand Axel and Ed come back to show generosity. Hell, I didn't know what kind of money they were making. An evening's show might not be a big deal or it might be a huge undertaking they couldn't afford. Regardless, the decision was theirs to make—and not mine to ask.

Renee narrowed her eyes. "So who the fuck overheard? The guy in your tent?"

"Well...yeah..."

Wait for it...

"Holy fucking shit." She grinned. "Ed? Because I've always gotten a bi vibe from him. And, oh my God, he's so hot. I like shorter guys—"

"Cope's—"

She waved me off. "So Ed. Those dreadlocks. Those soulful—"

"Not Ed."

That stopped her. "I don't think Big Mac's gay or bi. I mean—"

"Why did you skip over Axel?" I was going to tell her anyway, but I was curious why she didn't go for, what seemed to me, the most obvious.

"Well...he was your student."

"So was Ed." God, she'd been there, for Christ's sake. Had gotten an earful from me as I lamented the end of my disastrous marriage.

"Well, sure." She rubbed her belly. "They were both your students. But...Axel was special. You nurtured him even more than Ed. You composed those songs with him. You..." She hesitated. "I thought you saw yourself as a father figure to him."

Ed's father had long taken off, and Axel's father had been mostly absent. Both boys had been in need of guidance. And I'd stepped gingerly into that role. I hadn't been teaching that long myself and to wind up in such a difficult role...it tested all my abilities.

I sighed. *Another fucking sigh.* "I saw myself as a father figure to both boys—and I'm not sure that was appropriate."

"You took care of them. You nurtured their talent. And look where they are now. Other students have wound up in bands, orchestras, and singing in musical theater productions. You've had a hell of a lot of successful students—especially given what you had to work with."

"I know." I closed my eyes. "But you're right—it's a line I never should've crossed with Axel." Maybe that was as much of what the self-flagellation was about. Not just that he'd overheard my conversation—and taken everything out of context—but that we shouldn't have been in my tent at all. Hand jobs, blow jobs, kissing. So much kissing—

"Yo, Threadgold, pay attention."

I snapped my gaze back to hers.

"How old is he now? Twenty-seven?"

"He turned twenty-eight in September."

"Okay, so a bit beyond being a minor. Now, I'm going to ask a tough question and you better fucking be honest with me. I can always tell when you're lying to me. That's why the last two months have been so shitty."

She could tell.

And they had been shitty.

"Yeah?"

"Did you have an inappropriate relationship with him ten years ago?"

"No." The answer burst forth from me with vehemence.

"Did you think of him in that way ten years ago?"

"Fuck, no."

"When did things change?"

I drew in a sharp breath. I couldn't argue they hadn't...because obviously they had. Could I pin down a moment? Some time when I stopped seeing him as a young kid and instead a man?

"Their fifth album, I think. The one that came out last year. He did that video..."

Renee snorted. Yeah, she knew the one I was talking about.

The slick bare chest. The black leather pants with the top button undone and just a hint of what was to come. His smooth voice belting out love lyrics. About falling for the right person. About how love came on unexpectedly, but hit hard. The band hadn't played that song at Rocktoberfest, but they totally could have. One of their more popular tunes. One I'd played over and over again. "Not until recently and, frankly, not fully until he kissed me."

She sat up straighter. "Okay, this you have share."

"What does he have to share?" Cope stepped into the kitchen which was situated at the back of the house. He finger-combed his hair as he approached. "That snow's really coming down." He pressed a kiss to Renee's cheek.

Her squeal brought a smile to my lips.

"He's cold," she protested.

"Uh-huh."

Cope pressed a hand to her baby bump. So miniscule it could barely be seen. But clearly there. He focused his attention on me. "I got the new flooring in the back of my SUV. I hate to ask—"

"Oh, we definitely need to haul it in so that no one decides to break into your vehicle and steal it." Because, very likely, someone might try. I started to rise.

Renee pointed to my chair. "Don't even think about it."

Cope laughed. Then pointed to my coffee. "You want another one?"

Considering we'd be ripping up vinyl and putting down tiles for the next umpteen hours...? I held out my cup. "Yes, please."

Renee leaned forward. "Great, while he's brewing coffee, you spill the beans."

And so I did.

Chapter Fifteen

Axel

E d examined me as I sat at the breakfast bar in our condo, devouring meat lovers pizza. His own Greek vegetarian sat untouched. "What?"

He tapped the counter as he stood in the kitchen, facing me. "Janessa said a package arrived for you, and you sent it back."

"Janessa has a big mouth." She was also my favorite concierge. Or had been. "She's just mad because she had a big old crush on you, and you're obviously taken...even if you two haven't come out publicly." I returned Ed's examination. "It's been more than two months. He's spending as much time up here as in Portland. Why don't you, you know, make it official?"

"First, what does *make it official* even mean? Appear together in public? We do that all the time."

"Sure." I scratched my crotch through my sweatpants.

He winced.

"But like, not affectionate and all that. No one would know you're a couple."

He selected a black olive off his pizza, popped it in his mouth, then chewed thoughtfully. Finally, he swallowed. "Governments are complicated."

"You want to move to the States?"

"Fuck no." He winced. "And break up our band? Hard no. I believe we can be successful as a Canadian act. We don't need Los Angeles or New York—"

"Or Portland—"

"—or Portland, Seattle, or..." He waved his hand around. "Las Vegas—"

"Oh, oh." I waved my hand right back. "If Caesar's Palace offers us an in-house gig for a year, we're totally taking it."

He snorted. "Okay, now I know you're not taking anything seriously."

"I never do. That's my superpower." I took a big bite of my food and, at the last minute, remembered not to chew with my mouth open. After I swallowed, I took a swig of cola. "Are Big Mac and Meg spending Christmas together? She's got her dog, right?"

Slowly, Ed nodded. "She's now got full custody of Wren. Her asshole ex met some woman who doesn't like dogs—"

"Who doesn't love dogs?"

"—lots of people, and that's not the point. The point is between that and Meg hooking up with Big Mac, her ex finally realized he didn't have a right to keep a claim on her by demanding part-time custody of a dog he didn't love. He might've cared for Wren, but he didn't love her like Meg does."

"Where's the dog going to stay when we go on tour in May?" I bit into the pizza again, loving the tang of the spicy tomato sauce.

"Actually, Songbird's parents expressed interest. They babysat an elderly church member's dog when she was in the hospital, and they discovered they loved having a dog around for a short period of time. They can take care of Wren and give her back without any huge hassle. Songbird's mom is teaching the summer semester at the university, so they couldn't travel anyway."

"So win/win."

"Yes. And you're way, way, way off track."

"I didn't know we had a track." I picked off a slice of peperoni and made a big show of eating it.

Ed winced. A stint in a meat processing plant had put him off all meat consumption forever. Not dick, thank God. Or Thornton would be very disappointed.

"Are you going to Portland for Christmas?" I asked.

"No. Jesus Fucking Christ, Axel. Who was the parcel from? Janessa said a kid dropped it off. Since when do you refuse packages from kids?"

When they're sent by Hugo Threadgold? I'd made the mistake of opening the first one. Jesus, the gob smacking schlock that had dribbled off the page. Apologies I didn't want. An explanation that made no sense. I'd shoved the letter back in the envelope, taped it up—badly—then sent it back to his home address. With a three word note.

LEAVE ME ALONE.

That...hadn't worked. Three more letters and parcels had arrived. I'd sent all three back. "It doesn't matter, Ed. Trust me when I say, you don't want to know. Now, Portland for Christmas or Canada? And what do you mean about governments? If you two marry, doesn't that solve all your problems?"

"It...does not. Things are super complicated, Ed. Family reunification is a thing, and we'd be making a hash of things if we just get married." He closed his eyes. "If he can get a work permit and then..." He gestured for me to *forget about it*.

I made a note to check the website for myself. He was acting like he thought I was stupid again. That just pissed me off. "Again...am I planning a party for one or three?"

"You know, we might spend the holiday—"

I shook my finger at him. "Don't give me that shit. Why are you giving me that shit? Just be fucking honest."

"Who sent the parcel?"

I dropped the pizza to the plate, slid off the stool, picked up the plate, and moved to round the bar and go into the kitchen. Which would've put me in Ed's territory at the moment, but I wasn't going to leave a dish out. Especially with food.

"Hey." Ed snapped.

"I'm sorry, did you say something?" I put a hand to my ear. "I don't think I heard you."

"Canada." He scrunched his face. "Thornton's family said they're cool with it. He's going to spend New Year's Eve with them. He'll stay for a few days and then come back early January."

I slid back onto my stool. "So three or are we inviting everyone? Isn't Meg going to Big Mac's family? They're in Alberta, right?" I winced. "Are they conservatives?"

"Nope." Ed pulled an onion off his pizza.

Gross. Why doesn't he just eat it in one piece? What's going on?

"Nope they're not in Alberta, or nope they're not conservatives? Or both?"

Ed ate the onion, then appeared to contemplate his pizza. "They are in Alberta, they live in Edmonton, and generally support the New

Democrat Party, and I know you weren't going to suggest that they might have a problem with Meg's heritage."

"Uh..." *Shit*. "I just...she faces a lot of racism—which is total bullshit—and I'd feel really bad if she got it from his family." I considered. "So if she was facing that—"

"She's not."

"—but if she was," I pressed on, "Then we could insist she have to come here."

"Are you suggesting Meg needs us to protect her? That she can't hold her own?"

"Oh crap."

He laughed. "I wondered how long you were going to need before you realized what you'd done. Meg doesn't need us defending her. Yes, people discriminate against her for her Indigenous heritage. People treat us differently because we're Black."

"Oh dear..."

"Yeah. You wouldn't want Meg interfering on your behalf. You can fight your own battles. And you shouldn't have to. It fucking pisses me off that we still have to." He picked a chunk of feta off the pizza. "I was hoping if we did the documentary that people would just see us as like everyone else."

"We're rockstars, Ed. The fact Thornton's making a documentary about us kind of precludes us being like everyone else." I'd waited until he'd taken a full bite of pizza before delivering that retort.

He glared.

I shoveled in the rest of my pizza and chomped away at it. We'd eaten too much of the stuff lately, but he was always out with Thornton and...I didn't cook. Especially not for one person.

"Pauletta's bringing Mickey home to meet her parents." Ed managed to swallow first.

Apparently we were changing the subject.

"How's that going to go over? Mickey's..." I considered. Mickey was the director of the documentary. They were also non-binary and plenty of fun. Two things I wasn't certain Mrs. Magnum would appreciate. She'd been...downright hostile...to Pauletta's first girlfriend.

"Paulie's dad insisted. Apparently he's had a *chat* with her mom. Maybe he realizes how serious they are about each other."

"Yeah, they are that. For sure." I snagged my plate, then slid off my chair again.

"You're not having another slice?" He gestured toward the boxes.

"I don't feel like an interrogation. Big Mac and Meg are headed to cowboy country. Pauletta and Mickey are headed to the swanky West Vancouver. Songbird's going to be with her parents—and undoubtedly playing piano at their church—"

"Undoubtedly."

"So it's just you, me, and Thornton." I eyed my plate. "Fun."

"Is there someone you want to invite? Because we'd be happy to make it four—"

"No." I might've snapped that.

"We never talk about things anymore, Axel. What's going on? You've been different since we returned from Black Rock."

"Of course I'm different. Thornton is Kyesha's brother. We had to revisit her death. That trauma. Of course I'm different. Who wouldn't be?"

Ed reached for my plate.

I handed it to him. My appetite was a long-gone memory.

He put our plates into the dishwasher, wiped down the already clean counters, and turned to me. "Why don't we work on that song?"

"Well..."

Coming out from the kitchen, he hip-checked me. "I think this one will be good enough to release as a solo track. It's angstier than our normal stuff."

I cleared my throat. "I was thinking as an acoustic. Just me and the guitar. Maybe not even a formal release...just on the web."

He stopped short. "Yeah?"

"Like a song to whet their appetites. We've got the album coming out in April. This might...tide them over."

"Huh."

His stare nearly had me losing my nerve. I'd never released a solo song. Everything was always the band or, in the beginning, just Ed and myself.

Never alone.

Yet, in this moment, that was how I felt.

Alone.

Like I was calling out for something and a response wasn't coming.

Maybe because you keep sending back his packages? Ever thought of that?

Ed yanked his phone out from his back pocket. "Let me talk to Pauletta. She might agree to it. As an appetizer with the main course coming in April—"

"Food metaphor? Seriously?" My stomach, known for being rock-hard, just did a backflip. *Can I do this? A song all by myself? Something that's unlike anything I've ever done?* Likely Pauletta would veto the idea—

Ed held up his phone on the text screen. "She says we record in a studio. Full professional sound, even if it's just you and your guitar."

I blinked. *My* guitar? Did he understand how much this meant to me? Why it had to be me alone? I certainly hadn't said something—mostly worried about hurting his feelings. "Just like that?"

He placed his phone on the breakfast bar and pulled me into a hug. "Yeah, just like that."

Absorbing the comfort was easy. This was Ed.

Figuring out how to move on from the heartbreak was an entirely different thing.

Chapter Sixteen

Hugo

Nerves beset me from the moment I stepped into the Stanley Theatre, and they didn't stop. Thornton Graves's documentary about the rise of Grindstone was the reason for the crowd gathered in the theater. I had my own personal reasons, of course. I found my seat in the theater and plopped my butt into it.

I hated my uncomfortable suit. In my previous life, with Gavin, I wore tuxedos regularly. Often, before that, when attending charity functions with my parents. Since the day Gavin walked out, I'd purposefully avoided events that required some kind of formal attire.

A suit jacket is hardly formal attire. And you're not even wearing a tie. Stop whining.

Since the media had descended in full force, and there was an actual red carpet for some guests, I probably should've dressed up a bit more. I was standing on principle though—I wasn't a celebrity or invited guest. Much to my irritation, Merkerson had procured the ticket. Only one, of course.

Renee was on bed rest, but she totally would've given me Cope for a few hours. Her pregnancy was proving more challenging, and after some definitely heated arguments, she'd agreed to take sick leave from her job so she could take care of both herself and the twins. Whose gender I still didn't know. Neither did my friends, apparently. *Surprise us*, had been their attitude.

While secretly admitting to me that two healthy babies was all that really mattered. And gender was, especially to Cope, a continuum. In his practice, he saw a wide variety of clients who identified differently than the narrow construct of the binary.

A hush fell over the crowd, and then wild applause as the first notes of "Sunrise" played through the sound system. Eventually, the screen lit and Axel's face focused into view. "I have made a lot of mistakes in my day. I might not deserve to be forgiven for all of them, but I hope one day I'll find—" He gazed right into the camera. "—redemption."

And thus began a ninety-eight-minute odyssey into the myth and the legend that was Grindstone. Truthfully, I figured I'd known most of their story—having been there for the early, formative years. Their first guitars, their first lessons...and they both mentioned and thanked me.

That made heat rush to my cheeks. Especially when they showed a picture of the three of us. I shrank a little in my seat.

No one around me appeared to notice.

Truthfully, our four years together was just a fraction of a slice of their lives.

I'd known what had come before hadn't been good. I was right on that front. They only touched on it briefly—Ed's mother's suicide and the abuse Axel suffered at the hands of his parents. Parents who completely disavowed their son and, to the best of my knowledge, hadn't come around looking for a payout. Axel wasn't rich—yet—but that time could certainly come.

So many moments—mostly candid moments—caught me off guard.

The drug abuse was a known entity. The extent of it hadn't been reported.

Toiling away in some pretty sleazy venues was known. The struggle to get studio time and the compromises they'd had to make weren't, at least to me, something I'd been made aware of.

Finally, came Kyesha.

Thornton Graves's younger adopted sister.

Clearly, Ed and Axel hadn't been aware of that relationship before they'd embarked on the documentary. Just as evident was that this wasn't the hit piece Thornton had clearly envisioned. Without question, he'd expected to find two arrogant men who never thought of the young woman Thornton had believed—erroneously—whose death they were responsible for.

My heart ached for Axel and Ed as they recounted the painful circumstances surrounding Kyesha's death. A police officer from Vancouver even agreed to be interviewed to confirm Axel and Ed weren't even in the city when she died... and that someone else sold her the toxic drugs that killed her.

Wow. Just...wow.

Interspersed with the pain was the meteoric overnight success that took ten years to come to fruition. Well, more, if I calculated the time they spent with me. Fourteen years of hard work. Twenty-three years of an intense and intimate friendship.

Ed's admission he was bi didn't come as a surprise to me—but clearly it did for some in the audience. He and Thornton had been in pictures together at last week's launch party for the album—but no photographer had caught them in an intimate pose. Something told me, if the body language I'd caught earlier in the lobby was any indication, that was about to change. Oh, and the rings on their fingers. Whether engagement or wedding, I wouldn't speculate.

As the doc ended—with Pauletta letting them know they had a contract to produce an album with Grand Central Records—strains of "Sunrise" came up again. Now, of course, knowing the song was about Kyesha and the profound impact the woman's life—and death—had on Ed and Axel, the poignancy was even more profound.

I might've teared up.

A few sniffles sounded from nearby.

The ending credits rolled, and everyone got to their feet and applauded.

Mickey, the director, took the mic. They smiled at everyone. "Thank you for being part of the last leg of our incredible journey. I want to thank Thornton, Lydia, Kato, and everyone else who worked on the post-production of this film. Most specifically, I wish to thank Grindstone. Their openness with us made them vulnerable, but I also believe it's made us all better people for having watched this. For having been part of their journey." They pointed. "I've asked Thornton to say a few words, but he incorrectly said I'd be better with them." They rolled their eyes. "Drinks and food in the lobby."

More applause and laughter.

A technician took the mic from Mickey and then I noticed them go right up to Pauletta and kiss her.

Okay, so that's interesting. Because Big Mac and Meg were holding hands, the couple introduced as Kato and Lydia—sound and photography—were also close together.

Finally, as I entered the lobby, I spotted Ed tucked into Thornton's side.

Oh God, they're adorable. Complete opposites in looks, but obviously very similar in temperaments. Ed had always been the level-headed one. That trait was clear throughout the documentary. Axel tended to be more of a loose cannon. His impetuousness appeared somewhat curbed for the film. My memories of him sucking my cock assured me some of the spontaneousness from before still lingered.

And now, I had to find him.

A server passed by with a tray of champagne flutes.

When I hesitated, she smiled. "Non-alcoholic is on the table."

Not the reason for my hesitation, but I offered a genuine smile. "Brilliant idea. Thank you kindly."

She nodded, then headed off.

Truthfully, I didn't want a glass in my hand. I had something else I needed to do. Something burning a hole in my pocket that I needed to give to—

I spotted Axel.

He was speaking to two younger women I didn't recognize. He offered them a smile, but he didn't look thrilled to be there. Whether with the women themselves or this entire shindig, I wasn't certain.

Slowly, I approached.

One of the women spotted me and grinned. "The high school music teacher. Not so clean-shaven and short-haired anymore." She indicated my beard and long hair. "I love the sixties vibe."

"More like the lazy vibe."

The two women laughed.

Axel stared.

Okay, super lame. Yet I remembered how his fingers felt as he scratched my beard. How that level of intimacy had—

"Ladies, if you don't mind...I need to speak to Mr. Threadgold." Axel said my name with just the right amount of bite to have me on edge.

"Sure." The woman who'd spotted me grinned. "We can catch up later."

"Yeah." Axel pressed a kiss to her cheek.

The woman pinkened. Then she and her companion moved away.

I slid the CD out from my jacket pocket and attempted to hand it to Axel.

He cocked his head, but made no move to take it.

Distractedly, I noted his hair was much longer than the near buzz cut he'd had in October. Six months felt like a lifetime ago. "Please take it."

"What is it?" His attempt at disinterest failed as I caught the glint of something in his eye. Intrigue?

I could work with that. "These are a few of your old songs. I laid tracks and my students sang them—"

"I told you to burn those songs." He grabbed my arm and dragged me to a corner. Then, as if realized he was touching me, he dropped his grasp like he'd been scalded.

"You didn't mean it." We'd been joking around.

Hadn't we? He'd said something about a bonfire at Buntzen Lake, but I'd interpreted that as his just being silly. Judging by the look on his face—the one I hadn't seen in my tent that night that felt like a million years ago—I'd misjudged.

"You promised me." His voice carried almost a tone of menace.

"No, I didn't." I would've remembered agreeing to that. Mostly because I never would have.

"You..." He scrunched up his face, as if in distaste. "You used me. All those years ago, playing on my feelings—"

"First, I didn't know you had feelings. Second, I didn't use you." I sighed. "I kept those songs because they're meant to be out in the world. Yes, they're not something you might sing now, although "I See You" has shades of that old composition style."

"I will not be derailed." He glared. "Although I'm glad you like the song." Then, as if realizing what he'd said, his face hardened again. "You used me, Hugo. There's no other way to put it."

"No, I honestly didn't. Look…" I ran my hand not holding the CD through my hair. "Just listen to me. What you overheard isn't what you think—"

"Oh, so you didn't track me down on purpose?" He cocked his head with a disconcerting smile on his face.

"Well…actually…" I winced. "I did, but it's not what you think. And what we did has nothing to do with this—"

"It has *everything* to do with that. I trusted you. All those years ago *and* six months ago. You betrayed that trust." He moved closer.

As did I. I pressed the CD against his chest.

"I'm only going to say this once." His tone took on a menace I'd never heard from him before. "Fuck off. Just fuck right fucking off. Don't ever come near me again. Don't ever talk to me again. You're dead to me."

His words resonated in my chest and squeezed the air from my lungs. "Could you…just listen to me?" *I have to make him see—*

"No, I won't listen to you." He eyed me, as if taking my measure. "You wanted publicity? You're about to get it."

My breath caught. "What do you mean?"

His smile was malevolent. No other word for it.

"Axel—"

"No. You promised." Axel pivoted and stalked out of the room.

I started to follow him. I had to make him see—had to make him understand.

The silence, which I hadn't noticed, now became deafening.

Spinning, I found everyone in the lobby staring at me. Specifically, Ed, Thornton, Pauletta and Mickey gaped.

Well, I read Ed's stare as anger. If he was mad at me, I deserved it.

My cheeks heated and, even under the beard, they'd be red. I considered trying to make some excuse. To say anything. But words failed me.

And I fled.

Chapter Seventeen

Axel

I sat back and waiting for the fallout.

Terrified, but determined.

Hesitant, yet strident.

Afraid of losing everything...yet tired of not being true to myself.

In the end, because Thornton and Ed were in the shower together—for what seemed to me, a casual observer, like a fucking long time—Pauletta was the first to call.

"What the fuck, Axel?"

"Hello Pauletta, how are—"

"Don't give me that bullshit. You...you should've told me. I could've..."

"Could've...?" *Give her the rope to hang herself. No, too macabre. At least wait until she tries to talk herself out of this one.*

"Could've managed it. Jesus, Axel, I'm your manager. I'm supposed to know everything—your most intimate secrets. Your skeletons in the closet—"

"This isn't about Kyesha." I growled the words.

"No, it's not." She sighed. "I was in the process of setting up an interview with you and Ed...to give more context."

"The documentary gave plenty of context. We don't need to talk about her anymore."

"Axel—"

"No, Paulie. End of story." *She hates that name. Should you really be provoking her? Ah, fuck it. Today's the day to burn shit down.*

"You're going to listen to me. We can fix this. I've got an interview set up for you with Geneva Alvarez—"

My gut twisted. *That Gina Alvarez? I'm fucked.* "I don't need an interview, Paulie. The video speaks for itself."

"Stop calling me that." She snapped that.

I didn't give a shit. Burning things down meant not giving a damn who got hurt or what got fucked in the process.

"Look, Axel..." She drew in a deep breath. "Is it safe to assume you haven't spoken to Ed or checked the group chat?"

"Ed's fucking Thornton in their shower. They really need to get their own—"

"So you don't know that we're going to Rocktoberfest as a head-lining act in October? Prime spot in Friday night's lineup."

"Uh..."

"Right." She sighed. "So...as much as I support you coming out—because I assume that's the reason you posted the video and not some attempt at revenge porn—"

"It's not porn."

"Don't fucking argue with me. Clearly the person who took the video was wrong—"

"Thornton."

"Oh shit."

Huh. Apparently she hadn't known. I'd assumed Ed had told her months ago, and she was just respecting me by giving me distance. *Oops.*

"Well two wrongs don't make a right—"

"That's a stupid expression."

"It's the only one I've got." Another biting edge. "He shouldn't have recorded you. He shouldn't have given you a copy—he should have deleted it. Finally—and most importantly—you shouldn't have released it. Because—and I might be wrong, but I suspect I'm not—that gentleman didn't give you permission..."

"Uh..." I swallowed. Then sat up straighter on my bed. "It's not revenge porn."

"He's a high school teacher, Axel. He's *your* former high school teacher. Hell, he might not even be out at school—"

"He's not. At least not to the students."

"Jesus Fucking Christ, Axel. You fucking outed someone? Oh, my God. Do you know how wrong that is? In so many ways." Her breathing was harsh. "I want to fucking strangle you with my bare hands."

"I didn't out *you.*"

"I almost wish you had...if you'd felt the compulsion to try to ruin someone's life. Mickey and I are somewhat in the spotlight—especially after last night." She let that sink in. "Mickey's mature and responsible. They *might* be able to handle it. They also have a family who are completely unsupportive of them and how they've chosen to live their lives."

"So how would outing you two have been marginally better?" I wasn't getting this.

"Because neither of us are going to lose our jobs. Have you thought of that? Your old teacher might sue you if he gets fired. Hell, he might just sue you anyway. Have you thought of that? You don't have much, but you've fought for everything you do have. Do you realize you might lose it all?" She spit that out through gritted teeth. "I have taken care of you for almost ten years. You know all social media goes through me. For this exact—"

"Maybe no one saw it." I eyed my phone. "Maybe I can take it—"

"A hundred-thousand views, Axel, and counting. It's blowing up. Take it down anyway. I should've had you do that first. So do it now. I'll confirm with Geneva—"

"No."

"Axel, to be clear, this isn't optional. You've fucking made the worst decision ever. Well, aside from doing drugs. You fixed that mess. Now you're going to fix this one. Delete the video. I'll call you back in two."

The line went dead.

Reluctantly, I pulled up the site where I'd uploaded the video. As instructed, I pulled it down. Then I scrolled through the hundred or so comments. A few were homophobic, of course. Far more were supportive. That if I felt the need to come out that this wasn't the way to do it...but that I could be a role model.

My door opened.

Ed and Thornton burst in the room.

Thornton wore jeans that were zipped but not buttoned and his white shirt was open.

My friend had, at least, done up his jeans. But he wore no shirt, and he was towel drying his hair. I pointed to it. "Did you do your treatment?"

He glared.

"Whatever. If you smell later—"

He growled, spun, and took off back to his bathroom. He knew the rules—if you had dreads, when they got wet, you applied the treatment. Even in our darkest days of addiction, he'd always managed to do that much.

"Axel—"

"Don't start with me." I eyed Thornton. "In essence, you started this."

"I never should've given you the video."

"No, you're right. You shouldn't have."

"And I was never going to use it. Ever."

"Then why record it?"

He ran a hand through his blond hair. "Because I was worried. Clearly you were hiding something. I thought—"

"That you were worried about me?" I scoffed. "You still held me responsible for Kyesha's death—"

"That's not fair."

I pushed off the bed. "Am I not telling the truth? Does the truth hurt?" I got in his face. "I didn't kill her. I didn't buy the drugs that killed her. Hell, I didn't even introduce her to hard drugs—she introduced me."

Thornton winced.

I pressed on. "But I should've been there when she took the drugs. Instead, I was selfishly getting help for myself. I was fucked-up back then and...maybe I still am."

"Axel—"

"No." I slashed my hand through the air. "I just outed myself. Fine, whatever. I can deal. Maybe one day you and Ed will—"

"We only just told my parents, Axel. About us getting married. And we're still sorting through immigration stuff—"

"So fine. That's not the point. I didn't out you and Ed. I could have, but I didn't."

"Why did you out...Hugo?" He closed an eye, as if in thought. "Hugo Threadgold."

"Yeah."

Thornton nodded. "I wanted to interview him on background. He turned me down."

"But the picture—"

"Yes, we used a picture from the yearbook. Of you, Ed, and Mr. Threadgold. Now, with what you've done, there'll be speculation about your relationship back then."

"We didn't have one."

"People won't know that. Pauletta said—"

"You talked to Pauletta?"

"She left a voicemail. Said to get our asses in here and talk some sense into you—even though it's too late."

I pursed my lips. "What did Pauletta say?"

"Something about an interview so you can clear things up? So you can try to salvage the reputation of the man *you just outed*." His anger flared.

I'd never seen him like this. *Is he like this with Ed? Do I need to watch out for my friend?* Even as I had the thought, Ed returned.

He wiped his hands on his jeans. His hair was drier, and clearly he'd done as I'd asked.

Hoping he would be calmer clearly hadn't been the right thing to hope.

My phone rang.

I ignored it.

Ed snatched it from my hand and hit the button. Then he tapped it again. "We're all here, Pauletta."

"Axel?"

"Yes?"

"Thank you for taking the video down."

"Oh, I bet that was hard." She wasn't big on stuff like this. She was a get-shit-done type of person.

"You'll never know." She muttered that, but we all heard.

Thornton and Ed exchanged a small smile before putting their annoyed faces back on and glaring at me.

"Geneva Alvarez." Even just saying the woman's name put me on edge.

"Yes." Pauletta sent through a text. "At the pub across from the studio. She wants it informal."

"She got that set up?" I eyed my watch. "It's barely eight in the morning."

"Have you been up all night?"

"Maybe?" I'd drifted on and off, periodically checking the hits. I'd only been up to about a thousand when I fell asleep for what turned out to be a nap.

"Ed?"

"Yeah?"

"Get him cleaned up. I want make-up. I want him to look good. You and Thornton take him to the pub at noon. I'll be there as well. I'm still in full damage control mode."

"Seriously?" I waved her off. "It's over—"

"Axel."

Her imperious tone, as I liked to call it. "Yes?"

"I've only begun to fix this clusterfuck you've created. You think people didn't copy the video? That they're not sharing? It took a bit of time, but Threadgold's name is all over this. Have you called him?"

"Well..."

"Maybe..." She hesitated. "I need to talk to our lawyer. She can sort out this mess. After the interview, I want to issue a statement on your behalf, saying—"

"Pauletta—"

"Shut the fuck up, Axel. You're going to say that outing someone is never the right thing to do, and that you're sorry for any harm you might have inadvertently caused. I don't know if people will buy that, but we have to try."

"Uh..."

Ed met my gaze. "That's why we pay her the big bucks." He was right in one respect—we did pay her a lot of money. And she'd proven to be worth it year after year.

"Rocktoberfest?"

Yet another sigh. "Yes. But you have to fix this, Axel. You made this mess, and you're going to fix this." She cut the line.

Thornton eyed us. "I'm going to make pancakes. I'm hungry after last night."

I waggled my eyebrows. "I bet you are—"

"He meant the stress over the documentary." Ed glanced over his shoulder at the love of his life. "And we need to talk strategy."

"About coming out?"

Ed nodded. "It's your call."

"You're ready?"

He nodded again.

"Then we'll talk to Pauletta. Are you hoping this will blunt some of Axel's mess—"

"Hey."

Ed shot a glare my way. "A legitimate concern." He handed me the phone and turned to Thorton. They grasped hands. "Only if you're ready."

"I really am. I would've shouted it at last night's event. And most people there probably guess—what with you nearly tucked by my side." He smiled shyly. "But I like the idea of a coming-out thing."

"You realize it's going to create even more buzz for the doc."

"That's not why I love you."

I pushed past them. "I'm going to have a shower."

"Then pancakes and make-up. We're not going to be late." Ed caught my gaze. "Are you okay?"

"Do I have a choice?"

"Uh...no. Not really." Ed let go of Thornton hands, then pivoted back to me.

He pulled me into a hug.

I could've resisted. Maybe should've resisted. But this was Ed. He wasn't known for displays of affection. And as I settled into his embrace, the enormity of what I'd done hit me in the chest.

I'm fucked.

Chapter Eighteen

Hugo

I'm fucked.

As I watched the video loop over and over again, my mind whirled. I supposed I should be grateful Axel posted under his own name. That made it clear I hadn't been the one to do this.

I'm outed.

That had always been a risk. The school administration knew. Ms. Kenall had been supportive. She'd even liked Gavin—because she hadn't really known him. She'd given me space when my marriage ended and had even tried to set me up with her nephew.

We'd been...incompatible.

Mr. Merkerson also knew. And he'd used it against me a number of times. So often that I'd considered coming out just to spite him.

But I hadn't.

Because I hadn't wanted to jeopardize my career.

Well, so much for that...

For the first few hours, social media had been abuzz about who the redhead with the beard was. The footage wasn't great, and I was never directly facing the camera.

Trust one of my eagle-eyed former students to drop my name like a bombshell. The few other speculations fell to the wayside as everyone sought out as much as they could about Hugo Threadgold.

Not pretty.

My social media was almost nonexistent—except what I shared necessarily for work. I kept a low profile. Being Gavin's ex meant just wanting to be forgotten. We'd always been discreet while out in public.

He was not that way with his second husband and, once in a while, people would start to ask questions about his previous marriage. Fortunately, Gavin was good at shutting down speculation.

What's he going to say about this? Surely someone's going to make the connections. I've always been good at riding out storms—he has a tendency to make them worse.

For the thirteenth time, I played the video.

Watching it again and again didn't help me battle the warring emotions. Part of me remembered that kiss fondly. The emotion had been with wild abandon and passion. I hadn't initiated, but I'd certainly gotten into it. The rest of me watched in horror as I felt my career being flushed by the drain. That concern lay in the comments. Now everyone knew I'd been Axel's music teacher, the dialogue was mixed with questions about whether I'd seduced him back then and we'd been secret lovers for fifteen years or if I'd seduced him then, and we'd only just reconnected.

Several enterprising people suggested, since Axel was sex on a stick, that perhaps he seduced me. Then whether or not we'd been together all these years reared its ugly head again. The minority suggested maybe we'd only just reconnected and, since we were both adults, that maybe people should cut us some slack...? Of course, those posts were in the minority.

Then, to my horror, a photo surfaced from last night. One of Axel and me from the theater where we were clearly arguing. Thus began the speculation that we'd had a lover's spat and, finally—circling back to the video—that one of us must have released it as revenge porn.

Where the porn was in this scenario wasn't entirely clear.

Whether Axel or I released the video was of great debate. Yes, the damn thing was released on Axel's account. But what if I hacked it? What if he'd given me permission or access or something or—

My head ached.

Why would I out myself? That seemed to be what most of these people didn't get—that by one of us outing the other, we were also outing ourselves.

Someone finally suggested maybe neither of us released it. That someone at the studio—record or production—wanted the publicity and weren't they all just feeding into it.

We were trending everywhere.

A pounding on my door yanked me from my spiraling thoughts.

"Hugo, you fucking shit, open this door."

I raced to the door and flung it open.

A very angry Renee stood there, hand on her distended belly.

"Shit, Renee. Bed rest."

Still, turning her around and coaxing her back into her own bed was likely impossible—given the grim look on Cope's face as he held the knapsack she took with her everywhere *just in case*. She was seven-and-a-half months along. Preemie territory, but still with major risks.

I ushered her in...only to find a couple of photographers parked across the street with their cameras pointing right at me.

"Wave to them." Cope smiled. "Exact opposite of what they're expecting. You're not going to hide."

Because I figured the psychologist knew best, I waved.

The two women and one man shot their photos, and the woman waved back with a big thumbs-up.

I shut the door. "Media?"

"My guess." Cope handed me the knapsack so he could then help Renee off with her coat.

"Does bed rest mean an actual bed?"

"Your electronic recliner so I can put my feet up is sufficient." She glared. "Water retention. Fat ankles. Higher-than-normal blood pressure." She waddled into my small living room, sank onto the recliner, grabbed the control and, within moments, had raised her feet.

I wasn't *old*. That being said, the recliner was a gift to myself for my fortieth. Because I eventually would be *old*. "Water?"

"With ice."

"Great—"

"Not a chance." Cope grabbed the knapsack. He pointed to the couch. "Don't pace—it'll stress her. Just park your ass, don't argue, and we'll be fine."

I dropped my ass to the couch. "I almost wish today was a weekday."

"Why didn't you answer my call?"

I winced. "When my notifications started pinging a couple of hours ago—"

"The middle of the night."

"—the middle of the night."

She sighed dramatically. "You know you're supposed to turn them off at night."

"Do you want to hear this story? I keep the notifications on because my best friend might go into labor at any moment and, given I'm her birth partner—"

"It's going to be a Caesarian."

"Given I'm her birthing partner because her beloved partner, the doctor, can't stand the sight of blood—"

"I'm a psychologist." Cope stomped back into the room. "And I can *stand* the sight of blood."

"You just can't stay upright after you've seen it." I grinned.

Copeland's penchant for passing out at the slightest amount of blood was what, as an adolescent, finally convinced him he couldn't be a medical doctor. He'd wanted psychiatry anyway, but med school meant blood. So he'd focused on psychology and graduated with his PhD in clinical psychology at a mere twenty-five. He was a big believer in therapy, including some innovative versions. After the disastrous end of my marriage, he'd encouraged me to see a woman he'd mentored who ran a horse ranch out in Mission City that used equine and canine therapy. He'd thought that might appeal to me, trying to be helpful, but I hadn't wanted to hear about it. I hadn't wanted to see anyone.

Days like today—when I couldn't cope with the slightest upset—I wondered if I'd made the wrong choice. *Never too late.*

I went through that internal dialogue...or was that internal monologue...? I could ask Cope, but he was handing me a fresh coffee and settling on the other end of the couch.

Renee sipped her ice water. Clearly she'd been waiting for her husband to return before she started in on me. "You didn't tell us about the video."

"Really?" I cocked my head. "I'm sure I did."

She exchanged a look with Cope.

He shook his head, then pivoted his attention to me. "I admit hearing you'd had a...dalliance—with Axel Townsend, no less—kind of blew our minds. But I'm pretty certain we would've remembered hearing about a video. If only because I would've advised you to ensure the thing had been destroyed. Shit never reappears at opportune moments—it's always when you can be blindsided—"

"So what the fuck happened last night?" Renee glared.

"I saw the notifications and turned off my phone." I pointed to the thing as it sat innocuously on the coffee table. "I've been...obsessing over the laptop ever since. I'm exhausted—

"Yeah, boo-hoo-hoo." She gesticulated so hard she nearly tipped her water over.

"Honey."

She glared at Cope. "Don't fucking call me that. You know I hate that."

"Well, sweetheart, derailing you feels like a good idea right now. Direct some of that ire toward me, and we might actually get Hugo to talk." He again pivoted his attention back to me. "Renee found the photos of you and Axel from last night. That's what she's asking about."

Which I'd known. But I'd hoped to *derail* her with the explanation of turning my phone off which, in retrospect, had probably been a bad idea. "I was trying to give him a CD of the students performing some of his old songs. Stupid, I know, right? But...they did such a beautiful job with such wonderful material..."

Renee closed her right eye. Which meant she was either getting a migraine or was deep in contemplation. Neither boded well, but I preferred she unleash her anger on me rather than suffer one of her crippling, debilitating, but fortunately infrequent, migraines.

"Did you have his permission—"

"No."

"Did you have the legal rights—"

"No."

"So what you did is like, a copyright infringement? Violation?"

"Uh…" I winced. "We didn't actually publish—"

"Hugo." That warning tone she used with recalcitrant students.

In defiance, I crossed my arms. "They're fucking brilliant songs. Yes, a little…for a younger crowd… but still—"

"What does that mean?" Cope sipped his coffee. Then he frowned. "Like…juvenile?"

"Not exactly." I put my coffee on the side table, rubbed my face with my hands, then crossed my arms against my chest. "They're insightful songs. Mostly love songs. Pining, unrequited…that kind of stuff. A couple about how tough is for life as a teen. Including one about being poor and Black. But not melancholic. More…defiant." I glanced up at the ceiling. "Songs that will speak to kids his age as well as anyone with a heart. He's so fucking talented. Always has been. I think it would be good to show—"

"Hugo." Sharp and exasperated.

"Yes." I eyed Renee.

"You're attempting to justify the unjustifiable." She pursed her lips. "Did he take the CD?"

I blinked. "Uh…yeah…" I'd pressed it into his hands seconds before he fled. Then I'd faced the room of onlookers and had booted the fuck out of there as well. Not understanding that one, there would be cameras, and two, my behavior had looked suspicious as fuck.

"So he could listen to it and sue you."

"He won't."

"But he could."

"To what end?" I gestured around my pathetic house. Two bedrooms, one ancient bathroom, and falling down around my ears. I'd bought it just before Vancouver real estate had bounced back. My divorce from Gavin had given me only one thing—the down payment for this house. It might not be much—in a less-than-desirable part of town—but the thing was mine.

Well, mostly the bank's...but the thought was what mattered.

"He's not going to try to steal my house."

"But he could." Renee narrowed her eyes. "You need to get the CD back. Tell your kids...what did you tell your kids?"

"That they were recording songs from a previous student. Even if they might be curious, Axel and Ed's style is so radically different these days." I hesitated. "Except "Sunrise"."

Cope cocked his head, clearly curious by my tone.

"The documentary explains the song. It's complicated—"

Renee wiggled her butt to settle into my beloved recliner. "I've got all the time in the world..."

And so I told them everything.

Chapter Nineteen

Axel

Geneva Alvarez's beauty always stunned me. With her black, curly, flowing long hair. Her dark-brown almond-shaped eyes. Her bow lips, covered in a dark red lipstick that suited her.

What really turned me on, though, was her take-no-prisoners attitude. She approached every interview as an opportunity to break a big story wide open. As the entertainment reporter for the local Vancouver station of the Canadian National Channel—CNC for short—she vibrated energy.

Personally, I thought she was wasted in entertainment. Not that those stories weren't important. We entertainers needed exposure—of which she'd given Grindstone more than our fair share over the years. She also alternated between subtly hitting on Ed and me. Last night, though, I'd caught her sidling up to Songbird. Although Geneva was an unabashed and unrepentant bisexual, Songbird didn't—to my knowledge—swing that way.

On the other hand, I'd never sat and had a conversation with my bandmate about her potential bed partners. Life was complicated enough between keeping Ed's bisexual status on the QT and watching Meg and Big Mac *finally* hookup after Rocktoberfest last year.

Between Ed and Thornton, as well as Meg and Big Mac, we had two weddings in our future.

Ugh.

I eyed Geneva as she reviewed what I assumed were her notes on a tablet. The woman was better suited for investigative journalism. More like Lucille Forbes who wrote for our local paper and who always was finding some celebrity or titan of business to bring down a notch. Or six. Or right out of politics, entertainment, sports, or commerce. She'd brought the downfall of many a powerful person. Admittedly, mostly men. Arrogant men. Men who thought they were untouchable.

And the damn Forbes woman was texting and calling Pauletta incessantly—saying she'd run her story without our input but wouldn't it be better if I agreed to a sit-down interview?

Fucking vultures. Smelling blood in the water—

Wait. Sharks smelled blood in the water. Vultures ate carcasses of dead things.

Oh my God, so gross.

I winced.

Pauletta elbowed me. "Be nice."

"I'm always nice."

Thornton snickered.

I glared.

Ed shrugged. "Get over it. He's here to stay."

I wasn't certain if he meant in Canada, our lives, or just this moment in time when I was about to be skewered, spit roasted, and feasted on. I almost said that out loud, knowing Ed would be totally grossed out. My poor vegetarian friend.

"Axel." Pauletta whispered my name.

"Yeah?"

"Pay attention, for fuck's sake." That came from Ed.

In fairness, I'd discussed my ADHD in the documentary—and Thornton had kept that part... as well as found a couple instances where the shit manifested plus a couple of times when I used coping strategies to rein in the worst of the impulses. He'd mentioned, in the editing process, that he'd consulted a psychologist who'd given him guidance on how to portray the problem honestly. But with hope. That meant something to me. That he actually cared—both about me and about Ed. And about the millions of kids around the world—and adults—who went through what I went through. Or something similar. Basically that you could use it to your advantage and build on the gifts that came with it.

I'd learned early on, thanks to Ed, that I processed the world differently than other people. "I'm paying attention."

Even as I said the words, Geneva stepped forward, her hand extended. "Axel."

I grasped her hand. *Damn, her skin's so soft.* I liked most women's skin. I was a sensualist. What I liked more though, honestly, was a ginger beard attached to a man who got turned on when I scratched it. "Geneva." I shook with a firm grip, then released her hand.

She pivoted. "Ed, so lovely to see you again."

"Hello, Geneva. I believe you haven't met Thornton Graves. My fiancé."

Geneva's stunning brown eyes lit. "Am I breaking news today?"

Ed, to my utter shock, tucked himself into Thornton's side. "If you want."

"Oh, I want."

"With caveats." Pauletta stepped forward, not even bothering to offer her hand. "You saw the documentary last night, so that's fair—"

"You can't tell me what questions to ask." Geneva flashed a smile at Pauletta.

Malevolence? Or just ambitious? Either way, I was about to get nailed.

And I was right. Oh, Geneva started the questions easy. About the band, about my life before Rocktoberfest, and how things were now.

All things Pauletta warned me to anticipate.

Then came the one I didn't see coming. "Gavin McPherson says you and Hugo Threadgold were carrying on an illicit affair while you were still a teenager. In high school." She said the last bit as if I needed clarifying as to when I'd been a teenager.

I glared at Geneva.

Pauletta, far closer than I was certain Geneva was happy with, motioned her hand as if she were stuffing something down. Pushing something toward the ground.

Her way of saying, *Axel, chill the fuck down.*

"I don't know any Gavin McPherson. He's lying. I can't say it any more plain than that. He doesn't know what the fu—." I swallowed. "What the heck he's talking about."

"Gavin is Hugo's ex-husband. They were married back when you were in high—"

"The douchebag?"

At least one gasp reached my ears.

Not Geneva, though. No, her eyes lit with pure excitement.

I winced. "Am I allowed to say that on television?"

She waved me off. "We have censors. You just tell me why you think Gavin McPherson is a douchebag." Her voice was low and sultry. Whether to ping some lizard part of my brain that would react to that kind of enticement, or whether she was just showing interest, I wasn't certain.

Shoving my lizard brain away, I tried for the part that thought rationally. I might not use it as much as I should, but I certainly knew how to access it when I needed to. I smiled. A wide grin to show off my perfectly white and straight teeth. "I did meet Mr. McPherson. He made some wild, inaccurate, and frankly inappropriate comments. I'm only going to say this once—Hugo Threadgold and I were never involved. Ever. Back in high school he was a good teacher who helped a couple of poor kids get guitars and—"

"He helped you get guitars."

"Yeah, me *and* Ed." *Keep your temper in check.*

"Was he involved with Ed as well?"

"No." I tried to remember to breathe. "And he wasn't involved with me either. We didn't have that kind of a relationship. He was my teacher. My mentor—"

"You've seen the video."

"From October. Last year. There's nothing from ten years ago because nothing happened. You're barking up the wrong tree, lady. And maybe you shouldn't be believing everyone who offers up information. This Gavin dude obviously has a hidden agenda. Or maybe not so hidden. He's...I don't think he's a good person." *And when Hugo talks about him, he gets sad and mad and is...unhappy.*

"He's a pillar of the community."

"Doesn't mean he can't lie. Plenty of important people tell lots of lies. And the media figure it out because, like, it's in the public interest to know. So I'm suggesting you figure it out—that he's lying—and then you leave me and Hugo alone."

"So you are with Hugo?" More flashing triumph.

"I didn't say that. One kiss doesn't make a relationship."

"Much as you would want it to."

My heart squeezed. Yeah, I wanted that. More than anything. But he betrayed me—once in Black Rock and once last night. That shit needed to be resolved before we could move forward.

Wait. Did I want it to move forward? Could I find something redeemable about the relationship? About him? My parents had betrayed me over and over again. *We won't hurt you again. We didn't mean it. We were just drunk...* They were *upstanding* members of our community. And I'd never told the truth because I didn't want to be seen as the poor abused Black kid. And I didn't want people to think we were the norm. Plenty of kids had loving parents. Loving single moms. Not everyone got a shit sandwich in the form of abusive—

"Axel?"

I blinked.

Geneva's expression was of...concern. Maybe even genuine as her brow knit, which definitely wouldn't look good on camera. "We can stop—"

"No." I straightened. "Sorry. Just thinking about how people come across as pious and aren't really. This Gavin dude is one of them. Making shit up about someone he supposedly used to care about." Fuck the swearing now. "My parents are held in high esteem...but they're not good people. And I won't go into details because, you know, I've made a good life for myself." I looked into the camera. "I apologize to Hugo Threadgold for releasing the video. That was wrong of me. He had an expectation of privacy, and frankly, I'm a better person than this. I hope one day he lets me make it up to him."

Geneva cocked her head. "So you hope to see him again?"

"Vancouver's a small city."

Total bullshit. The Greater Vancouver District had upward of two million. One could easily get lost.

Something told me, though, that my future held more Hugo Threadgold.

Or at least I hoped it did.

With that thought, I plastered on a smile, and we concluded the interview.

Chapter Twenty

Hugo

My high school certainly wasn't the largest in Vancouver, but it did have an outsized presence. We were in the poorest neighborhood and yet had a robust arts program. Constantly under threat of having the funding cut, naturally, but we persevered.

I worried my actions might've undermined all that.

A fact nearly borne out when I finally turned my phone back on Saturday night.

Cope and Renee offered to hold my hand while I did it, but I sent them home.

Of course.

Renee needed rest. As much as I needed support, things would blow over, and my life would return to normal. If something happened to her or the twins, I'd never forgive myself.

Or Axel Townsend for bringing this chaos into my life.

Since I hadn't checked the laptop all day either, I truly felt detached. Like I'd spent the day in the studio and had no connection to the outside world.

As soon as I powered on the phone, it exploded. Not literally, but notifications buzzed through for a solid two minutes.

Need to change the settings.

Except I didn't know how and googling directions right now felt entirely too exhausting.

As I tried to sort through everything, Renee's newest message popped up.

—*CNC at 6pm. Axel and Geneva Alvarez*—

Jesus.

I dove for the remote, noting the broadcast would be half over.

Geneva and the occasional weekend anchor for the Vancouver News at Six for CNC flashed on the screen.

Momentarily distracted, I stared at Jake McGrath. A former war correspondent, he'd recently settled in Mission City and did spot reporting in Vancouver—mostly for the national nightly news broadcast. Breathlessly handsome—with his light-brown hair and stunning blue eyes. Also happily married. Him, I might've googled. Family man. Deeply committed to his wife and their son. Then I'd gone down a rabbit hole to delve into her tragic backstory and been overwhelmed with gratitude that sometimes happy endings existed.

Oh my God, that's what you're focused on?

I recorded this broadcast, so I could always watch it later. Maybe that's why my mind wandered because—

Geneva's words penetrated. "We're leaving in some of the expletives to provide context for Mr. Townsend's words."

Oh shit. He's so mad at me that he swore?

I eyed my phone, which just buzzed again.

—Call me this instant—

Merkerson.

Yeah, yeah. He could wait.

I barely held myself together as the interview began. Clearly this was just an excerpt because Axel was already speaking and *douchebag* came out of his mouth.

Gavin.

Geneva came back with Jake. "The full interview will air on Sunday night's national broadcast—"

Fuck a fucking duck.

"We reached out to Gavin McPherson to clarify his comments, and he maintains Hugo Threadgold was having an inappropriate relationship with Axel Townsend back when Axel was a high school student. Axel denies that vehemently and we'll let viewers judge for themselves tomorrow night."

Someone pounded on my front door.

Incandescent rage lit within me.

Fucking douchebag is the least of it. I'm going to kill him with my bare hands. Bad enough he was besmirching me. Horrific he was going after Axel. For all Grindstone's newfound popularity, they still didn't have the resources—

No, they just might. Pauletta Magnum's father was a scion in the business community. If he believed Axel, he wouldn't want the band his daughter represented to be dragged through the—

The pounding came again.

"Go away."

The media had knocked earlier, demanding a comment.

Cope sent them on their way.

Now I wish I'd said something. Although I would've been blind-sided and might've said the wrong thing. *God, do I need a lawyer? Yeah, I probably—*

"Hugo Theseus Threadgold."

Oh shit.

"Open this door or I'll assume you're in distress and in need of the police."

My father was blustering. No way in hell would he call the police and descend more chaos upon us.

Cope mentioned the media was still camped out when they left less than an hour ago.

The likelihood of them having packed up—especially if they knew Geneva's bombshell—was non-existent.

With great reluctance, I opened my front door, ensuring I stayed out of sight because, frankly, I didn't want a photograph of me and my parent showing up in the paper.

Surprise. My mother also stood at my father's side. Eugenia Threadgold, nee Iverson, didn't *do* conflict. She'd left the child-rearing to a series of nannies and the disciplining to her husband.

And had let me know—at every single turn in my life—how much of a disappointment I was.

My father's criticisms were tempered. Possibly because he'd learned early on that the more he leveled orders, the more recalcitrant I became. Instead, he opted for manipulations and veiled threats.

Most of the time, I responded to neither.

"Would you like a glass of water? May I take your coat?"

"A scotch on the rocks for me, and your mother will take a cabernet."

"I don't have alcohol in the house." *Which would you know if you'd ever visited.*

Not that I'd wanted you to.

"Speaking of houses…" Theseus Threadgold pushed against one of the wooden pillars. "Is it even safe?"

"I had a home inspection before I moved in—"

"Ten years ago—"

"Before I moved in." I gritted my teeth. "There was extensive termite damage, but the inspector figured I'd get about five years. So I'm pushing it at ten. It might fall down around us at any moment."

"Oh dear." Eugenia pressed a hand to her chest.

Theseus glowered. "That's not amusing, son."

I puffed out my chest. "I'm only ever your son when you want something from me. When you need to prove what a family man you are. Leonora did the right thing by moving to Europe years ago."

Eugenia held her hand to her chest. "My darling girl. Gone forever."

I snickered. "She married a Grecian, and you disowned her." She'd gone to Athens to study for university—her first attempt to escape my parents' grasp. Then she'd fallen in love with a *Greek God* and married him—the final straw in my parents' eyes and the permanent rift she'd hoped for. Three kids and pregnant with her fourth, she frolicked at the beach every day while her husband ran a successful hotel that catered to upmarket tourists. Leonora might speak the language of the ultra-rich, but she wanted nothing to do with them. I always assumed she'd burn in the sun—same fair skin as myself—but she managed to look stunning in every family photo she sent me.

I need to visit.

That'd been on my list for the summer. Truly. Until I'd nearly made love to Axel Townsend in a tent in Black Rock last October and my life had been turned upside down. "Leonora's very happy. Would you like to see the Christmas photo she sent? Your grandchildren—"

"We don't have grandchildren." Theseus stuck his nose in the air.

Something flickered in Eugenia's expression, though. *Ah, so not totally unaffected.* I never mentioned Leonora anymore. My parents might be indifferent, but I missed my sister terribly. We'd always been close.

Which made me think of Thornton Graves, his dead sister Kyesha, and...that landed me right back at Axel.

I glared at my parents. "Why are you here? You couldn't possibly have seen the interview with Geneva—"

My father met my glare. "I have...sources. I saw the raw footage about an hour ago. Naturally, we will stand by you—"

"Naturally." *Because otherwise people will think you believe Gavin's accusations and that would mean you have a pedophile son.* Of course, if proof emerged that I'd had inappropriate relations with Axel, then they'd light of out here like their asses were on fire and demand I be prosecuted.

But I'd never so much as touched Axel. Or any of my students. I'd been prodigiously careful. Accusations destroyed careers. I had too many students who needed my help. *Kids like Axel and Ed.* Which strengthened my resolve. "Why are you here, exactly? Because I know I didn't call."

"Don't be rude."

Rich. My father admonishing me.

Like I was ten and not forty-two.

"Say what you have to say, then feel free to walk right out of my life."

Eugenia gasped.

"Water or no water? Coats off or on? I honestly don't give a shit."

"May I sit?" Eugenia was *literally* clutching her pearls.

God help me. "By all means. I've got plenty of space."

As a unit my parents sat on the leather sectional, perched on the end.

Believing that meant no water—and their coats were staying on—I plopped into my recliner. I didn't put my feet up. I nearly did...and restrained myself because I needed to be able to show them to the door quickly and getting out of a reclined seat quickly just wasn't a thing.

"We believe you should see a lawyer."

"Your lawyer does corporate affairs." Damn competent woman whose name I couldn't recall. Eugenia had attempted to set me up with the poor woman after my divorce. Apparently my mother thought a lesbian and a gay man made the perfect couple.

Clueless didn't begin to touch that kind of ignorance.

"I'm not referring to Vanessa." Theseus straightened. "I'm talking about Wentworth Chamberlain."

"The divorce lawyer?" I snickered. I'd heard of Wentworth, of course. His name was whispered through the elite of Vancouver. If one needed a cutthroat divorce attorney, one called Wentworth. If one's soon-to-be ex-spouse hired Wentworth, one considered oneself fucked. Oh, Vancouver had a few other high-priced and perfectly competent divorce lawyers—but none as ruthless or as competent as this guy. He'd been on the way up when Gavin had divorced me. Neither of us had gone the acrimonious route, so neither of us hired Wentworth. "I don't understand why I want a divorce attorney. I'm already divorced—"

My father sliced his hand through the air. "He's also extremely competent in damage control. He has an excellent public relations team—"

"I don't need PR—"

"He can see you tomorrow at nine." Theseus looked around my living room and sniffed. "He said he could come here. Perhaps his office might be better."

"I don't need a divorce lawyer—I'm already divorced. I don't need a PR team—I didn't do anything wrong." I flashed to the multiple increasingly hostile messages from my boss. *Is some damage control in order?* Needing Cope and Renee's advice wasn't going to help. A psychologist and a teacher could offer their opinion, but they couldn't offer serious legal advice. "If I see Wentworth—and one hour of his time is about a mortgage payment for this place—"

"I'll pay." My father sniffed again.

I'd cleaned last weekend and hadn't spilled anything, so this room didn't smell. Honestly, he was just pissing me off. "Be that as it may...won't it look bad that I've hired a lawyer? Doesn't that make me look guilty?"

"Far from it. The hiring of a good attorney shows how seriously you are taking McPherson's accusations. That you intend to mount a defense—"

"I don't need a fucking defense. I didn't do anything wrong." I enunciated each word carefully.

"Your mother and I are issuing a joint statement that we stand behind you and believe in your innocence." He met and held my gaze. "Because you are innocent...right?"

"Fuck yes." I leapt from the chair. "I would never—could never—touch a child. Even a teenager on the cusp of adulthood. Axel is twenty-eight fucking years old. And yes, he's my former student. And maybe that crosses a line, but it's a fucking thin one that barely can be seen. I *never* thought of him in that way. Until we met as adults. Things...changed."

"Is there any chance you could change them back?" Eugenia still clutched her goddamn pearls. "I know a nice woman—"

"Oh my God, Mother. Gay. No women. No breasts or pussy. Those are very nice things—and women are wonderful. I prefer pecs, asses, cocks, and anal."

"There's no need—" My father rose.

"Great, you're halfway to the door. Don't let it hit your asses on the way out." I stormed to the back of the house, to the kitchen, and cursed that I really didn't have booze in the house.

My friends, when they visited, brough their own alcohol. I used to have a few things hanging around, but the bottles just gathered dust. No point in keeping them when they just went bad. So they all got tossed.

In defiance of both Renee and common sense—who both said don't drink caffeine after three in the afternoon—I cracked open a cola, poured it into a glass, added ice, and plopped down on a rickety chair at the kitchen table. Replacing the set was on my list. A very long list of improvements I'd make. Time, and more importantly money, always stopped me. My mortgage and helping the kids came first. Always had and always would.

My father clearing his throat pulled me out of my reverie.

I didn't bother to stand.

Gingerly, he stepped into the kitchen. He placed a business card and a thick envelope on the table. "Let me know if you need more. Our lawyer will issue the statement within the hour. You've hurt your mother, but I'm going to forgive as it's obvious you're under stress—"

"You think?"

"Be good." He snapped that. Then, in a conciliatory tone, "We do care. You think it's only about our reputations, but we do care." He cleared his throat. "If you could forward the photo of Leonora to my professional email, I would appreciate it."

Before I could respond, he was gone.

Sonofabitch.

How was I supposed to stay angry when he offered that small gesture of reconciliation?

I shot off a text to Leonora asking permission to share a photo.

To my surprise, she sent back a thumbs-up. *Well, that's not particularly helpful...but that must be permission.*

Knowing if I thought too long about it that I wouldn't do it, I yanked out my phone and sent the photo in an email to my dad's business account.

Then I shot off a text to Leonora letting her know what I'd done. Tactfully suggesting this might not mean anything...but letting her know I'd done it.

Given it was the middle of the night in Greece, I didn't expect a response.

And I didn't get one.

Instead, I fingered the business card.

Wentworth Chamberlain.

Fuck my life.

Chapter Twenty-One

Axel

E d stared at me from across the kitchen bar with a furrow in his brow.

Thornton stood beside him with an arm around his shoulder.

I blithely ate sugary breakfast cereal. More to piss Ed off than any desire to eat teeth-and-gut-rotting sugar. In fact, it didn't taste right. *Did you check to see if the milk is expired?* Dumb question—Ed would've chucked it. Nothing went past the expiry. We tended to have weird meals at odd times to prevent food going past the end date.

"I'll be fine." I shoved a mouthful in my mouth.

A drop of milk dribbled out of the corner of said mouth.

I wiped it away with the back of my hand.

Ed winced and Thornton chuckled.

Par for the course. Another dumb expression I'd absorbed somewhere along the way.

"We're just going for the weekend." Ed gazed up at Thornton.

"We don't have to go." Thornton made that offer.

"It's your mom's sixty-fifth birthday." I swallowed after having spoken with my mouth full of food. *Oops.* "You have to go. And isn't your sister starting wedding plans for you?"

Ed coughed.

Oh shit.

Thornton arched an eyebrow. "Okay, I didn't know that, so—"

"We need to be going." Ed snagged Thornton's hand and tried to drag him to the front door. "Be good, Axel."

I snickered.

Both men halted their forward motion and spun back.

I waved them off.

Ed moved so he stood directly before me with just the breakfast bar between us. "Damn, man. You fucked up that relationship." He shook his head. "You know there is such a thing as a telephone—"

"Eat shit and die. Leave me alone to my anger." I was *not* going to email or call Hugo.

Although I'd been damn tempted on numerous occasions. Usually late at night when my defenses were down. He was likely mad at me for uploading the video. I would've been, had he done that to me. Also, his asshole ex-husband had made the douchey accusation. So maybe Hugo owed me an apology for having married a kumquat.

"You're wallowing." He glanced at Thornton. "Maybe we should stay."

Thornton put his suitcase on the floor. "Your call, baby. Whatever you want."

"Fucking go." I leaned over to drop my bowl into the sink built into the bar along with the dishwasher.

Likely without thinking, Ed rinsed it off and put it into the dish-washer.

I rolled my eyes. "Just go already. It's a long drive to Portland."

"We can stay." Ed gazed at Thornton. "Or come back early—"

"Just fucking go." I might've growled that. "Pauletta's already checking up on me, like, ten times a day—"

"I think that's a bit of an exaggeration." Ed met my gaze. "Or maybe not."

I held out my phone. "Want to check my text logs? She hasn't been hitting up the group chat because she somehow believes I deserve privacy." I snorted.

Ed declined my phone.

Shrugging, I then put it back on the bar. "Have a good trip."

He held my gaze for another long moment. "I'm a phone call away."

"I know." I rose. "I'm going to nap. Later." I headed toward my bedroom.

Ed cut me off, stopping my progress. He pulled me in for a fierce hug. "I'll stay if you need me." He whispered the words with as much ferocity as the hug.

"It's been four days, Ed. I'm a big boy. Enjoy your long weekend. Put this all out of your mind." Reluctantly, I let him go. Then I spun him around and smacked his ass.

He glared, then appeared to relent. He moved over to Thornton, who kissed his forehead.

Thornton waved to me, the two grabbed their suitcases, then they were gone.

I snagged my phone and placed a call.

Twenty minutes later, Songbird arrived on my doorstep. Well, I called the concierge to let her in first, and then I'd called her.

As I opened the door, my neighbor Dante passed by.

He shot off a, "Great interview," as he headed to the elevator. After he pressed the button, he looked back. "You should come for dinner tonight. Evan's cooking and Kate's off work. It would be just the four of us. Oh." He seemed to register Songbird. "You're welcome too," he offered. "Just a small group of five."

"I'd like that." She grinned. "So would Axel. What time?"

"Say six? I'll let Evan know, and he'll make extra. Any allergies?"

"Nope." Songbird again. Way too sweet. For a woman who usually came off as reserved, she was certainly coming off as chatty with my neighbor. Who was in a triad relationship with two sweet people.

I always smiled when I saw the three of them together.

"See you tonight!" Songbird grinned, then spun to me and shoved me into the condo.

Well, I could've resisted and not let her in, but that would've been rude since I'd invited her. "What were you thinking, saying yes?"

"That you don't need to wallow."

I eyed her. "You talked to Ed." I might've leveled that as an accusation.

She grinned. "I messaged him that you invited me over and asked if there was anything I needed to know."

"Jesus Fucking Christ." I blinked. "And how did that parlay into a dinner invitation with my neighbor?"

"That's Dante, right?"

"Uh..." I blinked again. Had I just said the guy's name?

She grinned. "Ed got overtired one night and overshared about his BDSM Dominant neighbor, the man's Domme girlfriend, and the submissive bottom they shared. That would be..."

"Dante, Kate, and Evan." I rolled my eyes. "Ed's got a big mouth."

"And I get to eat dinner with these very intriguing people." She eyed me. "I'll keep their secrets—"

"They don't keep their relationship a secret. Well, Kate's a vet, so I don't think her clients know—"

"And you have to keep mine."

Again, I blinked. "I'm terrible with secrets."

"Geneva Alvarez and I are going for brunch tomorrow morning. So I can't stay out too late—"

"No way. No fucking way. You saw how she ambushed me—"

"Axel."

I snapped my mouth shut.

"You would've heard about Gavin Fuckface McPherson's accusation anyway, right?"

"Well, yeah." I squinted. "Fuckface?"

"What would you call him?"

"An attention-seeking douchebag?"

She waved me off. "You've already said at least part of that. We need to get more creative."

"Ugh."

"Now." She smiled. "Dinner's not for eight hours. What are we doing in the meantime?"

I almost pointed out I hadn't invited her to stay for eight hours, but it occurred to me that it might take us that long to lay down the track. "We're recording a song."

This time, she blinked. "Did Pauletta book the studio? Why are we not meeting there? Or are you driving—"

"We're recording it here. It's not an official track."

She placed her hand on her hips. "You don't have a recording studio in this condo. Unless it's well-hidden and you've kept it secret."

I grinned. "Ed's walk-in closet."

She arched an eyebrow. "And why not yours?"

"Uh..."

"Never mind. I doubt I want to know. You want me on the keyboard?"

"Yeah, I set it up after I called you. I have music written for an acoustic guitar as well, but I think just keyboard."

"This isn't going to have a professional sound. You planning to get an engineer involved?"

"Tim's going to run it a couple of times, but I want pure and raw. I don't want polished. You okay with that?

She chuckled. "I'm assuming this isn't an official release."

"Uh...no."

"Does Pauletta know?"

"Uh...no."

Songbird pursed her lips. "She has to approve it, Axel, or I don't want any part of it. You releasing the video was shitty enough. You put out a song without Pauletta's okay, and that could fuck with our relationship. The entire band's. Meg and Big Mac aren't going to care we didn't involve them—they're busy as fuck with their wedding plans."

"I don't need drums and bass with this anyway."

"Ed?"

I cleared my throat. "Need to know?" I offered a smile. "He's already in Washington State, I'm certain. On the way to Portland. We'll have the song released before he's back."

She threw her head back and laughed. "Oh God, to be a fly on the wall when he and Thorton find out."

Linking arms with her, I grinned. "Let's record the song, send it to Pauletta and Tim, and then go to dinner with my BDSM-obsessed neighbors. All good."

And so we did.

Chapter Twenty-Two

Hugo

"I'm still not certain this meeting is necessary, but I do appreciate you coming to my home." I clutched my mug of coffee.

Five days since the infamous video recording hit the airwaves.

Four days since Axel's interview with Geneva and the visit from my parents.

Three days since Merkerson put me on suspension pending an investigation.

Two days since Renee's doctor warned her again about her blood pressure.

One day since I caved and called Wentworth Chamberlain.

And now he sat at my kitchen table with his yellow legal pad and a grim expression on his face.

He didn't look quite like I expected a prominent lawyer to look like. His dark-blond hair was quite long, and I had to admit his hazel eyes mesmerized. Not the same as a pair of dark-brown eyes that haunted me, though.

Still no word. I didn't have Axel's email and worried about putting anything in writing. Hell, even sending innocuous texts and leaving generic voicemail messages felt precarious. I was still bitterly angry at what he'd done to me and wanting to connect with him on a one-to-one level at the same time.

"I'm glad you called." Wentworth sipped his coffee.

Sitting, we were on the same level. Standing, he had a couple of inches on me.

"We need an action plan."

"I need to get my job back." I winced. "My current and former students have left hundreds of messages of support."

"I saw that." He scrolled on his phone. "The website one of them created is...clever."

Ana Chung. Phenomenal flautist who now played for the Vancouver Opera and, to help pay the bills, created websites. Brilliant young mind and one of my best students. I was proud of all of them...but she was someone special. I wasn't supposed to have favorites. That being said, she was up with Axel and Ed with most accomplished and, more impressively, most humble.

"I try not to check it too often..."

"I don't blame you. There's a groundswell of support. Mr. Townsend and Mr. Markham's interviews were powerful. Your ex-husband is also coming under increased scrutiny."

After a moment, his words and tone sank in. I cocked my head. "What aren't you saying?"

For the first time, I got a ghost of a smile. "When I put out the press release yesterday that my firm was taking you on as a client and we aimed for complete vindication, a couple of...people...approached me. Off the record, so no names."

I nodded.

"Seems Gavin hasn't kept his nose as clean as everyone thinks. I've been made aware...of some shady dealings with his family's foundation. The one he's the chair of."

"What?" I scowled. "When did he become chair of the foundation?"

"When his father retired."

"Oh...I didn't know."

"You don't pay attention?"

"To Gavin's personal or professional life? Hell fucking no." I sipped my coffee, fighting a growing sense of unease. "That foundation does some really good work. They donate to my school's music program." At least I'd manage to wheedle that agreement out of Gavin during our divorce—and the foundation had upheld their end of the bargain for the past ten years. That money came in like clockwork. Money I relied on.

"Gavin's also been siphoning money without anyone noticing."

"Oh shit." My gut clenched. "But someone noticed. Obviously...they called you."

"What I'm about to tell you stays between the two of us."

"Of course." No matter what he told me—no matter how badly I would want to use it against Gavin—I would hold my tongue.

"The Vancouver police Commercial Crimes Division has opened an investigation. A subpoena is going to be issued Tuesday for the foundation's books."

"Oh God." A wave of nausea rolled over me. *Who can I approach to make up for the funding shortfall? Their donation is coming up next month...where can I go? Come to that, I might not even have a job anymore...did I think about that?* Yet even as I had that thought, I was honestly more concerned about the funding for the school.

"Hugo?"

"Hmm?"

"Are you okay?" Wentworth laid his pen on his notepad. "Is this distressing you?"

"You sound like Copeland."

"Copeland?"

"My best friend's husband. Well, he's my friend too. And he's a nosy psychologist who's promise to never analyze me and yet he does so on a regular basis."

Wentworth smiled. "Just like I promise to never get involved in my friends' legal issues...but can't help giving my two cents, even if the issue is an area of the law I know nothing about."

"You must be super popular." I snickered.

He smiled. "Yes, divorce attorneys are amongst the most hated of all lawyers—and that's saying something. We're also absolutely necessary. Mediation is great for couples who are honest, fair, and care about their ex-partners or, at the very least, about their children." He sobered. "Not everyone's like that. I've taken down more than a few abusers through divorce proceedings. I can be vicious."

"Have you ever had a client who was accused and innocent?"

"Unfortunately, yes. More often than you might think. Some soon-to-be ex-spouses think they can level accusations to be in a better position. I've also had a couple of clients who were guilty. I ensured they faced justice in those cases as well. I represented them—because everyone is entitled to a defense—but once they were convicted, I suggested they be generous in the division of assets."

"That's...gross."

"Well, it's also helped me hone my skills. I can't always tell when someone is lying to me—sociopaths can be very good at concealing things...but I'm wiser to the games people play."

"Oh."

"Which is why I'm here." He met my gaze. "I believe you didn't do anything untoward with Axel when he was your student."

"I didn't." I gripped my mug. "I don't understand Gavin's need to be vindictive. Or what he gains by dragging through my name through the mud."

"Donations to his foundation have increased."

"Okay, that's gross too." I rubbed my forehead. "I mean, if the money was going to charity, then I guess maybe that's... No, that's still gross."

"He's presented himself as the champion of abused young people. Those who are donating are overlooking the fact he stayed silent about the alleged abuse you were engaging in with your student."

My temper flared. "I didn't."

"I know you didn't. He knows you didn't. He's just using the publicity to enrich himself and, supposedly, the foundation." Wentworth quirked an eyebrow. "Here's the thing. I've got my accountant looking over all the public filings he can find. She's damn good—if there's something to be found then she'll find it."

"Isn't that up to the police?"

He met my gaze.

"Oh."

He nodded.

We understood each other. *Public filings* could mean many different things. And if people had approached him, perhaps he had access to other stuff. My father had called the man *ruthless*. I could see that in his eyes. Not avarice...but definitely something dark.

After a long moment, he picked up his pen. "I want you to take me through everything step-by-step. From the moment you graduated teacher's college until yesterday. I've got all day."

My mind flashed to the huge stack of cash my father had given me. I'd wanted to give it back, but even I could admit when I was outmatched. My family, including Leonora, had a stake in this. If I went down—even if I was innocent—it would stain all of us. In the end, I wasn't willing to take that risk.

I took a deep breath and started from the beginning.

A couple of hours later, I sat on a rocking chair in Renee and Cope's bedroom and gently rocked while watching my best friend.

She devoured the no-sugar fruit-on-the-bottom yogurt she loved so much. Well, she preferred heavenly hash ice cream with added marshmallows and extra chocolate syrup, but...babies... She rubbed her huge belly.

"How is it that the babies are still so tiny and you're as big as—"

Copeland cleared his throat.

I winced, then recalibrated. "A glowing, pregnant woman?"

Renee snickered. "They're still growing. How did it go with the shark?"

"Not sure he'd want to be called—" I reconsidered. "You know, I think he'd see that as a compliment." I sighed. "I was right. Today cost me a mortgage payment."

"Holy shit." Cope poked at the coffee ice cream I'd brought him. His favorite and one Renee didn't love.

Like that somehow would appease her.

To be safe, I was keeping my French Vanilla beyond her reach. "You know, I think I did a good job with the painting in this room."

Renee snickered. "Nice try."

"Well, I had to put in an effort." I pursed my lips. "Wentworth is meeting with Mr. Merkerson tomorrow. Informally. To let my principal know that the lawsuit comes next and to suggest that, although the investigation needs to be thorough, it also needs to be quick."

"That sounds fair." Cope poked at his ice cream. "It's super shitty that you were suspended at all."

"But I had to be."

Renee cocked her head. "That's a very mature attitude."

"That's all I've got." I tried to keep the venom from my tone.

My best friend's wince assured me that I hadn't.

All our phones pinged or vibrated.

After the past five days, I'd silenced everything except actual text notifications.

Renee held up her phone. "Why am I getting a text from Axel Townsend?"

Cope laughed. "Me too."

"I..." I wracked my brain. "I honestly don't know. I don't remember telling him about—"

"Renee posted on the website that you were her best friend, but that she was posting as a teacher who'd been with you at the school through the years in question and that she was one hundred percent certain nothing happened."

Slowly, I nodded. "You put your career on the line."

She shrugged. "I might've passed it by my principal and the school administration first. Plus, I know my nose is clean. You need defending. You shouldn't but you do. So I spoke up. Least I can do." She rubbed her belly. "I think the photo of me with this beach ball and a note that you're going to be the godfather had a bit of an impact."

Thinking of the hundreds of responses—including from many of her old students—had helped. Everything helped.

Cope waved his phone. "Okay, so assuming this isn't spam—"

I checked the phone number. "It's legit."

"So what is it?" He hit his screen. "It's a link."

Renee snagged his phone. "No way are you clicking on a link. Get my laptop."

I'd almost clicked as well. Even knowing better. Renee was right though. Safety first. And Axel's account might've been hacked.

Cope returned with the laptop and carefully entered the website.

Going out of my mind was a definite possibility by the time he finally hit play.

"It's an audio file."

Renee snagged the laptop and placed it on her belly. She patted the bed next to her.

Grateful she had a king-sized bed, I gingerly sat on one side of her while Cope retook his spot on the other side.

As we all gazed at the screen, she hit play.

As the piano gently played the first few notes, I was struck both by the mournfulness of the sound as well as the quality of the recording. Good equipment—but not professionally recorded. Most listeners wouldn't know the difference, but I could tell. This might've passed through a sound engineer, but we were still listening to a rough cut.

Axel's soft voice began to sing, and I was mesmerized.

Another text arrived and although the song pulled my attention, I still glanced at my screen.

—*You're an asshole*—

Yeah, I was. Yet he'd written and was performing this stunning song. Somehow, that brought me solace. I shot a text back.

—*Can we talk?*—

He never responded.

Chapter Twenty-Three

Axel

As I held my seltzer aloft, toasting Ed and Thornton, I managed a smile.

Thornton had asked the entire band to join the happy couple at The Georgian for an engagement dinner. He'd offered to pay—which was almost insulting given how good our album sales were. Then I glanced at the menu and was grateful Thornton had the dough to cover this. The band was doing well, but Pauletta still preached economy. We needed a lot more sales before we could look at anything lavish. That being said, she'd funneled a good chunk of my and Ed's share into our mortgage, and the condo was now ours free and clear. A good twenty years ahead of schedule.

So yeah, I could've paid for my meal.

This was for Ed, though. He'd thought this was going to be an intimate dinner with just Thornton. He'd been truly shocked to find all of us.

Hopefully not too upset at having his special dinner crashed.

This was, after all, the place where it all began.

The grand love affair.

A few things were different.

Kato and Lydia, members of Thornton's crew were here—all cuddled together and cooing.

Mickey, Thornton's director, was here canoodling with our Pauletta. Looking at their unrelenting sweetness should've made me nauseous...but I was so damned happy for them. Pauletta had been waiting her whole damn life for the right person. Who knew Mickey would prove to be that person?

Big Mac was trying to tuck Meg against him, but she was having none of that. Clearly she wanted the best view of the engaged grooms-to-be.

The surprise tonight was Songbird sitting next to none other than Geneva Alvarez. Who swore tonight was entirely off the record.

Pauletta hadn't looked thrilled, but in seven years with the band, Songbird had never asked to bring someone as a date. Had never told us she was seeing someone romantically. Had never even expressed her sexual preference. Or preferences. Ed and I were both definitely bi. Was she?

Although these days, a certain ginger kept popping me into my mind.

Why I'd sent him the video link was beyond me. He would've heard about it eventually. Sending it to his friends? Vaguely stalkerish. Both had responded with thanks and suggestions I might want to speak to

Hugo. Both had also sort of hinted that Hugo didn't know they were making that suggestion.

I'm glad he's got friends taking care of him.

Because I sure as shit wasn't.

Pauletta nudged me.

"What?"

Thornton cleared his throat. "Ed was just confirming you're going to be his best man."

Heat flooded my cheeks. I held up my glass again. "Of course."

"And my brother, Pietro, has agreed to stand up for me." Thornton grinned. "And all my sisters are planning a spa visit with Ed before the big day."

I raised my hand. "Can I get in on that as well?"

The entire table laughed.

I mock glared.

Thornton and Ed kissed, then sat back at the table.

Pauletta rose.

The happy couple—the ones we were celebrating—exchanged confused looks.

Still, our manager scanned the entire table, lingering her gaze on Songbird before finally landing on me. "I got a call from our record label."

I gulped. I'd done what Songbird insisted—passed the song by Pauletta.

She'd approved the release.

Panic engulfed me. We had another two records on our deal. *They're not going to cancel the contract...are they? Did I break clause 43-point-six? Crap. Should've read it closer.* Naturally, I'd trusted Pauletta and the lawyer her father insisted we use.

Paulie raised her glass. "One million views."

I gasped.

No one else did.

I gazed around the table.

Ed snickered. "You think we haven't been watching like hawks? We left it up to you whether or not you did. But we also agreed we'd share it if it hit a million. The song hit that mark three hours ago."

"Holy shit." I might've been a little louder than I should in one of Vancouver's swankiest and most expensive restaurants...but I sort of couldn't help myself. "Uh...crap...?"

"No, not crap." Pauletta held my gaze another long moment before breaking into a huge grin. "The execs decided that even though the song isn't *vintage Grindstone* that they want it on the next album."

"Yes." Big Mac pumped his fist in the air.

Meg giggled. "Excited much?"

"It's an amazing song and will be a huge part of the success we're going to have on the next record." Big Mac beamed.

His certainty disconcerted me.

But that was me—never quite happy enough. Never quite satisfied. Always worried about the next song, the next album, the next concert, the next tour... Hell, I still hadn't absorbed that we were going back to Rocktoberfest as a Friday night headliner.

"To Axel." Pauletta raised her glass. "May his angst earn us big bucks."

The entire table erupted in laughter.

I managed a smile. "Yeah."

The rest of the table toasted me just as our server, Tracey arrived with our meals. As she sorted everyone's order, the reality of the situation hit me like a freight train.

How did you miss this? It's so obvious. You're the only single person at the table.

Well.

Shit.

Fuck.

Up until October, we'd always attended events like this solo. Even if we were dating someone seriously—although that had only been Meg and her asshat ex—we always showed up alone. Solidarity. Yet, somehow, since October, everyone had hooked up. And yeah, Songbird was super new to the couple club…but she now belonged. If the looks she kept exchanging with Geneva were anything to go by, this might turn out to be serious.

I wish Hugo was here.

Which made precisely *zero* sense. I was mad at him. He didn't know anyone here. Except Ed. Okay, so he'd probably fit in just fine. He was that kind of a guy. And man, did he *know* music.

"Yes, he got his job back at the school." Geneva smiled. "Hiring that pitbull lawyer, Wentworth Chamberlain, really got things moving."

Her words finally penetrated. She was talking about Hugo. She glanced around the table. "Didn't you all know?"

Meg cleared her throat.

Geneva's eyes widened. She turned to me. "I apologize."

For the second time tonight, I plastered on a smile. "It's great news. I must've missed it. I've been busy writing music. As Ed can attest, everything falls to the wayside when I'm hyper-focused. Like bathing, cleaning, eating—"

Pauletta kicked me under the table.

Undeterred, I kept going. "I'll even forget to change my underwear. Music comes first, you know? Always has. I always had the love for music, but Hugo nurtured that." I swallowed, then blinked several times. "What they did to him was nasty. He didn't do anything wrong. He's never done anything wrong." I pushed back my chair. "I have to go." I directed my gaze to Thornton. "Apologies. Thanks for the meal, sorry I couldn't—" I coughed to cover my choking.

Ed rose.

I waved him back down.

Then I fled.

Right out to Georgia Street.

I nearly bumped into a group of women who I assumed were tourists. They all had their phones pointed at The Georgian's stunning façade. Something I never took the time to look at because Vancouver was *my* city. The good, the bad, and the ugly. I'd seen the seedy underbelly, and I'd also been toasted by some of the elite at a charity function Pauletta dragged me to last year.

Before Rocktoberfest.

Before my career took off.

Before Hugo broke my heart. Or maybe I did.

I stalked down West Georgia, headed back to the condo. Ed would find me there, of course. And he'd have Thornton with him.

They're getting married.

Ed let me know they were planning a Christmas wedding. So the craziness of Rocktoberfest would be behind us.

Thornton's family had reserved a floor at The Georgian for a freaking week. I couldn't even begin to fathom what kind of money that took. Even with the group-discount rate, that kind of money could feed a serious number of kids.

Except both Thornton and his parents donated tons of money to charities as well. Mostly in Portland, but Ed let it slip Thornton had sought out a couple up here as he felt a new kinship to Vancouver.

God knew, we had plenty of people needing help. Canada's most expensive city. Unbelievable wealth and unfathomable poverty. All residing within less than a mile of each other.

I halted, nearly knocking into a couple of guys holding hands.

One glared, but then his companion yanked on his arm. "That's Axel." He smiled. "Oh God, so sorry, man."

Typical Canadian. I stopped abruptly, and they were apologizing.

"All good—" I started to walk away.

"Could you..." The first man met my gaze, looked at his companion, then back at me. "My husband's a huge fan. I am too." He added that quickly and so transparently, I had to smile.

His grin turned rueful.

"What can I do?"

"A selfie?"

His husband started vibrating. "But you look busy and—"

I waved off the objection. "Always time for a fan."

Carefully, I positioned myself between the two men and—

"Hey, would like me to take your photo?" A gorgeous redhead tugged her companion over with her. "Because I'd love to take your photo."

"And then one with yourself?" Wild guess, but—

Her friend squealed.

My thought of heading back to the Downtown Eastside—back to my old neighborhood—got completely derailed.

Probably for the best.

Yeah.

That.

Chapter Twenty-Four

Hugo

"I'm not certain why I'm here." I glanced around the sunny, bright yellow office of one Justin Bridges.

Counselor.

PhD psychology student.

Coworker of Copeland's mentee Dr. Kennedy Dixon.

Dr. Dixon would've seen me, but one of her seven sisters had some kind of medical emergency and she, along with apparently the rest of the Dixon sisters, had descended upon the hospital.

Justin's comment had been simply, "Kennedy's sorry, and the hospital has no idea what they're in for with the sister invasion."

By necessity, he'd given me the tour of Healing Horses Ranch. Apparently that was normally the job of Rainbow Dixon—Kennedy's younger sister and the manager—but she was...with the other pile of sisters.

My head spun. One sister was enough. Truly. And remembering the names of my now four nieces and nephews was plenty. Healthy baby Mia made the fourth and, Leonora swore, the last.

I didn't have to worry about my family's legacy. Leonora might no longer carry the Threadgold name, but she'd ensured the security of the next generation.

And had given me permission to send along the baby photo to our father.

Small steps.

I gazed down at the yellow labrador retriever at my feet.

Tiffany was the ranch's official comfort dog. Her services were completely optional.

Right...like I was going to say *no* to those gorgeous dark-brown soulful eyes and the happy grin as she panted.

Now she rested against my leg as I petted her head.

"Sorry about that." Justin stepped into the room, closed the door, then made his way over to me.

I'd dropped into the oversized couch and made myself at home. I figured that was okay.

He handed me a bottle of water, then sat himself. "Denise, another counselor, has an open slot, so she'll handle anything that comes up. I'm not certain I ever realized how much Rainbow actually does around here until she took a break." He winced. "Not that having a sister in the hospital is a break—"

I held up my hand. "I get it."

The man smiled and my breath caught.

Cope had obviously never met Justin.

And clearly Kennedy had never described him.

Or someone might've thought to warn me I was meeting my twin. Red hair, red beard with gold flecks...only Justin's eyes were a lighter shade of blue than my own.

Well, almost my twin—I had a few white whiskers, while Justin, clearly more than a decade my junior, didn't have any.

"I'm gay." I wasn't certain why I felt the need to blurt that out, but I did.

Justin smiled. "I was aware. I am too, if that makes any difference."

"It doesn't."

"That's cool." He uncapped his water, took a sip, recapped it, then put it on a table next to his high-backed chair. "I researched you after Kennedy asked me to help you out today."

"Oh." I frowned.

He held up his hand. "These days, it's just the prudent thing to do. I might not always tell my clients, although I believe honesty is important. You seemed like a guy who wants it straight."

"I do."

"And I'm someone who likes to work with as much information as possible. Without making judgements."

I eyed him. "The video was a pretty hot kiss."

He coughed. "Uh, yes it was. And I understand it was released without your consent."

"Well, the kiss was consensual."

"I would agree it certainly appeared consensual. But coercion can be powerful—"

"He didn't coerce me. And neither of us knew we were being recorded. And yes, the person who taped us admitted he shouldn't have done so, and everyone seems to agree the recording should've been destroyed. But it wasn't. Here we are."

"You got your job back."

"Thanks to a very high-priced attorney." I winced. "Oh, and the fact I didn't do anything fucking wrong." I winced again. "Sorry."

"No apologies necessary. Everything that gets said in this room stays in this room. Unless you admit to abusing a child or being a danger to yourself or someone else."

"No, no, and no." I stroked Tiffany's soft fur. "She's very...mellow."

Justin smiled. "Yes, she is. I think she carries the heaviest load in the place. She doesn't just take care of patients...she takes care of us as well." He gazed outside. "Of course, the horses do their fair share as well."

"Yeah. I read up on this place. After Cope suggested it."

"You've come a long way."

"Vancouver's not so far. My parents own a chalet in Whistler, so we left the city regularly. The drive out here was less treacherous than the Sea-to-Sky highway."

"That's true. The highway to Mission City's pretty tame, and our back roads are well-maintained."

"Right."

"But that's not what you're here to discuss."

"No." I eyed Tiffany.

She met my gaze.

I tried really super hard not to think of another pair of dark-brown soulful eyes. "I always wanted a dog as a child. My parents wouldn't allow it."

"That's unfortunate. I have a mutt my husband and children adore."

"You do too, I suspect." I caught his gaze.

"Yeah." He smiled. "Have you ever considered getting a pet yourself?"

"I'm never home. Between school, my volunteering, my best friend who's about to give birth any day..." I shrugged. I wasn't going to mention my old feral rescue.

"That's fair."

"I suppose I could get a pair of cats." I scrunched my nose.

"What's that look for?"

"Just thinking about how much my ex-husband loathed animals—cats in particular. Which should mean that I could get one just in retaliation...but that's not fair to an animal. I mean, I'd love them all on their own..."

"Your ex-husband?"

"The douchebag."

Justin tried, but failed, to hide a smile. "Okay."

"That's what Axel calls him. Or called him. Like, on national television."

"Ah. I didn't have time to watch that interview. I will, though, before you come back. If you come back," he added. "No pressure. We're always here."

"I appreciate that." I gazed around the soothing room. "He won't talk to me."

"Your ex?"

"What? Oh no. Axel. I tried to explain to him that what he'd overheard was a misunderstanding, and then I thought if I gave him the CD that would make up for what he thought he overheard, and then..." I sighed. "He released the video and won't take my calls." Despite my despair, anger rose in me. "Why won't he fucking talk to me? He did this to me, not the other way around. I'm begging for a chance to explain, and he's the one who blew up my world."

I'd been angry.

He'd made the video.

I'd reached out.

He'd blocked me.

"That sounds...complicated." Justin smiled. "Why don't we slowly unpack this?"

That didn't sound like fun to me but, as I pulled out of the driveway two hours later, I could acknowledge feeling mildly better. We had *unpacked* everything about my complicated relationship with Axel. Or acquaintance? No, we'd nearly fucked. That constituted a relationship.

Then Justin gave me a tour of the ranch and I met the horses—Briar, Sugar, Sienna, and Fallon. They were just as placid as dear Tiffany who followed us around everywhere.

As Justin was seeing me to my car, an SUV pulled up.

A stunning brunette emerged and, upon noticing me, came over. She apologized as Justin introduced her as Dr. Kennedy Dixon.

I waved off her apologies, complimented Justin's counseling skills, then drove away after having made the man blush.

Something that brought a smile to my face.

I was nearly to the bridge that would take me back to Vancouver when my phone rang.

Without looking, I hit accept on the steering wheel. "Hugo Threadgold."

A heavy sigh. A sigh I recognized. A quick glance at my dash confirmed my suspicion.

Should've declined the call.

Might've been Axel.

Yeah, but it wasn't.

"How can I help you, Mr. Merkerson?"

"We have a problem."

"I can't imagine what that might be."

"Fucking hell, Threadgold, you know what it is. We're in the news again."

I sighed as I merged onto the bridge. "I hadn't heard. Anyway, you wanted publicity." *So go suck rotten eggs.*

"Not because my fucking male music teacher had his tongue down a former male student's throat."

"Are you trying to insinuate something? Weren't you the one who suggested I get down on my knees—"

"No! I didn't say that. I didn't mean that."

And yet he had said that, and he had meant that. Perhaps not literally—he hadn't known Axel was gay—but he'd wanted me to secure Axel's agreement to perform. That felt...very quaint. Almost like a lifetime ago. But that was all beside the point. Merkerson was a homophobic asshole—and we both knew it. "What do you want?"

"The McPherson Foundation has pulled their funding."

I sighed. "Their books were seized by the police, and their assets have been frozen pending an investigation of the foundation's financial..." I tried to remember what I'd heard in the news versus what Wentworth Chamberlain had shared. "Shenanigans."

"I'm cutting your budget if you don't make up the shortfall."

Fucking hell. "You know, I'm certain Geneva Alvarez would love to do a story about how funding from the music department is being pulled even after the music teacher was vindicated and found—"

"Are you threatening me?"

"I'm suggesting you might want to find somewhere else to cut—"

"You think any department wants their funding cut?"

I sighed. "Of course not."

"So get Grindstone to do a charity concert. I bet it'll sell out."

"You did not just suggest—" *Fucking hell. This was what got you into the mess with Axel in the first place! Goddamnit.*

"Your funding, your decision." He cut the call.

I nearly drove into the next lane.

A sharp horn had me yanking the wheel back just centimeters from catastrophe.

I waved.

The woman flashed me the bird.

Which was also so, so, so very Canadian. Polite as a shit in person, but rabid demons behind the wheel.

I sighed.

There has to be a way to fix this.

You know there is.

Yeah, but I'm too chickenshit.

Instead of going down that road, I grabbed three salads from a fast-food chain not known for making very good salads and I headed to Renee and Copeland's.

Chapter Twenty-Five

Axel

E d continued to stare at me.

"You're telling me that wasn't the cheesiest song ever? In the history of all cheesy songs?"

He squinted, as if in thought. "Well, first, I'm not certain I was supposed to hear it."

I glared. "He gave *you* the song to give to *me*."

"Yes."

"Hugo."

"Well...yes." Ed scratched his elbow. "He said something about unread messages and unanswered calls and that it was super important that you get this."

I rolled my eyes. The *super important* song was a cheesy, mopey song about a pretty prince who got his wires crossed and got angry at the wrong person. "Ed."

"Yes."

"You realize I'm the pretty prince."

He snorted. "Yeah, I know. That's imagery I could do without."

"Why are you defending him?"

"Axel—"

"Don't start."

"Okay, but you just said—"

"I know what I said." I might've snapped that.

"Oh, sorry—" Thornton's voice reached us.

Ed and I sat on the couch, but Thornton wouldn't have been able to see us from his vantage point.

"I'll just—"

"It's fine." Ed and I might've said that at the same time.

"Right." Thornton moved to the kitchen. "I'm just grabbing a ginger ale. Do either of you want one?"

I gagged.

Ed raised his hand. "Thanks."

"Axel? You want a cola or something?"

I sighed. "Sure, Thornton. Since you're already there."

Moments later, he returned with two cans of ginger ale and one glass bottle of cola. I maintained soda tasted best out of a glass bottle.

Thornton humored me.

Ed rolled his eyes.

I took the bottle.

Thornton began to move away.

"No, stay." I glared at him.

He winced. "I really didn't mean to interrupt. I was working and not paying attention and—"

"Was thirsty and wandered out into the living room of the condo where you live." I offered a smile that I didn't feel. "It's fine."

"It's not, but we'll leave it at that." He nodded toward the television. "Were you watching something?"

"Play it for him, Ed," I commanded.

This time, Ed winced. "Uh, I'm not sure—"

"*He* gave it to you. *He* knows you're engaged to Thornton as well as my best friend. *He* really didn't have a right to expect privacy."

Thornton's eyebrows shot up. "Uh—"

"It's fine." Yeah, I snapped that.

After a long moment, Ed hit play and the sound of Hugo singing a song filled the air. His musical talent was phenomenal. His voice...not so much.

A couple of times, Thornton chuckled.

Yeah, at the cheesy parts. The same ones that made me laugh out loud and yet wince on the inside. Hugo's message couldn't have been clearer—I was acting like a spoiled brat. Or at least that was how I interpreted it.

The song ended.

Thornton cleared his throat. "That was..."

"Adorable and sweet?" Ed grinned.

"Cheesy and sappy?" Couldn't let my best friend get the last word.

"Uh..." Thornton scrunched his nose. "Yes."

Somehow, I was certain he meant all of the above.

"You going to respond?" Thornton eyed me in a way I often found disconcerting. Ed knew me, so when he looked at me *that way*, I knew he did it because he had some insight. Thornton, however, hadn't even known me eight months. As far as I was concerned, he didn't have the right to claim knowledge of me—of my soul. And yet, he gave me looks that assured me he knew more than he was letting on.

Which meant he was either fucking intuitive, or Ed was feeding him private information.

Or both.

Neither of which sat well with me. "When are y'all getting married?"

Ed blinked. "Christmas. After Rocktoberfest." He cocked his head. "Are you okay?"

I pushed up off the couch. "I'm fine. Send the CD back. He should be sending you digital files."

"He doesn't have my email."

"Oh, I'm certain he could find it if he really wanted to." I stalked off to my room. Once inside—with the door firmly closed and locked—I called Geneva Alvarez.

"Axel Townsend. Lovely to hear from you."

The sound of a door closing reached my ear.

"Is this a social call?" She paused. "Is Songbird okay?"

Confirmation, if I needed it, that the two women were still together and going strong.

"Song's fine. We're all doing well. Could...would you be interested in doing an interview with me?"

A long pause ensued. "Is Pauletta aware you're calling me?"

"Pauletta's not the boss of me."

Geneva laughed. "Yes, that's true. But I have a working relationship with her that I'd like to maintain."

This time I hesitated. *She has a point.*

"But perhaps you let me know what's on your mind and we can figure something out?"

I chuckled. "I like how you think." I took a deep breath. "I just...there are still lots of rumors swirling—"

"Hang on a sec, do you mind if I record this? I'm big on accuracy and my shorthand sucks."

"Don't they teach that in journalism school?"

She chuckled.

I steadied myself.

"I'll take that as positive affirmation on the recording. Now, you were saying about rumors swirling?"

"Yeah." I cleared my throat. "I don't want you to think that I think that I'm hot shit—"

"Okay."

"But I've seen social media. And a few reports on websites. Well, more like blogs and—"

"I get it, Axel." Her soft voice hit just the right note—likely as she'd known it would. "You want to set the record straight."

"Yes." I drew in a deep breath. "On the record. Hugo Threadgold was my high school music teacher. I'll always be grateful for what he did—for both Ed and me. But that's as far as it goes. He's no one special to me. I need you, and fans, to know—I'm not in a relationship with Hugo. Or anyone else. I'm taking the time to be true to myself. To figure out who I am. And what I want."

"And that is?"

"To make music. To sing songs that fans can relate to. That they can say, 'hey, he gets it' or 'he's going through what I'm going through' or, best of all, 'he went through something rough and came out the other side—maybe I can too'."

"That's laudable. You want to make a difference in the world."

I laughed. "Geneva, I'm just a rock singer. I'm not going to change the world in any perceivable way. But when I get a note from a fan that my song impacted them, then I know I've done something right. I always want my songs to be a force for good in the world. To give people hope."

"Like "Calling for Help"." She paused. "Like "Sunrise"."

"Yeah."

"Off the record?"

"Sure." I squinted, wondering where she was going with this.

"I think you did a good thing. With the documentary. People have responded positively to it. For the most part."

Yeah, like except those few people who condemned Ed and me for not being there when Kyesha died. As if we could've somehow saved her from tainted drugs. We couldn't have, of course, but that didn't stop the critics.

"There are days I wonder."

"You shouldn't. I've heard a few stories of people going to get help with their addictions since your story came out."

"And Ed's."

"Yes, and Ed's. But yours has a greater impact, Axel. You're the lead singer. You're the frontman."

"Shouldn't that be front person?"

She laughed. "You calling me out on sexist language—that's priceless."

"I know what you mean. I don't necessarily agree with it, but I can respect it." I wiped my sweaty hand on my jeans. "So you'll write the story?"

"I will. Would you consider letting me do some stills to go with it? Human interest pieces always do better with something unique to go with them."

"Uh..." Crap. *This is getting way more complicated and...I might be losing my nerve. Maybe this was a bad idea.* "You know—"

"I'm going to co-ordinate with Pauletta."

Oh shit. "That's not really—"

"This is a good story, Axel. About how people can have healthy relationships with themselves and not always need to be with someone."

"Well, I'm not certain that's what I meant."

"But it's a conclusion readers can draw. Being alone these days is common. We can talk about the importance of friendship..."

Damn. She had me. Because Ed meant more to me than any woman ever had and any future partner might. He was my rock. My foundation. My world. "Yeah, okay."

"Great!"

And so, three days later, I found myself at a café, having *casual* photos taken by a professional photographer and tons of equipment. So much for *not a big deal*—which was what Pauletta promised.

She'd liked this idea...thought it was one of my better ones in this entire clusterfuck that just kept going.

I'd taken down the kissing video right away but, as Pauletta predicted, people had downloaded it and were still sharing it.

Hugo was back at work, of course, but that didn't fix the rest of the mess.

Perhaps the article would.

So you hope.

Chapter Twenty-Six

Hugo

"Advance copy—this will be released in three weeks." Ed Markham stared at me.

Slowly, I took the CD from his hand. "Do you mind meeting up like this?"

He snickered. "This time I'm not going behind his back. He gave this to me. And told me to tell you—"

"Advance copy and it'll be released in three weeks." I scratched my beard. "Why is he giving me notice? I thought..." I swallowed. "The article made it damn clear we were nothing to each other."

Ed glanced around the A&W on Hastings Street where we were meeting. The place was deserted in the middle of the day. I was on my lunch break, and Ed was...

Huh.

I didn't know what Ed was. What he was sacrificing to come here. What he might otherwise be doing.

He tapped the CD case. "My personal email is in there. If you have any other *files* to send me, you can use that. If it's too big to send, use a drop-box." He shrugged. "Or we can meet again. It just…"

"Feels weird?" This was the first time I'd seen him…well, talked to him…in ten years. The launch party certainly hadn't counted. All the times I'd watched Grindstone perform hadn't either. I glanced at my watch. "I have a couple of minutes. How are you?"

After a moment, he offered a rueful smile. "Happy as all fuck because I'm in love and feeling guilty as all fuck because I'm in love."

"Ah." I let those words sink in. "I'm really happy for you. And, I don't know, proud that you were finally in a place where you felt you could come out. That's a big deal—for a lot of people."

"Seems weird to people that Axel and I have been best friends for almost twenty-five years and yet I didn't know he was bi."

"But he knew you were."

"Right." He tapped the table. "So it's not like I would've judged. I could've been supportive. He's hidden that part of him away for so long that I…I feel like he doesn't know what to do about it."

"What do you mean?" *Do you really want to open this can of worms? Yep. I do. If only to torture myself.*

"I mean that he's still walled himself off. Since Kyesha, he's never saw any woman more than a few times—no matter how smart, attractive, or attentive she'd been. Now, of course, I wonder if that was because he would've preferred being in the company of a guy."

"And right now?"

Ed narrowed his eyes. "He's not dating or fucking around, if that's what you're asking."

"I'm not." *Fucking liar.* "I just…did I mess things up for him?"

He pushed out a laugh. "Uh, he kissed you. Unless I read the video wrong—"

"You didn't." Heat rose to my cheeks.

"And he released the video."

"Okay, that's true."

"Which was a super shitty thing to do. You never out someone. Ever. He knows better. Just..."

"I hurt him."

"Yeah."

"And you want to know why."

"I'd like to know how." He held up his hand. "But it's none of my business and I'm so not getting into the middle of this. Between the two of you. Y'all need to sort out your own shit." He looked me over. "Because something tells me you're not handling this any better than he is."

Not looking at myself took some effort. The day was hot, sticky, and gross for this early in May. Despite the laboring air conditioning, I wasn't much better. "I'm surviving, Ed. This just...wasn't where I thought I'd wind up."

"Being outed on the internet by a former student."

"Sure."

"Falling in love with that former student...?"

I blinked, winced, and ducked my head. "Sure." I sighed, then—after what felt like a monumental effort, met his gaze. "I can't be *in love* with Axel—"

"Why the fuck not?" Ed made the demand just as a woman with four kids came into the restaurant.

The chatter from the children was indistinguishable, but clearly none were happy. In this weather? I didn't blame them. Just thinking about heading back out to my SUV filled me with dread. Let alone going back to my classroom with no air conditioning.

"You mean aside from the optics of him being my former student?" I winced yet again. "Well, the fact we've barely spent any time together as adults." Again with the fucking heated cheeks.

"He won't tell me what happened in Black Rock."

Which made me feel very guilty for having told Renee and Copeland. Oh, and Justin, my new therapist. I'd ventured out to Mission City twice more. He'd offered to give me sessions over the phone—now I'd opened up more. Yet, despite being expensive and time-consuming to drive that far out of the city, I chose to make the trek. I knew I wouldn't be as honest if I wasn't looking at him—or if I was looking at him through a computer screen. Truthfully, he needed to see my body language. To know if I was lying to him. I tried not to...but I wasn't telling him the entire truth either.

"Mr. Threadgold?"

I blinked. "It's fine to call me Hugo. If you want."

"Hugo." He said the name as if trying it out. "Okay, well, I'm sure you need—"

"Did I screw him up? By...doing what we did?"

Ed sighed. "I'm working off the assumption you did more than kiss."

Damn cheeks. Must be as red as Rudolph's nose.

"Yeah, that's what I figured. So I'm not going to try to guess because more than kissing leaves a lot of wiggle room, but Songbird said Axel came back around dawn. She heard him—none of the rest of us did. Now I understand why he snuck out."

"We, uh, went back to my tent and, uh, made out."

He cocked his head. "Okay, TMI, but that helps. So yeah, Axel might date a lot, and he might not always select the best bed partners—"

Wince.

"—but he takes care of himself. And his partners. He's not cruel. Which is why his behavior to you is so aberrant."

"He misunderstood something."

Ed arched an eyebrow.

I blew out a breath, counted to ten, and contemplated my next move. "My principal wants you and Axel to come back to the school and to do a charity rock concert. He sees dollar signs." I sighed. "He always sees dollar signs."

"That's it? A concert?"

"Yeah." I rubbed my forehead. "The guy called me before dawn, demanding to know if I'd spoken to Axel yet. I might've been angry and said some stupid things. But I didn't mean them and, out of context, they sounded really bad."

"You've tried to apologize, of course."

"Yes." I tapped the table. "At the time, of course. And I hoped the CD I gave him—"

"At the premiere."

"—at the premiere...would be a gesture of sorts." *Go for broke.* "He wrote some songs, back when you both were my students."

Ed cocked his head.

"And they were damn good songs. Perhaps a little juvenile, but that's what high school is." I blew out yet another breath. "My students recorded them, and I was trying to give the CD to Axel."

"He did take it, right?"

"Yeah."

"He hasn't let me listen to it."

"He claims he's embarrassed by them." I scratched the top of my right hand with my left. "The thing is...I think he should put them out there. Whether he lets my students sing them or he does it himself, I think they're worth being published."

"Many artists never publish their first few attempts. Plenty of paintings, sculptures, musical scores, and manuscripts are sitting in the back of peoples' closets for a reason, Hugo."

I held his gaze as he said my name. Then sighed. "You're right. But...to see where he is now and where he came from—where you both came from. That's remarkable, Ed. Surely you see that."

He narrowed his eyes. "I do. But I don't see what good could come of old songs getting out in the world."

"If I send you the songs, will you listen to them? They're rough cuts, of course, and I would never publish them without permission."

"Glad to hear it." He scoffed. "Copyright's a thing."

"I know."

"AI generated fakes are bad enough. We're constantly worried someone's going to try to take our sound."

"That's a legitimate concern these days."

"It's why Pauletta has a lawyer on retainer."

Slowly, I nodded. "I'm glad she's taking care of you."

He chuckled. "Someone has to herd the musician cats. She'd love if we were all obedient dogs."

"Ah, yes."

He eyed me. "What?"

"What, what?"

He pointed. "You're thinking of something."

I snickered. "Ed, my mind never turns off, you must know that." I was forever bringing new ideas to the classroom.

"Axel's the one with ADHD. Now—"

"There's a therapy dog at the ranch where I'm going for counseling."

He sat up straighter.

"Yeah, I admit to needing help to sort through this mess. Between my principal, the misunderstanding with Axel, and my lack of truly dealing with the terrible marriage I'd been in..." I scratched my cheek. "Frankly, I needed help. Still need help," I was quick to add. "But I'm making progress. Maybe one day I'll forgive myself." I clutched the CD in my hand. "Three weeks?"

"Yeah. Pauletta knows about this one as well. The last one was more official. This one..." He tilted his head. "Straight acoustic. Just him and a guitar. He's going to release it straight to the internet."

"Why tell me? Why not just release it?"

"It's going to coincide with our official announcement that we're going to Rocktoberfest this year."

"Oh, wow, that's amazing."

"And under wraps for another little bit. Swirling rumors make Pauletta happy—if they're good ones—because it means we're getting traction. We're making a name for ourselves. Increasing our fan base. That's a win in her books."

"Well, I won't say anything about Black Rock." I checked my phone. "Shit, I have to get back to school."

He held out his hand.

We shook.

I rose from the booth and headed out the door into the furnace-like heat.

Exercising self-control I barely knew I had, I waited until I was home from school that night. I planted myself in my living room, in front of a portable a/c unit. I slid the CD into an external player hooked up to my laptop and played the song.

Axel's haunting voice filled both the room and my heart. Tears pricked my eyes as I listened to a song about shattered dreams. About longing. About endless pain.

I played it over and over again.

Eventually, I wept.

Much later, I slept.

Chapter Twenty-Seven

Axel

"Okay, seriously?" I sat next to Ed as he played Hugo's latest song on his laptop.

They'd stopped exchanging CDs apparently, and my former music teacher had sent his latest cheesy song via a file sharing app.

"Do you want to hear it again?" Ed cocked his head. "I thought the song was...charming."

"Oh, my God. All the *I love a man who doesn't believe in me*. Or *if only the man could see*. Or, Jesus, *he could see his dreams are real*. Did you hear that shit? With the *ooo waah wahh* thrown in?" I winced. "Cheesy is generous. It's...bad."

Thornton snickered. "Only you would see it that way. I think it's charming."

I shot him a glare. "Who asked you?"

"I asked him," Ed shot back. "He was the one who said I had to play it for you—and here we are. And what did you expect? You wrote that heartbreak song, which is releasing in four days, I would like to remind you. Then we're announcing our triumphant return to Rocktoberfest. You thought he'd just...take it lying down?"

"Well, not with me, he doesn't."

''What?" Ed might've snapped that.

"I think it's sweet." Thornton offered his shit-eating grin.

"Thank God he's not going to release it." I eyed Ed. "He's not releasing, is he?"

"You mean like some acoustic solo on the internet?" He tapped his lips. "He didn't say. He would get a ton of hits, though. There's plenty of curiosity about him—even after all this time."

Which sort of bothered me. Hugo had never wanted the spotlight. He'd always wanted to be behind the scenes. Even though he was incredibly talented, he never performed. Well, perhaps in private. Certainly not in public.

That you know. Ten years is a long time, and you haven't kept track of him, have you?

"Would it be the end of the world if he did?" Ed eyed me. "We'd get more attention for sure. And since it's pretty harmless, I think even Pauletta couldn't object."

"Tell me you did not just invoke our manager's name." This I did snap.

Thornton chuckled.

"Who asked you? Why are you even here?"

Hard to say who appeared more shocked and then hurt—Ed or Thornton.

Eventually, though, Ed's hurt turned darker. "He's my fiancé, Axel. He's here because I love him and want him here. I'm lucky he's willing to do that, given this isn't even his country."

I should've felt contrite—but I didn't. "You once said you loved me and wanted to be here with me. Has that changed?"

Ed and Thornton exchanged a look.

My heart sank. I rose. "Fine, then. I'll move out. I think Big Mac's spending all his time at Meg's these days. I'm sure I can crash—"

"Big Mac's lease was up last month." Ed held my gaze. "He moved in permanently with Meg. I mean, they're getting married in a couple of months."

Meg had her preventative breast removal surgery a month ago. *And you haven't even asked how she's doing.* As she was our drummer, we were taking a break. The record execs had wanted us touring after the album, but even they admitted Meg's health came first. Ed had told me they found a small lump and it might've eventually become cancerous. Meg was so damn young, but I understood her choice to choose better health than keeping, as she put them *ticking time bombs.* Genetics sucked—but she'd had the tests and they'd given her some hard truths.

"I'm certain I can share a bed with Wren." Wren being Meg's very spoiled dog. "Or Pauletta. She's got that big—"

"Mickey's there all the time." Thornton eyed me. "We're not asking you to leave the condo, Axel. This is your home."

And just like that, the pieces fell into place. "You're not asking me to leave...but you're going to."

Ed winced. Then straightened his shoulders. "I'm going to give you my share. You'll pretty much own it free and clear."

"That's hundreds of thousands of dollars." I spun on Thornton. "You're just gifting him the money?"

"It's a loan." Thornton slowly nodded. "We've bought a small house in Kerrisdale—"

"Kerrisdale?" My head ached. "Even the smallest of houses in Kerrisdale costs well over a million dollars."

"Over two." Ed murmured that, but I heard him clearly.

"Throwing your money around?" I glared at Thornton. I hated White savior shit. I didn't want him *saving* Ed and I sure as shit didn't want Hugo saving me—even if only from myself.

"I'm not *throwing my money around*." Thornton laced his hand in Ed's. "I'm making a life for us. I've rented out my loft in Portland. I've secured a work visa for Canada."

"Just that easy?"

"Far from it." Ed fidgeted. "He'd be giving up a lot to come here."

"Not really." Thornton brought their joined hands to his lips and kissed Ed's knuckles.

Don't gag.

I wouldn't. Because the gesture was sweet. And so…Thornton. He wasn't the detached man we'd met nearly eight months ago. He was kind and gentle. His thoughtfulness knew no bounds. And, most importantly, he made my best friend so fucking happy. Ed was incandescent with joy.

I was happy for him. Truly. Except…we'd had a really good thing going for a long time. I didn't know how I'd cope without him. "We can sell the condo." Inwardly, I winced. Outwardly, I held my ground.

"Axel—"

I waved off his objection. "You should be able to contribute to your new life…even if he is richer than…" I floundered.

"Axel—"

Another slash of my hand through the air. "Yeah, it's rude to talk about money. Except because of his money, you don't need me anymore—" My voice caught. "I have to go."

I bolted.

Well, I went to the front door, shoved my feet in my shoes, and searched for my keys.

"Axel, we need to talk." Ed's voice was laced with concern.

"No, we really don't. Ah here they are." I grabbed my keys, double-checked my phone was in my pocket, then unlocked the door.

"Axel." This time, Thornton spoke.

I blinked several times before meeting his gaze.

"Are you okay? Should you be driving?"

Shooting back a comment about it being none of his business died on my lips. He loved Ed. He would give a shit about me because if something happened to me, Ed would be devastated. Even in my muddled brain, I was able to piece that much together.

I took a deep breath. "I'm fine. I just...need some time. I've got my phone, okay? I'll be back...later. Don't worry."

"Axel." Ed's voice carried a worry I remembered well. I hadn't heard that tone in a long time because I'd been okay for a long time.

"I'm okay, Ed." I met his gaze. "I don't feel the need for a drink. Or a hit. I'd never endanger my sobriety." I blinked, then met Thornton's concerned gaze. "I swore on Kyesha's grave that I'd never...and I won't." I opened the door, not waiting for a response, and left.

The elevator ride down felt like it took forever. I'd never actually been to Kyesha's grave in Portland, but I knew Thornton would understand I wasn't being literal. And hopefully he and Ed would understand.

I waved to our concierge as I headed out into the warm day. Cursing my stupidity, I strode to the first sunglasses store I could find. I paid way too much, but the relief was instantaneous as I stepped back into the bright sunshine. Looking dorky was the least of my worries, and I made my way down Hastings Street. The homeless situation was still bad in Vancouver, even as the city had attempted to sweep people off the street. Without anywhere for them to go, however, they kept coming back.

Passing Carnegie Library on my way through the intersection of Hastings and Main, I smiled to myself. Carnegie had been closest to our home, but Ed always dragged me to Library Square because, frankly, a different caliber of people. Rarely did the homeless congregate in Library Square. Instead most of the patrons were student, seniors, children, and people who lived nearby. Lived on the Westside of Vancouver. A million miles from the Eastside. At least wealth-wise. I continued down Hastings Street, trying to ignore the drug addicts, homeless, and those who were simply destitute.

Over and over, I thought about the song I composed back in high school. About feeling at home with the inhabitants of this part of town. A song, apparently, that Hugo still had.

I hadn't listened to the CD he'd given me. I'd managed to look through the song list and had cringed over and over again. A couple of the songs I didn't even remember. Most, though, I had. Memories of the unrequited love songs hit the hardest. They'd been the cheesiest. Because they'd been about Hugo. Only I hadn't known he was gay. Or married to a man who turned out to be a douchebag.

Are you any better with what you've done with your life?

Ouch.

True.

But ouch.

Eventually, I stepped beyond the Downtown Eastside and made my way through to East Vancouver. The west was mostly towers with a smattering of homes between Cambie Street and Stanley Park. The east was some low-rise buildings mixed with plenty of houses. Small houses as well as ones torn down and replaced by monstrosities.

Still, I walked. When I'd left the condo, I hadn't been certain where I was going or what I was going to wind up doing. By chance I'd grabbed running shoes instead of a more stylish pair of boots. As my legs ate up the miles, that choice felt providential.

Eventually, I turned off Hastings and headed down Victoria Drive. Just a couple of streets later, I hung a left and continued eastward down Turner Street. I'd never been here, of course. Never would've had a reason to. Vancouver itself was a sprawling city. Add the other cities close by and the Vancouver region was substantial.

I stopped on a patched sidewalk that really needed complete replacing and stared at the small house thirty feet away.

The squat, one-story house was slightly elevated with stairs leading up and basement windows visible. The garden was neatly trimmed and the one tree appeared to offer shade. The yard was fenced in with an adorable gate. The stone stairs showed a little wear, but the house carried a certain charm. A house I would've done anything to live in during my childhood. Our two-bedroom three-story walk-up had been...awful. Barely affordable with what my father made. My stay-at-home mother had been...well, not very helpful.

I tried to wipe out the memories I always did my best to repress. Thanks to Ed, I'd survived. Thanks to him and Pauletta, I had a new life. And yeah, Ed was leaving. For a better life. But he wasn't leaving Grindstone. He wasn't abandoning me—no matter how I chose to frame this departure. I could wish him well and help him pack or I could sulk and be a baby about it. Although the sulking option was tempting, in my heart, I knew I wouldn't. I loved him too much to make this all about me—no matter how much it felt like it was.

The gate swung open when I undid the latch. Carefully, I closed it up again. Slowly, I took in the entire space. Small. Cozy. But charming.

I ascended the stairs and stopped at the door. I wasn't expected. I didn't even know if anyone was at home. If there might be a guest. Or even if my presence would be welcome.

Still, I knocked.

And waited.

I had my hand raised to knock again when the door opened. "Can I come in?" If someone else was here, I'd just deal with the consequences.

"This doesn't mean anything."

And maybe if I repeated the words enough, they might actually be true.

Yeah, right.

Chapter Twenty-Eight

Hugo

This doesn't mean anything.

Axel could tell himself that. As I closed my front door, I could tell myself that.

But it'd be a lie.

This meant *everything*.

Axel stood in my living room, slowly spinning. Taking in the couch, the recliner, the television, and the bookcase.

Maybe he's interested in my reading preferences. Mysteries, thrillers, literary masterpieces, and a couple of gay romances. Most of the ones I read were on my eReader. Occasionally, though, I came across a book I loved so much that I needed a paperback to admire.

None of which would be of any interest to him. "Would you like a drink of water?"

"I want you to fuck me."

Well, okay then. Nothing like bluntness.

Finally, he met my gaze. "Or I can fuck you. Except I wouldn't know what I was doing. I mean, I've fucked—" He winced. "I've made love with plenty of women. So that part I understand. I mean, and I obviously understand gay sex. You don't live with a closeted best friend and roommate without learning a few things. I mean, I never slept with him, or—"

I raised my hand in an attempt to halt his rambling. "Did you walk here?"

Slowly, he nodded.

"Then you need a glass of water. It's a warm day and you're sweating."

He sniffed his pits. "Shit."

I laughed. "Axel, I don't care. But you need to replenish fluids. Especially if we're going to...do other things."

"Can I borrow your shower?"

"As long as you take a bottle of water in with you." I was dead serious about this. I really didn't care how he smelled—but there was a sweaty sheen to his skin, and I'd worry continuously if he didn't replace fluids. "Or do you want some juice or something? Hell, I don't even know if you have a medical—"

Within moments, he was right in my space. "I'll take a fucking shower and I'll drink fucking water and then one of us is fucking the other. I've waited..." Something flashed in those dark-brown eyes. "A fucking long time."

"Yeah." October felt like a million years ago at this point. Every night I'd dreamt of this moment. Many times I'd masturbated to the memory of his skin, his moans, and the memory of his hand wrapped around my cock. But, much as I wanted to, I couldn't just throw him down on the mattress and fuck him.

Could I?

"We need to talk."

His gaze turned feral. "I'll leave." He poked my chest. Hard. "I'm not here to talk. I've done enough talking. And enough thinking. Either fuck me or I walk back out the door."

To what? What are you running from? Because as much as I wanted to believe my song had driven him here, I didn't. Believe. No, something had happened. And if I chose to ignore that and just—as he put it—fuck him, I'd be contributing to the problem. I certainly wouldn't be making it better. "Axel."

He shook his head. "Either you find lube and a condom while I shower, or I walk out the door and you never see me again."

Something tells me you're going to do that anyway. The whole not meaning anything made that a strong possibility.

But, in the end, I knew I'd give in. Even if we only had today, I'd take it. "Lube and condoms." Tentatively, I stroked down his cheek. "But water and shower first." I didn't care about the shower, but clearly he did. "And if you give me your clothes, I can wash them." *Because that'll keep you here longer.*

His eyes flashed with triumph. He toed off his sneakers, then pulled his soaked T-shirt over his head and tossed it at me. He unbuttoned his jeans, lowered the zipper, and removed them—along with his underwear—in one fluid move.

No missing the cock that already stood at half-mast. Apparently this discussion had just been foreplay to him.

Blood rushed to my own cock as I snagged all his clothes. "Grab a water bottle from the fridge. Bathroom is the last door on the right. My bedroom's across from it. I'll be waiting." I didn't know if taking charge was the correct thing to do—but it felt right.

He licked his lips. "Yeah, I can do that." He stalked into the kitchen, offering me the most wonderful view of his glorious ass. All round, firm, and with just the right amount of jiggle. I'd seen that ass encased in leather pants or jeans quite a few times over the last few years, but I'd never felt the longing and need that coursed through me now. For just a moment, I took a deep breath.

I can do this. I can make it good for him.

And hell, I might just make it good for myself as well.

After the sound of the bathroom door closing reached my ears, I hustled down to the laundry. I emptied his jeans pockets, carefully gathering everything to bring back upstairs with me. I tossed in a few of my own dirty clothes to make a full load, then I set the washing machine. As soon as that was done, I scurried back upstairs. I found an extra charging cable and plugged in Axel's phone. I wouldn't ask if Ed knew he was here. I'd also resist the urge to ask if anyone might worry if he stayed longer than a few hours.

This doesn't mean anything.

Yeah, except it meant everything.

You need to be naked.

Yet I had a momentary hesitation. I didn't have the body of a twenty-eight-year-old man who kept himself in shape. Tipping over forty had encouraged me to do more exercise, but I focused on stamina rather than body sculpting. *Stamina might stand you in good stead. If he cared what you looked like, he would've bolted in Black Rock. Or not come here at all.*

I removed my T-shirt, jeans, and underwear. Carefully, I also set my phone on the charger. It might be Saturday, but I was always on call. Especially with Renee nearing her due date.

The shower shut off.

I grabbed the box of condoms and the lube. Didn't have to brush off the dust—but only because I'd swapped out the old stuff when I'd returned from Nevada. I couldn't have explained it—but I had zero regrets. The fact I had expired condoms was not a conversation I'd wanted to have.

I hopped onto the bed with my barely used bottle of lube—because masturbating hadn't really been a thing recently—and a single condom. This was presumptuous as all hell, but better that I take the *fucking* part of the conversation seriously.

Axel entered the room and stopped short. He had a towel, turban-style, wrapped around his head. "Uh, sorry, my hair got a bit wet."

His hair had grown so damn much since the summer. He was now able to put it in dreads. They gave him a very different feel. His hair more resembled Ed's. The look was...more...mature? Definitely sexier. But way more work, as I'd learned over the years from students who embraced the look at even younger ages these days. I respected that kind of dedication. I shook away my thoughts. "I have a blow dryer. Uh, somewhere." Wait...maybe I didn't. Gavin had taken his, and since I never used one, I likely hadn't replaced it.

"Uh, Hugo, I don't think you do. At least not in the bathroom. Unless there's another bathroom—"

I barked out a laugh. "Two-bedroom, one bathroom. What you see is pretty much what you get. I've crammed a single bed in with a desk into the second bedroom. The single bed in case I ever have a guest."

"Do you ever?" His eyes lit with amusement before they flickered. "I'm sorry, that was rude."

"To imply I don't have anyone close enough to me to need a spare bed?" I waved him off. "Everyone close to me lives in Vancouver, so they never need a place. I hosted Renee's third cousin once. Lovely man, surprisingly straight."

Axel cocked his head.

I laughed. "Renee swore he was gay and that we'd make a lovely couple." I snickered. "He wasn't even closeted. But he was dating a refugee from Bangladesh and afraid his family wouldn't approve."

"They're bigots?"

"Some random family member on his mother's side. So not Renee's branch. By the end of the weekend, I convinced him to be honest." I grinned. "They've been married five years, and she was able to bring her kids to Canada a couple of years ago."

"Oh. That's amazing."

"Yeah. I've never been so happy to be sort of set up with a straight guy."

Axel burst out laughing. "Yeah, okay. You did good." He lowered the towel. "But I didn't come here to spend my time drying my hair."

Knowing all the bad things that could happen if he didn't had me holding up my hand. "You take all the time you need. Or I could run and get a blow dryer." London Drugs would have several for me to pick from, and the store wasn't far—

Axel held up his hand. "This doesn't mean anything."

"Right." *This isn't going to happen again. And since blow drying your hair makes it frizzy, why would you want to spend the money on it?* "Except I might have guests—" At his amusedly arched eyebrow, I desisted. Amusedly? Sarcastically? Could eyebrows be sarcastic? *Focus on what's really important.* "I'll do whatever you need."

He left the room.

Well, okay then.

He returned. "I was not going to drop a wet towel on your genuine wood floors. Are these original to the house?"

"Uh, yeah. I had to sand and polish them when I moved it, but yeah, they're original." *We're talking about flooring?* "Thanks for the consideration."

His eyes flashed with something I might've thought was pain, but the look was gone too damn fast for me to put my finger on it.

"Ed might not say I was considerate."

Ah. So...pain. "Do you want to talk about—"

"Hugo, I want to fuck. My hair's fine. My cock is starting to get interested. I figure you've got tricks to get me fully engaged." That might've come out on a leer.

My cock perked even as hesitation ate away at me. "We *should* talk, Axel." Yet my mouth salivated as his chubby turned into a semi. He took himself in hand and tugged a couple of times.

Memories of October flooded back—shoving thoughts of talking to the back of my mind. We always had afterward...right?

This doesn't mean anything.

He might not stick around.

That was a chance I had to take. I grasped my cock, giving it a couple of good strokes.

It sprang to life.

Axel grinned. "This is going to be so good." He spotted the condom. "So...are you good with fucking me?"

I wasn't a huge fan of the word *fucking*. First, Gavin had used it a lot. Second, on the few hookups I'd had, that word circled in my mind as I'd gone home with men to get my rocks off. Slowly, I shook my head.

Axel's face fell and his brow knit.

"I'm going to make love to you, Axel. That's what I want."

Slowly, a grin spread across his face. "Yeah, that works for me."

I waited for him to repeat his *doesn't mean anything* comment, but he didn't. Instead, he pointed to the lube. "So are you going to, you know? Or am I?"

A slow heat rose from my chest and settled in my cheeks. I might've hoped hidden under my beard, but Axel's knowing smile assured me I wasn't fooling anyone—least of all him. I cleared my throat. "Uh...I enjoy preparing my partners." I also preferred doing it so I was certain they were adequately prepared. Some guys weren't interested in that and didn't mind a bit of pain. Me? I was all about pleasure.

Inch by inch, Axel approached the bed.

I scooted over to what I thought of as my side. Farthest away from the door, but facing the window, I could lie in bed and gaze out over my garden. That simple act was one of my small joys in life.

He cocked his head. "What were you just thinking of?"

"Lying in bed and looking at gardens, trees, and backyards."

"Oh." He smiled. "Not what I was expecting. Certainly nothing I've ever had experience with." He winced. "All concrete jungles for me."

I wanted to promise him a lie-in one day. With the sun shining in through the eastern window and the sun-drenched south-facing garden.

But he didn't want to hear that. *This doesn't mean anything.*

I could hope he was wrong...but something warned me this was a onetime thing.

Chapter Twenty-Nine

Axel

Hugo's discussion of gardens nearly derailed me. As I gazed into his backyard, though, overcast skies greeted me. The day had turned dark, and we might get a spring rainstorm. I'd have to ask him for a ride when the time came to leave.

No, you'll take a fucking taxi.

Right.

"Are we, uh…" I pointed to the empty side of the bed. The side I preferred. And judging by the stuff on the nightstand next to Hugo's, the other was his side. Of course…the view out to the garden.

Focus. I could blame him for derailing me, but part of this was my fault. I was nervous. Uncertain. Questioning all of it.

No, not all. I didn't question coming here. Just when I'd be leaving.

I knelt on the mattress, and then slowly crawled to Hugo.

Our gazes met.

"This is going to be so good." My cock perked at the promise of something amazing.

He licked his lips. "Yeah, I think it will be."

I eased myself over him.

He shifted his thighs open to accommodate me.

I held his gaze, only closing my eyes as our lips met. *As soft as I remember.*

As I took his mouth, he ran his hands up my sides, around my shoulders, and then to grasp my neck, holding me steady. He thrust his tongue into my welcoming mouth.

This. This. This. I'd tried to obliterate my memories of him several times over the past months, but I'd failed every time. Aside from a few kisses—ones that hadn't even aroused me—I hadn't been intimate with anyone. In my most fervent dreams, I hoped Hugo hadn't either. That he'd pined for me like I'd pined for him. That he'd meant what he'd said in all those cheesy songs.

His grip on my neck increased.

I pulled back and met his lust-glazed deep-blue eyes with pupils blown wide. "Grab my hair. I've dreamt of you grabbing my hair."

He hesitated.

"It's okay." I grinned. "I can sort out the mess later." It'd be a pain—but *totally* worth it. Some partners didn't like the feel of my hair, but Hugo grabbed it and tugged.

My cock jerked. And suddenly found his.

They brushed.

Little tingles of electricity shot through me, and my chest tightened at the thought of him in me. "This is going to be so fucking good." My voice croaked a little, but I wasn't even embarrassed. The need coursing through me obliterated everything that had come before.

"Why don't you roll onto your back?" One hand still gripped my hair while his other trailed down my flank, and eventually grasped my butt. "You really have the most exquisite ass."

"Do you..." I swallowed. "Are you going to fuck me while I'm on my back or are you going to drill me from behind?" Both held appeal—but I knew which I preferred.

"Facing for the first time." His eyes softened. "I need to see you. To gauge how you're doing. That's harder from the, uh, rear."

I cocked my head.

"All right. It's less personal. That was how—" He stopped abruptly.

"How douchebag preferred it." I completed the sentence with absolute certainty.

"Uh..." He blinked. "Yeah."

"Then we don't ever have to do it that way." *Which sort of implies this will happen again. What happened to* this doesn't mean anything, *huh?*

I tried to tell my inner monologue to shut the fuck up. Damn thing was right, of course. I'd implied this was a onetime thing. And I'd meant it...half an hour ago. Now, though, things felt less certain. Like maybe we might do it more than once.

"Making love that way feels really good, Axel. Although that might feel more like the *fucking* you're asking for. Less personal...but amazing. And I don't want to deprive you of that experience. Although maybe with other guys—"

I grabbed his hair and tugged. "Just you." Whether I meant he'd be the only one I planned to be with now or forever, I wasn't certain. Not wanting to examine my words too close, I rolled away from him and onto my back.

After a nerve-wracking hesitation, he pushed up.

I opened my thighs, inviting him in.

He positioned himself between them and grabbed the lube.

Meeting his gaze—and holding it—I grasped my knees and pulled them up to my chest.

His grin lit the room as he squeezed lube onto his fingers. "I'm going to make this good for you."

I blinked. "You already have."

He cocked his head.

"You let me in." I wanted to say more. To apologize for being a jackass. To promise to end this mini tug-of-war we were in the middle of. I couldn't, though. I didn't know what tomorrow held, and as much as I wanted to promise to be a better person, I couldn't do that either. I knew myself too well. I was the best grudge-holder on the planet. And given Ed was my best friend and Pauletta loomed large in my life, me claiming top spot for not being able to let go of things meant something.

"You'll always be welcome." Then, as if realizing what he'd said, he winced. "Sorry. I know this means nothing—"

I let go of my knees, letting my feet fall to the bed. Awkwardly, I tried to push up. I needed to silence him with my lips—to show him I couldn't stand to hear my words used against me. That I'd maybe—just maybe—been wrong.

As if understanding my clumsy motion—and the motivation behind it—he leaned forward and pressed our lips together. A broken kiss. One we could barely maintain with our awkward positions—but one that meant everything.

Slowly, as he pulled back, I eased down to the mattress.

"Perhaps less talking and more doing?" He snagged the lube.

"Yeah." I blinked, all the while hoping he understood the emotion I was trying to convey.

He put more lube on his finger.

I grabbed my knees again and moved them out of the way. In one sense, I'd never been so exposed. Not even the first time I'd slept with Janelle Phong when I'd been all of sixteen. I'd known I'd made a mistake before we'd even finished. I lacked maturity. Enough to wear a condom, but not enough to have dealt with the consequences if the condom failed. I'd waited nearly three years after that before trying again. With an enthusiastic fan who followed us from Portland to Vancouver.

Kyesha.

"Axel?"

My gaze shot to Hugo. I took a breath. "I'm okay. Really." I meant it. In a way, I'd been preparing myself since the moment he'd called my name at Rocktoberfest.

He nodded and scooted closer. He held my gaze as his finger skimmed the rim of my entrance.

I clenched. I couldn't help myself.

"Uh...have you ever...?"

I shook my head.

"Okay. So we go super slow."

Great. Except I didn't want slow. I wanted him inside me so badly that I honestly thought I was going to explode. "Please, Hugo."

He nodded, slowly finishing his leisurely exploration. Then, with exquisite care, he pressed one finger inside.

My every instinct was to pull away. I wasn't hurting or anything like that. Just that this felt weird. Odd. And, in the world I'd grown up in, wrong. Knowing Ed did this with other guys—and now just with Thornton—didn't make me more comfortable.

Hugo paused. "I can stop, Axel. You say the word and we're done. No recriminations. No hard feelings."

"Just do it." I grit my teeth. "I need you to do this."

Slowly, he nodded. "Yeah, okay."

I supposed he realized he'd have to trust me. That I'd be honest with him. And I planned to be. Too much had passed between the two of us for me to not be.

He wiggled his finger.

Breathing deeply, I forced myself to relax. To concentrate on how fucking good this felt.

After I nodded to his questioning gaze, he added a second finger.

I continued to focus on those blue eyes—lasering on me with breath-stealing intensity.

He scissored with growing intensity. Then, he pushed in farther.

My breath stuttered as he did something, and—

Holy hell.

He grinned. "Prostate."

A wonderful feeling overtook me. Little shocks of electricity followed by a warmth I struggled to describe. My cock leaked precum. "Uh."

He tapped it again.

I fought the overwhelming urge to buck. "Jesus, Hugo, you're killing me."

That grin widened. "Think of all I can show you."

If we do this again.

Well, that likelihood increased every moment he touched me. We hadn't made out. We hadn't sixty-nined or given each other hand jobs. Part of me wished we had, while the rest of me was excited at the prospect of having him inside me.

We have all night.

I'd text Ed, promising I was okay, and then I'd stay.

What if he's expecting someone? What if he's got plans to go out?

I wouldn't ask. If he ushered me out after this, then at least I'd have this memory.

He withdrew his fingers.

I moaned.

Somehow, even with slick fingers, he managed to roll on the condom. He applied more lube and then again met my gaze.

Nodding to him, I tried to put everything I felt into my expression—eagerness, desire, and...a touch of fear.

As if understanding, he leaned in for a long, languid kiss. As he pulled back, he smiled shyly. "I'll take care of you, okay? Just so you know, this is new for me as well. I've never deflowered a virgin."

I burst out laughing.

Likely as he'd planned.

He lined himself up.

I nodded.

With maddeningly slow speed, he started to press into me.

Knowing it would hurt and actually remembering to breathe through the pain were two different things. Still, as the crown breached me, I tried not to wince. *Don't give him any reason to stop.*

To his credit, he didn't stop. He didn't ask how I was doing. Instead, he scrutinized me with an intensity I'd never endured. Even Ed, when probing into my soul, didn't carry this attentiveness. Concentration furrowed his brow as I adjusted to his girth.

Admittedly, I hadn't been paying much attention to his cock. I blamed the mesmerizing blue eyes. The assurances I'd sought that had been given back tenfold.

But I remembered having been impressed back in Black Rock. That, at the time I'd given him the blow job, how I'd thought he was pretty big. Again, though, I'd had other things on my mind—like that

I was giving my high school crush a blow job ten years after the last time we'd met.

"Axel?"

I blinked.

"You with me?"

I wanted to snicker, but this didn't feel like the moment. "Uh, yeah, I'm okay."

"My head's in. It's going to feel weird, but bear with me, okay? I'm going to try to make this good for you."

"Just do it, Hugo." *Jesus, you sound like a freaking commercial.*

He grinned. "I love...your enthusiasm."

My breath caught. Had he been about to profess his love? Did it count if you were in the middle of fucking? I just didn't know.

Centimeter by centimeter, he pressed into me.

I kept breathing and trying to relax. *You can do this. This is Hugo.* I blinked back tears. Not of pain. Not of joy. Not even of relief. Just tears ten years in the making.

Hugo sighed. "I've bottomed out. I'm all the way in."

I blinked again, this time with surprise. "That wasn't as bad as I thought it'd be."

A laugh burst out of him. "I don't know how to take that."

I clenched.

His eyes closed for a moment, and he let out a long breath. "Keep that up and it'll all be over sooner than both of us want."

Demanding he fuck me was on the tip of my tongue, but I held it in. "Make love to me, Hugo. Show me what it can be like." *What it can be when two people love each other. I love you and I'm going to pretend you love me back.*

"Yeah, I can do that. Hold on."

I grasped his shoulder.

Inch by inch, he withdrew. Then he pressed back in.

Those sparks arced through me once again. "More." I might've demanded that. "I know you're worried about hurting me, but I trust you. To know how much I can take. To make it good for me while also taking care of me."

"Uh, okay." He withdrew again, almost to the top, and pressed back in.

I wrapped my legs around his hips, using my heels against his ass to encourage him to pick up the pace.

He grunted as he apparently got the unspoken message. He continued to thrust, but his movements hit a steady rhythm as he snapped his hips.

I continued to grip his shoulders.

His gaze never left mine. "Your cock. Can you jerk it?"

"Uh, okay." I grunted as he thrust into me. I snagged my shaft and tugged at it with a rhythm and intensity that matched his. I used the little bit of precum as a sort of poor man's lube. That was enough because I didn't mind friction and I certainly had no problems with everything he was doing to me. Then, without warning, my balls drew up. I hadn't expected an orgasm so soon, but I barely managed an, "I'm coming," through gritted teeth before I erupted.

"Thank fuck." Hugo thrust twice more, held himself still, and arched his neck back, exposing his vulnerability to me. He let out a long moan.

I wished he was actually coming in me instead of the condom—which was completely unlike me. I'd never had sex without a condom. Never would've taken the risk of either pregnancy or disease. But here? I knew I was negative. Two negative tests in the past ten months and no sexual partners meant I was neg. I was damn sure he'd be as well. He just wasn't the reckless kind of person. Someone who would endanger himself or others.

He gazed down at me.

I reached my cum-covered hand around his neck and coaxed him to lie down on top of me.

As he did, his cock slid out with a pop.

I laughed.

He grinned against my shoulder.

All felt right in the world.

Right until the moment his phone rang.

Hoping he might ignore it proved to be a wish in vain.

He elbowed me in the ribs as he scrambled for the phone. He swiped and then, breathlessly, said, "Renee?"

Right. His friend. The one I'd messaged. Completely inappropriately.

"Now?"

The panic in his voice had me snapping to attention.

"Uh...I need a shower, but—"

A long pause.

"No, not because of sex. You know me better than that." He didn't meet my gaze.

Well shit. I hadn't thought he'd be quite so literal with my *this doesn't mean anything*. More fool me.

"Women's hospital. When is the c-section scheduled? I thought they wanted to wait—"

I held my breath.

"Yeah, that's a good reason. I'll get there as fast as I can. I mean, I can't ask them to wait for me—"

My brain screeched. They might hold surgery for him? He was that important to her? She was married. Right? My sex-scrambled brain couldn't figure this all out.

"I love you. Tell Copeland to hang in there. Bye." He jabbed the off button. Then he met my gaze. "My best friend's water broke, and they're doing a C-section to protect the twins, and I have to—"

"Go." I eased away from him. "Toss the condom and go. I can, uh, go—"

"I'm not kicking you out." He unrolled the condom, knotted it, then tossed it in the trashcan. "The back door locks on its own if you flip the lock. No one will know the deadbolt isn't thrown."

"I could wait."

He shook his head. "This will probably be all night. If not longer. I'm..." He hesitated. "I'm sorry."

Awkwardly, I pressed a kiss to his cheek. "Go."

And he did.

Chapter Thirty

Hugo

Scarlett Rose and Matthew Hugo were born within mere minutes of each other with little fanfare. They were quickly held for Renee and me to see and then whisked away. Neither cried lustily, and their APGAR scores were lower than we would've liked. But they were alive, tiny, and with functioning lungs.

The neonatal specialist had warned Renee of all these things. But as I held her hand while they stitched her up, tears ran down her face.

"I should've tried harder."

I pressed a kiss to her temple. "Renee, you did everything you could. Your water breaking was not your fault. But those beautiful babies have a fighting chance because you stayed in bed and took care of yourself."

"But the ice cream—"

"Did not increase your blood pressure or induce premature labor." My heart ached. "And you're going to be in Cope's arms in a short time, and he's going to tell you this wasn't your fault."

"They're so tiny—"

"They're almost three pounds." I knew the survival statistics, but wasn't going to quote them. Nothing was one hundred percent, and each pound less than normal birth weight decreased the odds. Still, three pounds was respectable. She'd done a hell of a job. The rest was up to the universe.

I wasn't a praying man, but I'd sure uttered more than a few over the last two hours and would continue to do so.

"Your hair's dry."

I didn't want to talk about wet hair, but she was the new, panicked mom. If she wanted to go there, why the hell not?

This means nothing.

Inwardly, I winced. Outwardly, I smiled. "Yes, I got lucky. Yes, we were done when you called. Yes, we enjoyed ourselves."

Axel hadn't said as much—but I hadn't given him time. I'd bet simultaneous climaxes generally meant enjoyment, though.

"Who?" Her brow furrowed. "Did you undelete the dating app?"

"I don't think you can undelete an app." Of course, not being tech savvy, I didn't actually know.

"You can re-enable your account." And Renee, being perfectly tech savvy, would know this.

"I'm pretty sure I deleted the account entirely. Remember Wally?"

She winced. "He had such a cute name."

"And a small dick. Which was, honestly, the least of his problems. I mean, I'm not a size queen by any extent of the imagination—"

"Gavin."

"True."

My ex had a small dick as well.

"But Wally..."

"Yeah, okay. But there are thousands of single gay guys in Vancouver. You must be able..." Her eyes widened. "You had sex with Axel Townsend?"

The doctor appeared. A dark-skinned woman with a beautiful smile. "You did great. The NICU reports the twins are doing well. You're all stitched up and ready to go to recovery where you can see your husband."

The woman was aware I was the birth coach...Cope's blood phobia and all...

With a smile she left, Renee snagged my neck, grabbing my hair.

Hard.

"Hey."

"I want fucking details, Hugo. Because you said—"

"I know what I said." I sighed. "There's been a lot of back and forth and—"

The curtain between Renee's head and belly came down.

A nurse with a nice smile and kind eyes approached. "Let's get you moved and settled."

Renee cast another glance at me. "This isn't over. But I want a gown and some feeling back in my lower half."

"There'll be pain." I didn't want to issue the warning, but she deserved the reminder. Right now, she was clearly flying high on happy drugs.

And, true to my word, a couple of hours later, she was miserable. "Fucking hell."

"Major surgery." I reiterated this as she sat in her hospital bed, clutching her still distended belly. "There aren't babies in here anymore. So, like why—"

"Renee." Cope clutched her hand. "I don't care what you look like. You're so beautiful." He brushed a stray lock of hair off her face.

I'd run a cold cloth across her face once she'd settled a bit. After all these years, knowing what soothed her helped in situations like this. One I doubted we'd repeat. Twins? Not likely at her age. Although, with Renee and Copeland, I'd learned to never say never.

A nice, young woman in a bright pink shirt and blue jeans arrived with a massive arrangement of flowers and two teddy bears. One blue and one pink. Which made me wince a little because Renee didn't tend to like the *gender shit* as she put it. Still, Cope's effort was appreciated.

"Thank you." Renee beamed as the woman put the arrangement on the window sill. "They're lovely."

The woman grinned. "Congratulations."

Renee's smile faltered. "They're preemies—"

"But going to be fine." I snagged the hand that Cope wasn't holding. "They're going to be okay." I gave the young woman a smile. "She's going to see them shortly."

"That's great." Her smile didn't falter. "Best of luck." She gave an odd wave and headed out.

Renee managed a watery smile at me. "Thank you for the flowers."

"I didn't."

We both turned to Cope.

"Uh, shit. When I tell you it wasn't me, I'm going to look bad, aren't I?"

"We haven't told anyone." Renee frowned. "We agreed we were going to wait until we've seen the babies."

"Well, I saw them as they were taken away—"

"But you didn't call anyone." She glared. "Did you?"

"Oh, hell no. We agree to do it together—"

"Because if you did..." Her glare didn't lessen.

"Why don't I check the card?" Gently I released Renee's hand. I laid it on her belly and made my way over to the stunning—and clearly very expensive—bouquet.

Congratulations to the new parents and best of luck. AT.

"Son of a bitch."

"Hugo." Renee's warning tone had me walking the card over to her. She read it and cocked her head.

"AT. Axel Townsend. I mean unless you know another—"

"Holy shit." Cope's eyes went wide. "The lead singer of Grindstone sent us flowers and teddy bears?"

"How did he know one girl and one boy?" Renee eyed me. "*I* didn't know until they came out."

Cope laughed. "And I found out even after that. It's only been a couple of hours and, as you can tell from our heated discussion—"

"Argument."

"Discussion." Cope eyed Renee at the interruption. "Anyway, we didn't tell anyone."

"I don't know." I shrugged. "Maybe he just figured two of the same kind would be confusing. I'm kind of surprised he chose pink."

"That might've been the only color choices." Renee frowned. "I'm a little tired of the binary."

"And yet after healthy, the next thing you wanted to know was gender." I winked.

She mock-glared.

I always knew the difference between the pretend and the real thing.

A hunky nurse appeared at the doorway with a wheelchair. "Do you think—"

Renee was already trying to scoot off the bed.

I grinned at the gorgeous guy. "Yeah, she thinks."

Twenty minutes later, Cope was sending me photos of Renee holding each little tiny bundle.

I asked if I could forward it to Axel.

Cope said yes.

I forwarded the photos to Axel.

Renee would hate me for it. Her hair was a mess, and she looked pale and pinched. And also tremendously relieved.

Axel shot back teddy bears and eggplant emojis.

I smiled tiredly.

Yeah, today was one to remember.

Chapter Thirty-One

Axel

E d eyed me. "Okay, why the goofy grin? I know you got laid—"

I smacked his chest.

"Oof. Hey, that was uncalled for."

I glanced over at Pauletta and Thornton who sat at the dining room table, poring over some kind of administrative something or other. Something to do with Rocktoberfest. Something I should've been more interested in. Instead, I kept imagining the two photos of Renee and the babies. I didn't know kids, but they looked so tiny. Like, scary tiny.

Hugo assured me they were of a good weight and expected to survive.

Expected to survive.

That still unnerved me. I didn't know how someone would live with the fact their newborn baby might or might not survive. All that being said, humans had a finite life. Since none of us knew which day we were going to die, we just needed to make the most of each day.

You're getting sappy.

Yeah, I was. Because I wasn't certain if I'd see Hugo again. If he'd want a repeat.

This doesn't mean anything.

I rubbed my hands against my closed eyes. Why? Why the fuck had I said that? Because, if Hugo'd said that to me—no matter what came next—I'd assume our fucking was a onetime thing.

Making love.

He'd said that. Then he'd started to say he loved me. Or he loved something about me. Or he loved rainy days. I had no fucking clue what was supposed to come after that.

And I'd almost told him that I'd never truly gotten over my crush. But that now, all these years later, something more powerful had taken its place.

Ed glanced down at his laptop, sitting on the coffee table.

Mine was in my room. Attached to the charger because, of course, I'd forgotten to charge it. In the last four days, since I'd been abandoned in Hugo's house, I'd been oblivious to everything. Given my normal state of chaos, this was even worse.

He didn't abandon you. His best friend had to deliver premature twins. This isn't about you.

Okay. Fair. But he had yet to call.

And have you called him?

Fair question. I'd sent the flowers and teddy bears, though. That had to count for something...right? A way for me to show I didn't want things to be over with just one fuck.

I'd lain in those cum-covered sheets that smelled like him for hours—waiting in vain. Hoping he might come home and be happy to see me. Eventually I'd realized that wasn't going to happen. I'd put my clothes in the dryer and then, in an act of consideration, I put the dirty sheets in the washing machine. I didn't generally do laundry these days—but I remembered how.

Naturally, I had to wait until the sheets were out of the dryer.

Still, Hugo hadn't come home. He hadn't texted.

I'd called the hospital and sort of bullshitted my way into finding out about the babies. Either I was super charming or the person I'd spoken to wasn't big on privacy. I wanted to believe the former was true—that people just couldn't resist my sunshine ways.

I snickered.

Ed arched an eyebrow.

I shrugged.

He pointed to his laptop. "New song."

I rolled my eyes.

"What new song?" Pauletta's voice rang clear.

Ed and I twisted to find her standing directly behind us as we sat on the couch.

"Let me check." Ed squinted.

"Honey bunch, my BFF needs his glasses." I said the words in a sing-songy voice guaran-fucking-teed to piss Ed off.

He glared.

Pauletta snorted.

Thornton appeared moments later with the reading glasses Ed swore he didn't need. Yet, somehow could always see better when he wore them.

Ed cast me one more caustic look before turning back to his laptop. "Axel's paramour sent a song." He moved closer to the laptop. "There's a message." He turned to me. "Do you want me to forward this to your phone?" His gaze flickered between Thornton and Pauletta.

For a hot second, I considered taking him up on his offer. In the end, though, I waved for him to just read it. Unless he either professed his love or said he wanted to fuck me again, I didn't figure it couldn't be read in mixed company. Plus, he had my phone number. He could've texted. He'd known, when he sent this, that Ed would see.

My best friend cleared his throat. "Dear Axel—"

I snorted.

He glared. Then continued. "I wanted to find you at Rocktoberfest last year for two reasons. The first was to ask you and Ed to consider doing a concert for the school's anniversary. That was what you overheard that morning. Me telling my principal I wouldn't abuse my friendship with you to ask that of you and Ed. He didn't take it well, and we exchanged words. I said some inappropriate things, and he was a jackass. Not my best moment. For that, I apologize."

Ed glanced at me—as if trying to gauge my reaction.

I rolled my hand. "He said two things..."

"Yeah." He again cleared his throat. "I also wanted to find you so I could ask your permission to record a song you wrote eleven years ago." Ed glanced at me.

I couldn't read his expression.

He continued. "The singer's name is Marley, and she's from your neighborhood." Ed hesitated. "I know you didn't give your permission. So this is wrong of me. But I wanted you to hear what my students are capable of—with the right music."

I sat in silence, seething at Hugo for putting me in this position. "So much for burning them—"

"What?" Pauletta asked the question sharply.

"I said so much...never mind." I waved for Ed to continue.

"He just says he hopes you're not mad and..." Ed scrolled. "Maybe a bit of personal stuff you won't want me to share—"

"Oh, I can I see?" Thornton moved to the couch and tried to push Ed toward me so he could plant his ass.

"Just play the song." I reached around Ed's back to tweak Thornton's ear.

Hard.

He yelped.

I didn't really mind. He was family.

Pauletta laughed at his exclamation.

Suddenly, a full orchestration began.

What the...?

After the introduction—which was no more than fifteen seconds—a girl's voice came through Ed's not-so-great computer speaker.

Thornton, Ed, and I all leaned closer.

Pauletta scooted around and knelt by the laptop, trying to get a better listen. "Start it again."

"Uh, yeah." Ed mumbled the words even as he fidgeted with the machine.

The orchestration began anew and, as Marley's voice rang through clearly, my heart seized. I recognized the song. "Can We Be True?" *Jesus...he still has this?* Another song I'd written for him. Only I barely recognized it. Because between the orchestration and one of the most powerful, pure, and gorgeous voices I'd ever heard, I couldn't believe this was the same song. Yet it was. For all of my memory fog from trying to forget that time in my life—and failing—the familiarity sank deep into my bones.

With a grand finale and a great crescendo, the song ended.

Slowly, I sat back.

Ed whistled.

Thornton pointed, as if asking him to play it again.

Pauletta stilled his hand when he tried. She met my gaze. "You wrote that?"

"Yeah."

"You own the copyright for that?"

I shrugged. "I certainly never filed a claim for it. Hell, I thought I'd thrown out all that old shit. He was the one—"

She held up a finger. "That's not shit, Axel. That's...fucking brilliant." She glanced at Ed. "I fucking want her. What's the girl's name?"

"Marley."

"Great." She bit her lower lip. "I'm going to assume she hasn't got representation. I want her. I fucking want her." She met my gaze. "And I want her singing that song. And I want every other fucking song you've written. Not just to protect the copyright—you did the work, you deserve the credit—but because I want to see what other hidden gems are tucked away." She cocked her head. "This the teacher from the video."

Ed snorted. "Oh yeah. And Axel saw him recently."

Pauletta held up her finger again. "Do I want to know?"

Simultaneously, Ed and I said, "Probably not."

He caught my eye.

For the first time in what felt like forever, I smiled. I'd released three new songs since my blowout with Hugo at the launch party. He'd sent me two shmoopy songs as well as this phenomenal song by a protégée who was clearly a diamond in the rough.

His friend Renee's twins would grow stronger.

I might find the courage to message Hugo.

To proposition him—of course.

And to maybe explain that *this doesn't mean anything* really meant *this means everything*.

Chapter Thirty-Two

Hugo

As I carried Scarlett Rose's car seat into Renee and Cope's house, a feeling of rightness settled over me. The twins had spent thirty-seven excruciating days in the hospital. My frequent visits to the NICU to visit Renee and the twins were greeted with gratitude, but she struggled with everything.

Her body didn't bounce back the way she hoped it would.

Cope and I empathized and specifically didn't point out that forty-two wasn't old, but it wasn't young either. Although Renee had been in peak condition before she got pregnant, a series of complications, including the extended bed rest, had taken their toll on her.

Her babies weren't thriving as much as she hoped.

The doctor kept assuring her they were doing well, but little things kept cropping up, and Renee's ability to cope was declining by the minute.

Her husband had to go back to work.

Yeah, no one could prevent that. He had patients who needed him. Renee and the twins would always be a priority, but sitting around waiting for the twins to gain weight wasn't helping the clients who relied on Cope to get them through their own crises.

Her best friend had to, you know, work.

Despite her attempt to pile on the guilt, I took three days off work. Days when she literally couldn't cope and had needed me more than anything. Calling in sick those days hadn't been ideal, but I would've been useless at school anyway.

Somehow, we'd weathered the storms.

Somehow, the twins were home.

Somehow, I'd managed to *not* see Axel for thirty-seven excruciating days.

Fuck my life.

Renee held the door while Cope and I entered carrying precious cargo. Mercifully, both had slept during the short drive home. As much as the nurses had tried to get them on the same schedule, they were never awake at the same time. Which meant they never slept at the same time. Which meant Renee was in for some brutal days ahead until she could get everyone sorted.

Or so she believed.

That she could get everyone sorted.

I loved her dearly, but was pretty certain the little angels in cute sleepers held all the cards in this relationship.

Even as I had the thought, Matthew popped his eyes open. And howled in displeasure at...whatever.

Not to be outdone, Scarlett started fussing.

Renee, recovered enough to use the second floor again, pointed upstairs.

Cope and I climbed the stairs.

At least the stifling June heat stayed outside, and the central air in the house blew a gentle coolness. My place, without such luxuries, was brutally hot. Southern exposure was lovely for plants but liable to turn a nice little house into an oven.

Hence my being happy to spend plenty of time at Renee's.

Upon arriving in the twins' bedroom, I sighed. Two rocking chairs. Two cribs. One dresser and one changing table. If one or both babies hadn't made it—

Breath caught in my chest. Cope and I would've fixed the room, of course. Or they might've closed it off entirely. Instead, two beautiful and very healthy babies were now going to take over this space, and life was never going to be the same.

I placed the car seat on the ground and crouched.

Scarlett was nearly the color of her name as she howled in rage.

Matthew was even louder.

I chuckled. All the years of Renee being a loudmouth were going to be paid back in spades by these two.

Having zero infant experience meant watching Cope closely as he unbuckled Matthew and gently removed him from the car seat.

With gentleness, I replicated his actions. Cope was the eldest of a passel of kids and so had helped with diapers, scraped knees, and general child raising.

With my sister and her brood so far away—and with no close cousins—I hadn't been exposed to any of that.

Gavin had several younger siblings. He'd made it clear we weren't having *brats*. Somehow, I'd internalized that and decided I wasn't going to have them either. My douchebag ex had been gone from my life for ten years—double the time I'd been in the ill-fated marriage—and his opinions on everything still permeated my life.

As I held Scarlett, though, I didn't feel anything but gratitude for her health. I didn't look at her and wish for this responsibility for myself. I'd hadn't thought I would, but I did. I'd thought I wanted kids of my own. The last thirty-seven days had shown me I didn't need to be a father to be fulfilled. I had my kids at school. That had always been enough. Enough stress. Enough sleepless nights. Enough worry to push me into an early grave. That was truly all I needed.

But does Axel feel the same way?

I pushed the thought aside. What did it matter? Somehow our one-off had been just that. No repeat in sight.

Pauletta had come to the school to meet Marley and her dad.

Some kind of negotiations had taken place, but I hadn't been party to them.

During her visit, she'd also demanded all copies of everything of Axel's. The original songs—including the paper they were written on—as well as any recordings I'd created. She also took copies of the orchestrations I'd created.

She might've said something about compensating me.

I might've argued and said she could have them.

She might've said something about legal documents.

I might've tried to scrub the conversation from my mind.

Axel didn't come. He sent his manager. Which pretty much told me everything I needed to know.

"I think they need to be changed." Cope sniffed. Then wrinkled his nose. "Oh, yeah."

At Renee's insistence, I'd leaned diapering at the hospital. The idea still terrified me because I always seemed to have one less hand than I needed, but if I was going to remain in her good graces, then diaper duty was the least I could do.

By the time we had two clean infants, time for lunch had arrived.

Cope and I hustled downstairs, slightly less fussy babies in our arms, to find Renee in the kitchen, making a batch of bottles.

"Sit in the family room. I'll be there in a moment."

Knowing better than to disobey, Cope and I headed to the family room. I dropped onto the couch—gently—and arranged a pillow beneath my arm.

He sat on the chair.

My phone buzzed in my back pocket.

I ignored it.

It buzzed again.

I ignored it again.

A third time, it buzzed.

Renee swept into the room. She handed Cope a bottle.

He immediately stuck it in the mouth of the still disgruntled Matthew.

My phone buzzed for a fourth time.

Renee dropped onto the couch next to me and indicated I should hand her Scarlett.

"I can feed the baby."

My phone buzzed for a fifth time.

Renee glared and held open her arms. "It might be, you know, important."

Reluctantly, I handed over my bundle. I didn't want Renee to think badly of me. "Nothing can be that important. I'm here. The four most important people in my life are—"

A sixth buzz. "Jesus Fucking Christ."

No one admonished me for my language. But heat raced to the tips of my ears as I dragged my phone out of the back pocket of my shorts. Pretty soon I would have to worry about my language. I did at school, of course, but never in my private life. In essence, when I wasn't under the microscope, I let loose.

Gavin had always hated that.

My phone buzzed again. I'd lost track how many times this was.

"What the hell, Hugo?" Cope laughed. "You're damn popular today."

I pulled up my messages app and started scrolling. "Pauletta Magnum."

"Really? Drink, sweetheart." Renee tried to cajole Scarlett into taking the bottle.

The recalcitrant infant wasn't interested. Instead, she just wanted to squawk.

Smart kid. I can't imagine formula tastes good.

"What is it?" Cope gestured to my phone with his chin. "Don't keep us in suspense."

"A ticket."

"Oh?" Renee's interest was clearly piqued at the exact moment Scarlett spit up. "Jesus Fucking Christ."

I chuckled. "Where's the mouth soap? We're all in trouble, aren't we?"

Cope laughed. "Speak for yourselves—I'm a virtuous saint."

"You got me knocked up." Renee spat that, but without true venom.

"I seem to recall the day the Canucks lost in game seven of the playoffs." I just had to point that one out. Cope was a way bigger hockey fan than I was, and his curse words had been *epic*.

He pursed his lips.

"Ticket?" Renee gestured for me to take Scarlett back.

Oh great, so she can spit up on me? I glanced at my ratty band T-shit from the late nineties. Yeah, small sacrifice. I put my phone down and gathered my goddaughter in my arms.

Renee handed me the bottle, and I didn't hold out much hope, but apparently whatever Scarlett had been working on was gone and now she was positively voracious.

Her mother, upon seeing this, huffed. She left the room, stomping as she went.

I arched an eyebrow at Cope.

He shrugged. "We're feeling our way through this. For some reason, two adults in their early forties believed getting pregnant would be the biggest challenge."

I blinked.

"Right?" He pointed to each twin with his chin. "We spent so long trying to get pregnant that we never really talked about how it would work if we actually succeeded."

"Not putting the cart before the horse?"

"Exactly." He offered a weary smile. "Now we're absorbing this lifetime commitment."

"Yeah. I think I'd rather get a dog."

"Dogs are huge commitments as well." Renee trudged back in the room carrying three water bottles and still swiping at a spot on her blouse. She went to hand one to each of Cope and me, realized our hands really were full, shrugged, then put them within reach. She dropped back to the couch and eyed me. "You didn't tell Cope what the ticket was for yet, did you?"

Cope snorted. "And risk you cutting his balls off? No."

That image was vaguely distressing, but I was also in the company of the two people I loved most in the world. Well, the four. That thought shot through me like a bullet as I held Scarlett. As did the fact I wished Axel was here more than anything in the world. I sighed.

"Ticket?" Renee gestured for me to...spit it out? She always was terrible at charades.

"A ticket to Rocktoberfest. And an airplane voucher."

Cope whistled. "That's a good chunk of money."

"There's more."

"Of course there is." Renee angled herself toward me and nodded her head in some weird way.

"I told you about Marley—"

"Your student. The one we've seen perform. Keep talking."

I didn't point out I would've completed the thought if she hadn't interrupted me. She wasn't in a tolerant enough mood to deal with me kidding. "She's going to be performing at the show."

"What the fuck?" Renee's mouth dropped open. "Are you kidding me?"

I gestured to the phone I'd abandoned when she'd thrust Scarlett back into my arms.

She clicked a button and held the screen to my face.

It illuminated.

She winced. "I told you that my cop friend said it should be password only."

"Renee."

She met my gaze.

"Who the fuck wants to see my phone? There's nothing there."

"No sexting between you and Axel?" She arched an eyebrow. "And why haven't you seen him?"

I snuggled Scarlett closer to me.

Renee narrowed her eyes. "You're using your goddaughter and son as excuses for not seeing the hottest man on the planet?"

"Hey." Cope whined that.

"Nice try, honey." She turned to him. "You know I love you, but you're not in the same league as Ed Markham and Axel Townsend." She tapped her lips. "Or Thornton Graves. When are he and Ed getting married?"

Before I could answer, she waved me off.

"Okay...Marley's singing at Rocktoberfest." She held my phone up again because the screen had gone black. This time, she actually scrolled.

"Burp time." Cope tossed me a receiving blanket. "Good luck."

I grinned as I put the blanket on my shoulder. I'd done this a few times at the hospital as well.

In fact, the nursing staff commented how helpful I was. I'd overheard two of the nurses wondering if Cope, Renee, and I were in a triad relationship like that actor Cole Hamilton, his girlfriend Caressa—a nurse, no less—and their third, Michael. Since I barely knew who Cole was, I just tiptoed right past the nurse's station. I could've set the record straight, but I'd had more fun telling Renee the story. She'd snickered, pointed out Cole and Michael were bi, and then moved the conversation along.

I'd googled the famous triad when I got home and got a laugh. No, I was never going to be a third to Cope and Renee. God, no.

"Okay." Renee finally stopped scrolling. "So ticket to Rocktoberfest, voucher for airfare. You just need a rental car and a tent."

Cope snickered. "We know what you do with tents."

"I..." I tried to purse my lips in annoyance, but ruefulness took over. "Good point." I pivoted back to Renee. "I can afford all that. Getting the time off school—"

She waved the phone. "Grindstone is donating part of the proceeds of their PNE performance this year to the school. They're also throwing in one hundred tickets to be auctioned off, one hundred tickets to be raffled off, and one hundred tickets for students."

I blinked.

"So if Merkerson doesn't give you the time off work—well, he can go fuck himself."

"That's not his jam."

"Are you sure?"

"Uh..."

"Homophobic people can also be gay, Hugo. Even you know that."

"He's just...very straight."

"If you say so." She continued to scroll. "Oh."

Scarlett belched and spit-up dribbled down my neck.

I couldn't have been prouder. *Take that, world. I made my god-daughter spit up. Fucking awesome.* "Oh, what?"

"She says Axel's going to be really busy...for the next three-and-a-half months."

My heart sank. "Well...it might've been nice coming from him...but at least I know." I'd messaged several times over the past few weeks.

He hadn't responded.

Now I knew why.

"Hey." Cope winced.

"He just spit up on you? Because Scarlett did a doozie on me."

Renee snagged the cloth she'd been using to try to clean her nice shirt and attacked my neck with vigor, gently moving Scarlett's head aside so she could get at the congealing goop. Renee had worn something pretty for the *coming home from the hospital* picture. I suspected she wouldn't do that again anytime soon.

"Matthew didn't spit up on me." Cope continued to pat his son's back. "I meant, *hey* don't assume you know the reason."

Renee stopped cleaning, and we both turned to Cope.

"Maybe…" He cleared his throat. "Maybe he's got as much shit to deal with as you. I mean, how many more appointments do you have with Justin out at Healing Horses?"

I squinted. "He said he figured two or three more. He's taking me through some self-talk exercises."

"Thank Christ. You're your own harshest critic." Renee licked a corner of the cloth and stuck it down my shirt.

That was possibly even grosser than Scarlett's spit-up, but silence was truly the better part of valor.

"So maybe don't assume it's you." Cope held my gaze.

Right up until Matthew burped.

"Fuck."

Renee and I howled with laughter at Cope's letting the expletive rip.

Maybe he's right. Pauletta didn't have *to send me a ticket to the concert. Huh. Maybe I should try positive self-talk instead. Four months isn't that long to wait.*

Or so I told myself.

Chapter Thirty-Three

Axel

I glanced at my phone for the millionth time at the text I'd sent.

—*Meet me by the Greek food truck at ten—*

He'd responded with a thumbs-up emoji.

Seriously? We don't talk for nearly five months and you give me a thumbs-up? Did he even realize I meant ten in the evening? Like, tonight? Pauletta confirmed he was here. She'd seen him with Marley and her dad. Paulie had rented a camper van for those two. Maybe she should've done the same thing for Hugo.

But that would've meant more money. I would've paid, though.

Five fucking months. Too much time. I let too much time go past. He's forgotten about me. Forgotten how good the sex was between the two of us. He's moved on and is just here for Marley. He's—

"Hey." Hugo's voice snapped me back to attention at the exact moment he tapped my shoulder.

I whirled.

He stepped back and held up his hands. "Sorry, didn't mean to scare you—"

"You didn't." I swallowed. "Okay, maybe a little bit..." I pressed my hand to my chest. "I was just—"

He rested his hand above mine on my chest.

I wasn't uncomfortable—far from it—but I was disconcerted. I'd expected a wave and maybe a handshake. Certainly not his hands on me so soon. Or so... intimately. I blinked. "Uh, how are Renee, Cope, and the twins?"

He'd sent me a few pictures every week.

At first, I wondered if he was trying to drop a broad hint and I was just too dense not to get it.

Then he captioned one of the photos that being both a godfather and an honorary uncle was the best job in the world, and thank God he got to give them back at the end of the day.

I remembered *that* photo. He'd been shirtless with two little pink bundles pressed against him. Something about skin-to-skin contact being good for their health.

"They're great." Hugo grinned. The lighting might be crap where we were, but a bit of his blue irises showed around his large pupils. "You don't have to keep sending gifts."

"Uh..."

"Renee and Copeland have lots of great people in their lives, but only one person who sends something on the thirteenth every month."

"To celebrate their birthdays," I pointed out.

Belatedly realizing what I was admitting to.

"They're not fancy things." Because now I felt defensive.

"They're not...they're considerate gifts. But Axel, sweetheart, there's only a finite amount of space in the house."

"Hey, I sent chocolates for Renee last month. That wasn't for the kids."

He laughed. "You should've been a lawyer."

I straightened. "I'm good with arguing. Ed will tell you that.

Slowly, he nodded. "Ed contacted me last week."

"That shit."

"Yeah, I figured you didn't know. He wanted to know if I was coming or not. And that if I wasn't, to be honest so he could prepare you."

"That shit." I might've put less vehemence in that.

"He's watching out for you."

When he went to pull his hand away from my chest, though, I snatched it. "Don't let go of me, Hugo. It's been...hell."

He stilled. "Okay, well I can tell you I've been in therapy to deal with some of my shit leftover from my crappy childhood and my ill-conceived marriage. It's funny—I wasn't deprived of anything material. I was very well-off. But I lacked love."

"And I had love from Ed, but no one else in my life." I winced. "The whole world knows that, thanks to the documentary."

"Your friendship with Ed—the bromance—shows the world that even kids who grow up in horrific circumstances can find acceptance and love. And are deserving of that love." He glanced down at his shoe and sort of crushed it against the ground. "You deserve all the love, Axel."

"Do you know why I asked for time?"

He met my gaze and slowly shook his head.

"I needed to get my head on straight. And that comes directly from Pauletta, Ed, and Thornton. My life changed a lot in a very short period of time, and coping with all that took all my strength and focus." I smiled ruefully. "And I also did some counseling. With someone who understood the specifics of my particular trauma. A word I both hate and embrace. I've sworn to do better. I've had long conversations with everyone in the band. Coming clean about some stuff. Apologizing for previous insensitive—"

He held up his hand, as if to stop me.

I kept right on going. "Insensitive comments and actions. When I quit the drugs and alcohol, I didn't have nearly as many people in my life—"

His expression read pure panic with wide eyes and a gaping mouth. *Shit.* "No, nothing like that. I didn't turn back to drugs or booze."

He pressed a hand to his chest and took a deep breath. After a long moment, he indicated I should continue.

"But someone can owe an apology for callous and insensitive behavior. I wasn't so much high on myself as just slow to recognize other people and their problems. I was...sometimes I was self-centered. Coming to grips with that's been tough."

"I can imagine." He waved. "Well, I have trouble picturing you as insensitive. You were always a sensitive young man."

I drew in a deep breath. "Something..." I wiped my brow with the back of my hand. The temperature had dropped precipitously as night set in, but I was still sweating. "Something broke in me when I was seventeen." Despite my fervent wish to look away, I held his gaze.

"Me." He swallowed.

"Yeah, you. Not your fault by any means. But yeah, I felt betrayed. And shoved away any notion I'd had of coming out to you. Of coming out to anyone. I hid that part of me away. For what I believed would be forever." I drew in a deep breath. "Then you came back into my life."

"I'm sorry."

I tried to wave him off.

He indicated he had more to say.

I lowered my hand.

"Sorry for what you heard after our amazing night together. Merkerson—"

"Is a jackass."

"And yet you raised over a hundred thousand dollars for the school."

"Half of which had to go to the music department." I shrugged. "That jackass was right—we owe everything to the school. Except a straight-up invitation from him would've been the right thing to do. Sending you down here to play on our relationship wasn't fair..." I chuckled. "But it brought us together. I had my first experience with cock and, I have to say, I kind of got hooked."

"Oh?" He arched an eyebrow, not looking as pleased as I wanted. "Really?

I smacked his shoulder. "Yours. Just yours."

He smiled. A genuine smile. "You've forgiven me?"

"Ages ago." I scrunched my nose. "But I've had to come a long way to forgive myself. Making amends to your friends—"

"You owe them nothing. You owe me nothing."

"—seemed like the least I can do. But if you want me to stop, then I'll open university funds for both of them. This album..." I sucked in a breath. "I'm not mega wealthy or anything, but for the first time ever, we hired our own tour bus. Thank God we don't have to pay Mr. Magnum back for his generosity over the years...we would've tried, but...well, he came to see us and said how we'd made Pauletta happy all these years and this was the least he could do. Something about his wife that only later clicked in with me."

Hugo cocked his head.

"Not accepting of Pauletta's bisexuality. In fact, Mr. Magnum left her after she refused to accept Mickey as the significant other in Pauletta's life. Apparently dating someone nonbinary was as bad as dating a woman." I winced. "So Mr. Magnum offered the woman a generous divorce settlement and wished her well. She moved to Toronto and is dating some famous guy. Having money buys access."

"Yuck."

"Right? I'd rather be broke and have principles than be homophobic and rich."

He smiled. "Yeah, I get that about you."

Okay. Now's the time. "So, uh, I need to warn you..."

"Warn me?"

"Yeah." *Breathe.* "Thornton's doing a follow-up documentary this year. Way shorter than last year's beast." I chuckled. Well, forced a laugh from my chest. "Anyway, Ed wants me to talk about my bisexuality. He plans to as well." I bit my lower lip. "And I think there'll be a shot or two of Pauletta and Mickey as well. A whole *love is love* thing."

"And Songbird?" He toed the ground again. "Because even I've heard the rumors about her being seen about town with Geneva Alvarez."

I chuckled. "Yeah, who knew Big Mac and Meg would wind up being the token straight people?" *And they're hoping to have a baby now Meg's recovered from her surgery.* "They're doing great. Meg's even doing the drumming competition this year. She's...embracing her life. Despite slow healing from reconstructive surgery, she's still the best drummer out there."

"That's great." He met my gaze. "I watched the rehearsal tonight. And met with Marley and her dad afterward. I admit I worried this might all go to her head—"

"She's the most grounded teenager I've ever met."

"Yeah. Growing up in a single-parent household can do that." I considered my next words. "Her dad's only using a bit of the money so he could take a leave from his job and come down here. He's got Pauletta putting the rest in a trust fund for when Marley's older, college money or whatever she needs. A couple of music schools have already come poking around. She'll be able to go anywhere she wants."

"She's talking Julliard. Secretly she's always wanted to get into their vocal arts program. Of course, coming from near-poverty, she'd known that would be impossible. Even with scholarships, she could never afford an American school."

Hugo's eyes widened. "I had no idea. She never said—"

"She was afraid you'd try to make it happen for her. And that she wouldn't be able to go."

He cleared his throat. "I didn't realize she was making that much money."

I laughed. "Oh, we're paying her well, but we're not *that* big yet. This weekend's going to cement our reputation and the album we're releasing—including Marley's song—"

"Your song."

Another laugh burst from me. "Un-fucking-relenting. Jesus, you just don't give up."

He grinned.

I waved him off. "What I'm trying to say is Mr. Magnum's been looking for a new place to put his money. He might not be able to write off Marley's education as a charitable donation, but he's damn pleased to send her wherever she wants to go." I rubbed my neck. "She's not even obliged to keep Pauletta as a manager."

"She's going to though."

"For now? Yeah. I recognized talent, but I wouldn't have immediately thought to pair Marley with us."

"Or to use your old songs."

I glared.

Which had precisely zero effect on his smile. "You know."

"About the new album geared toward younger fans? Yeah, word's gotten out." He shrugged. "Sorry."

"Yeah, you're so *not* sorry."

"No, I'm not. It might've been questionable to keep your original compositions from back then—and I'd had no idea they were about me—but I can't bring myself to regret it."

"And not just because of Marley and the opportunity this has afforded her."

"No, not just because. That's an added bonus."

"You care about your students."

"Always have and always will."

"But don't want to have kids of your own?"

"I'm old—"

"Men older than you have become fathers." I added a touch of humor.

"I'm turning gray—"

"Men older than you have become fathers." I smiled. "And gray makes you look distinguished." He still had a full head of flaming red hair, but the gray at the temples and the flecks in his beard that caught the light were fucking sexy. Got my libido going.

"I don't want kids of my own, Axel. I have Scarlett and Matthew and, truly, I don't need more than that in my life. I don't even think I'd be a good father. God knows, I had one of the worst examples possible."

"How is your dad?"

"Still pissed at Gavin for lying to the press about us." He indicated between the two of us. "The *I must have misunderstood what I saw, but really, he shouldn't have been alone with a student* non-apology apology bought him forgiveness from the upper crust of Vancouver society, but that shit didn't fly with my dad." He smiled. "And his troubles with his family's foundation and his inappropriate appropriation of funds has him in trouble with the tax authorities and the law."

"Oh dear. Couldn't have happened to a nicer guy." My voice dripped appropriate sarcasm. Then I considered my next words. "Are you closer to your parents?"

"Oh, fuck no. I'm grateful for their help, but their reasons were all about them, so no, not much closer.." He scrunched his nose. "But...things are thawing between them and my sister."

"You spent two weeks in Greece this summer."

He cocked his head. "Oh, social media. I didn't post."

"No, but your sister tagged you."

"Okay, which was so not cool, *and* speaking of not cool, Greece is brutally hot in the summer. She's coming out here next summer."

"Hopefully not staying with you."

"With her four kids and husband in that house? Oh, hell no. But my parents have a mansion and a newfound desire to meet their grandchildren." He winced.

"They might do better at that than actual parenting."

"Maybe." He clasped his hands. "Leonora will have no problem turning around, heading back to Greece, and never speaking to them again if they blow this." He squinted. "But I don't think my sister is the reason you wanted to meet me behind the food truck."

As if on cue, my phone buzzed. This time, I winced. "No. And my time's almost up."

Chapter Thirty-Four

Hugo

A *nd my time's almost up.*

For a fraction of a second, I thought Axel meant he was dying or something like that.

He held up his phone. "Ed and Pauletta have me on a tight leash until after tomorrow night's performance. Well, maybe even longer than that—we'll see what's negotiated. They don't want a repeat of last year when I almost missed the rehearsal."

I eyed him.

"They want me to stay out of trouble."

"And I'm trouble?"

Slowly, he advanced toward me. "You're the best kind of trouble." He grasped the front of my T-shirt and yanked me toward him.

I went willingly.

Our mouths crashed together.

His grip loosened, then he ran his hands up my chest. Farther still to my cheeks—all the while eliciting little shocks of electricity arcing through me. He scraped his fingers through my beard, then reached behind my neck to snag the hair at the back of my neck. He tugged.

I thrust my aching cock against him. Seeking friction. Seeking satisfaction. Seeking more than I had the right to ask for—yet doing it anyway.

His grip tightened.

Remembering how much he'd liked this before, I replicated his actions. I gently grasped some of his hair and tugged—careful to not mess with his gorgeous dreads.

In turn, he thrust his hard cock against mine.

A soft whistle had us pulling apart.

"Guys, there's event security hovering ten feet away, get a... Axel? Axel Townsend? Oh hey, I'm Griffin. I'm looking forward to your show tomorrow night. Big fan."

I didn't know this middle-aged guy—and wasn't thrilled about the interruption—but I had been about to offer to blow Axel again. Behind the food truck no less. Or better, I would've dragged him back to my tent.

Axel's phone buzzed. "Oh, shit." He glanced at me.

I read his expression as rueful, regretful, and a little lusty.

He turned back to Griffin. "You're performing Sunday, right? We're sticking around to see all the shows. Can't wait to see you, and Chaser Lost, of course."

The guy grinned. "Thanks. Well, uh, sorry to interrupt. I just figured y'all wouldn't want to have security find you..."

"We'd have kept our pants on," Axel assured him. "Well, probably."

They laughed.

Heat crept into my cheeks. *Wait, fuck, is that Griffin Marsh?*

Griffin waved and sauntered off.

I let out a breath.

Axel's phone buzzed yet again.

"That seems excessive."

"Well, I kind of haven't responded." He tapped away for about thirty seconds. "That's bought me time."

"Does having them on you all the time feel restrictive?"

"Oh, I usually have plenty of latitude. Just...like I said, last year I almost missed rehearsal because I ran into you. They're...concerned."

"Because they know I'm here."

"And that I'm still hung up on you." He eyed me. "Yeah. Okay...one more for the road."

This time, he took me in an embrace, wrapped his arms around me, and pressed a kiss to my cheeks. The touching embrace felt more intimate than anything we'd ever done.

Tears pricked the backs of my eyes. "This feels like goodbye." I barely recognized my hoarse whisper.

"This is *hello again*." He released me gently and took a step back. "You'll be the ruination of me." Lasciviously, he looked me up and down. "But what a way to go. Stick with me, Hugo. Trust me. This is not an ending. We'll talk soon." With that, he slipped between the trucks and was gone.

My phone buzzed.

Curious, I pulled it out of my back pocket.

—You get laid yet? —

Fucking Renee.

I sent back a flurry of nonsensical emojis—very careful to leave out eggplants and peaches—and followed my nose and growling stomach to find a late-night snack.

Less than twenty-four hours later, I stood near the front of the crowd, having sought out this spot early. Although the sun was long gone, the press of bodies kept me plenty warm. Flightless had just given an electric performance, and the crowd buzzed.

The Kiwi band had been truly remarkable, and the fiddle music had gone over great with the crowd. And the last song? When Jared had kissed Owen's hand? My mind had been a little blown. The open show of affection. The love clearly returned.

As the band had sung, the sun had slowly started to set. It hung with a particular red glow that was just stunning. I remembered my final morning here last year—that awful, horrible, terrible morning. And the stunning pinks and purples of the dawn. Might we get something like that tonight for sunset? Pink-hued clouds to round out what was turning out to be a pretty fucking amazing day.

Grindstone's roadies, along with a couple of people I'd pegged as stage crew, swapped out equipment.

My stomach clenched. Yes, I was going to see Axel perform again. I'd attended the performance at the PNE in early September. Would've been weird for the music teacher of the school for whom the money was being raised not to been there. Axel and I kept a significant distance that night. Like at no time could a photographer have gotten us both in the same picture. Pauletta had ensured that, and Merkerson, although annoyed, had gone along with her demands.

He wanted publicity.

She wanted sanity.

Thank God, she won.

The stage sat empty for a moment before the band took their positions.

The crowd went nuts. Hoots, hollers, cheers, and shouts percolated up around me. People were so excited for this act. That enthusiasm nearly took my breath away because I remembered the two gangly teenagers who'd shown up in my grade-nine music class.

"Hello Rocktoberfest!" Axel's voice rang out.

"Hey Canadian!" Some voice from behind me shouted back.

Axel grinned. "See, our reputation precedes us. You remember from last year. Since all Canadians know each other, we should meet up later."

"I love you!" A woman's piercing scream carried clear across the audience, and everyone laughed.

"Ah, a genuine fan." He grinned. "I'm sorry to tell you that everyone on this stage is taken."

Boos rang out through the crowd.

Axel held up his hands as if to stem the tide of criticism. "But you can always keep us in your fantasies."

Big Mac strummed a chord on his bass, and the band broke into a raucous new song I hadn't heard before.

Murmurs broke out across the crowd as they realized the song wasn't a familiar one.

Once Axel started singing, though, we were all captured under his spell. His voice held a melodic quality that I'd rarely heard. He enunciated each word clearly, and yet also hit the notes with strength. The words registered with me. Fantasizing about someone. Worrying about whether they would live up to that image. Meeting them and discovering they did.

Then his previous words hit me. *Everyone on this stage is taken.*

I *knew* Axel. No way would he have kissed me like that last night and then trotted off to someone else's bed. So was he just delivering a line or did he mean he was mine and I was his?

The end of the song brought more loud hoots and shouts from the crowd as well as thunderous applause.

This time, Ed stepped up to the mic. "Now, Black Rock, we need you to be kind."

"We love you too!" Another disembodied voice.

"My fiancé will be happy to hear that." He turned toward offstage. "Thornton, baby, you want to come on stage?" After a brief pause, he turned to the audience appearing dejected. "He's shy."

The audience roared with laughter.

Ed stepped closer to the mic. "So, recently some treasures from Axel's past came to light."

"That he's gay?" A woman's voice rang out. Her tone was enthusiastic rather than unkind.

"Bi," Axel quickly corrected. "I'm an equal-opportunity guy...even if I am spoken for." He scanned the crowd and his gaze settled on me.

Or at least it felt that way to me. Surely with the tens of thousands of fans, he couldn't possibly have spotted me. That only happened in the movies.

"Axel's past can be a dangerous thing." Ed grinned. "But this surprise shows his sweet side."

Several *aw* and *sweet* carried through the crowd.

"Axel's high school music teacher kept all of his compositions from back then."

My heart seized. I hadn't seen this coming.

"Anyway, with the help of some professionals—"

Meg beat her drum, Songbird hit a key, and Big Mac strummed a chord.

"—and others..." Ed pointed to himself. And scanned the crowd.

Me. He meant me. And the orchestrations I'd written. Wow.

"We're debuting one of the songs tonight and in order to do it properly, we've invited a young woman from our old high school to sing for you tonight. Her name is Marley, and we promised you'd be kind to her."

The audience erupted into cheers as Marley stepped onto the stage with a mic in her hand.

She glanced at Ed who gestured she should wave.

This was all for show. She'd been performing for years. Hell, I knew her—she likely wasn't even nervous.

Obligingly, she waved.

The audience waved back.

When the noise died down, Meg started a beat.

Then Songbird added her keyboard.

Finally, Big Mac and Ed added guitar.

My heart caught in my throat. I'd played this song over and over again during the past ten years. Adding and taking things away...trying to make it perfect.

The version the band played now wasn't quite what I'd envisioned. Truly, their performance of the material was better than anything I could've imagined.

Marley sang the first line.

The crowd lost their collective shit.

Her voice carried clear across the chaos.

The audience, judging by the comments around me, realized this young woman had genuine talent. That she wasn't just window dressing or nostalgia for a song. She was the real deal.

My mind flashed to her father who was backstage. The pride he must've been feeling for her daughter threatened to bring me to my knees. *This.* This was why I taught. This was why I showed up every day. This was why I was okay with not having kids of my own.

The song ended with Axel, Big Mac, and Ed bowing toward Marley as she held the last note.

When she finally cut the sound, the place shook with the applause Even she appeared momentarily startled at the noise.

My ears rang—and probably would for days.

And I didn't give a shit.

She waved, bowed, and booted it off the stage.

The conversations around me were all about this dynamo and how cool was it that she'd come to Black Rock and...a bunch of other stuff. I tried to grasp onto the threads of the conversations, but Ed strummed a chord and the band was off with "We Need to do Better". Soon, Big Mac was performing his amazing guitar solo. They followed that with "Day's Pay for Day's Labor". Another crowd pleaser and back to their rock roots.

When the reverb ended on that song, Axel grinned. "We have a new song for you tonight."

More cheers. More laughter. More shouts.

"This is "In Another Life"."

Ah, so not one of his teenage angsty songs. Good to know.

I was just a boy when I first met
you everything was a blur
caught in the noise in need of rescue
wishing to be heard
you held out your hands of course I took them
thinking is this meant to be
if only you knew how much I needed you
or what you meant to me

A rock lodged firmly in my throat. Someone on the outside might not know, but I didn't have a single doubt he was singing this for me.

For us.

Audience members held up lighters and cell phones. This torch song obviously was touching more than just my own heart.

I know you meant, what you said
it's not the time
but in another world or a different life
you are mine

is there something I'm not understanding
about how this all works
if love is a story some are happy
and others left to hurt

Jesus. He was killing me. I longed to run onstage and give him a hug. Tell him I wish I'd known then what I knew now. I might not have been able to soothe his pain, but I could've given him a safe space to vocalize it.

Except I would've been the last person he would've wanted to speak to. I'd lied by omission to him for four years.

you're stuck in my head like a melody
or some kind of catchy tune
alone in my bed I'm humming memories
that always rhyme with you
Frozen in time, you're a raindrop on my soul
our stories entwined I don't want to let go
of this destiny made out of none but flesh and bone
tell me you are mine and I'll finally feel at home

I know you meant, what you said
it's not the time
but in another world or a different life
you are mine

Ed, who'd played acoustic guitar while Axel sang, held the last note. For just a moment, the audience held their breath.

Then the noise grew deafening. Without an iota of a doubt, the audience clearly loved this new song.

Tears stung my eyes.

In another world, or a different life...you are mine.

Did that mean he didn't consider me his? Or that I couldn't claim him as my own? Or was he speaking about past pain? Here?

"Now we're going to rock this place!" Ed nudged Axel, who appeared as stunned, with his wide eyes, as I was.

His gaze scanned the audience and lasered in on me. Tens of thousands of people and he somehow found me?

That felt fanciful.

Yet he pressed his fingers to his lips, pointed them my way, winked, and then grabbed his mic again. "Yes, we're going to rock your world."

A woman nudged me. "You're the teacher."

I winced.

Out of the blue, she gave me a huge hug.

Uncertain what to do, I eventually relaxed into the embrace. I wasn't keen on strangers accosting me—and I certainly never did it to other people—but she got it. Not just who I was in Axel's life...but that my life had just profoundly changed. Ninety-nine percent of the audience missed that exchange.

But I hadn't.

"No, my bad." An accented voice hit me as someone bumped into me.

I turned to find— "Owen? Of Flightless?"

He looked surprised I'd called him by name, and then grinned. "Sorry, still getting used to be being recognized. Yeah. We've snuck down here because we're huge fans of Grindstone."

Jared, who clung to his hand, also grinned. The dark-haired man was damn handsome. "What better way to enjoy the show?"

"You guys..." I sought the right words. "Your kind of talent..." I tried to keep my voice low so I wouldn't attract attention to them. They were about Axel's age and were beaming.

Owen cocked his head. "Hugo, right? You were Axel's teacher?"

Heat raced to my cheeks as I nodded. "We weren't involved—"

He waved his hand. "We read the stories. So you're Canadian?"

I managed a smile. I'd likely never stop being defensive about whether or not Axel and I had been involved back when he was a teenager. "Yes. Very Canadian."

"And you also taught Marley? Wow." Owen had a clear avid curiosity.

I grinned. "Yeah, Marley's my student."

"We heard her as we were coming down. She's seriously talented."

"She is."

"Do you think she'll be playing with them regularly?" Jared asked.

A question I'd only asked myself a dozen times. "I honestly don't know. If the song went over well with the crowd tonight, I do know they might put it on the next studio album."

"We already own all their albums." Owen nudged Jared. "But we're going to have to buy their next one when it comes out." They exchanged a look.

I couldn't help thinking that they were getting lucky tonight. Or something. That kiss might've just...no, the chemistry and affection between the two was unmistakable. "The band will appreciate the sale."

"We're hoping we might run into them at some point this week. We've only been able to exchange a few words.."

Despite not having any idea of how the interaction had gone, I could confidently say, "I'm sure they'd love that. They're...really down to earth."

"And Axel's in love." Owen's smile didn't diminish. "If that new song was any indication."

Heat flooded my cheeks and, fortunately, I was saved from having to answer because the song ended and the audience cheers drowned out anything I might've said.

We didn't resume our conversation, but I was fine with that. The two men appeared completely enthralled with each other.

Yeah, that's what love feels like.

I should know.

Yeah, I really did.

And I didn't know if my life would ever be the same again after tonight—whatever the evening held.

Chapter Thirty-Five

Axel

Did she find him? Did she find him? Did she...?

My mind wouldn't stop obsessing, even as Jenny, Mikhail, and the Rocktoberfest tech crew swapped out our equipment for the next band's.

Our band glowed with happiness as the crowd chanted our name. *Grind-stone. Grind-stone.* We couldn't do encores here because the schedule was jam-packed with amazingly talented groups. Didn't mean I wasn't tempted to head back out.

I started to remove my T-shirt.

"Uh, no you don't." Ed grabbed it. "You're not throwing it into the crowd. Nor the towel. That gives away your DNA."

"Never know what that might uncover." Songbird hip checked me.

Since I'd been prodigiously careful with condoms, I was pretty sure I didn't have a kid out there. Surely the woman would've spoken up by now.

Thornton indicated Lydia should turn off her camera.

Damn, how'd I forgotten they were filming tonight? Nothing like the complicated setup they'd done last year for the documentary. This year was just a way to memorialize our new songs and, more importantly, Marley's first performance in a venue like this.

My mind also kept flitting back to Flightless. How the two guys, through the simple gesture of kissing a palm, sort of proclaimed their love. And they'd been affectionate backstage. I'd been too nervous to congratulate them on their first time. I was pretty sure Ed had said something. About how we'd been newbies last year and how that performance had changed our lives.

Songbird slung an arm around my shoulders. "We have to clear out."

"But—"

"She'll find him. And then you can say anything that the song didn't." She held my gaze. "The song's brilliant, Axel. Even better than "Sunrise"."

The song we'd debuted last year we had put on our first album with Grand Central Records, and it had topped charts for months.

The song our fans, and even our critics, really liked.

"We're moving." Jenny, lugging a speaker, pointed in the direction of offstage and out of the area.

I gave another hard look, all the while knowing Pauletta would find me if she found Hugo. And would likely spend hours looking if she didn't.

Then as we hit the area beyond the stage set-up, Pauletta stood there with a rather nervous-looking Hugo.

My heart skipped a beat. Yes, I'd seen him only twenty-four hours ago. Yes, I knew his every feature. Yes, I'd found him in that crowd and winked at him.

The red hair shone in the bright lights.

Or a magnetic force had drawn me to him.

Whatever. He's here now.

Ed nudged me, none too subtly, toward the love of my life.

Together, we stepped to the side.

"I'm sorry." Hugo met my gaze with those stunning blue eyes. "I didn't do right by you and I'm sorry. I should've seen the pain. Should've recognized the suffering. That's on me that I missed it."

"Hugo—"

"And I want to say I'll make it up to you—but that's got to be your decision. I can't just ram into your life and expect you to accept me."

"Hugo—"

"I'm trying to say I love you—"

I yanked him into my arms and pressed my lips to his. If he insisted on pretty words, then I'd listen—later.

He melted against me. He again grabbed my hair as he pulled me flush to him. Our bodies fitted together like they always did. Like they were always meant to. Like we could do this forever.

A *yo* drew us apart.

"We're going to watch the next few acts. F-holes are playing and they're fucking amazing." Ed grinned. "Then we're having ice cream on the bus."

I grabbed Hugo's hand and started dragging him toward the rows of band buses.

"I don't—"

"You're going to fuck me in the shower." I kept yanking. "Or I'm going to fuck you in the shower." We made some progress, but a group of women—all wearing Grindstone T-shirts—spotted us.

At the last moment, though, one of them pointed between Hugo and me. She said something.

All her friends smirked—in a good way—and they veered out of our path.

Hugo waved to her.

She waved back.

Have to ask him about that.

Later.

When we arrived back at the bus, we were able to get inside with minimal fuss.

"Holy crap." Hugo stopped in the living area and looked around. "How many of you?"

"All the band members except Pauletta. Oh, plus Thornton—but he and Ed share a bunk. Economy and all that."

Hugo made his way to the bunks and pulled back a curtain. He whistled. "That's a tight fit."

You have no idea. I might've, uh, enjoyed the company of a groupie once or twice over the years. Or maybe ten times. Used to drive Ed nuts. Now he had Thornton in his life, he complained a lot less. *Huh. Guess that's a good thing.*

I slapped Hugo's ass. "Bathroom. There's just enough time and space for us to strip, get in the shower, fuck each other, and dry off before the rest of the band comes back.

He laughed. "No friends are going to call this time because their water broke."

I shoved him toward the bathroom. "Glad to hear it. Turn off the damned phone anyway." I yanked my T-shirt over my head, tossed it in the dirty laundry hamper, and grabbed a fresh one from my drawer. Then I nabbed jeans and fresh underwear as well. I dropped my phone on my bed, toed off my shoes, and continued stripping.

Hugo stood in the doorway to the bathroom.

Making a shooing motion, I laughed.

"You're stripping naked out here."

"Nothing they haven't seen before, and if you'd seen Big Mac's scrawny, lily-white ass, you'd understand why I'm not shy. But they've given us about half an hour. Go." I nabbed my lube and a condom from my drawer as well. I'd been optimistic when I'd packed these. Apparently with good reason.

"I'm naked, Axel. Do I turn on the water?"

I snagged my pile of clean clothes and headed into the bathroom. I locked the door—then checked it twice. I added my stack of clothes to Hugo's haphazardly piled ones on the closed toilet lid.

After giving him a quick kiss to the lips, I pressed the condom and mini bottle of lube into his hand.

He grinned.

Just before I stepped into the shower, I grabbed a plastic thing to secure my hair so it wouldn't get damp. I eyed Hugo.

He held up his hands. "I'm not going to comment about how my grandmother had one of those."

I snagged his cock and gave a hard tug.

His Adam's apple bobbed as he swallowed. "You have my attention. No more grandmothers."

"Good." I put my hair in the plastic thing whose name I could never remember. Then I flipped the shower on. We had a limited amount of hot water but I knew, from Ed and Thornton's shenanigans this time last year, that one could manage a quick fuck and not run out of hot. I grabbed Hugo, pulled him into the tight confines, and shut the shower door. I gestured to the lube and condom. "You good with…?"

He grinned. "Yeah, I'm good." He leaned in for a kiss.

I met him with an ardor of my own. I wanted him. My cock dripped a couple of drops of precum that mixed in with the shower spray. "While you glove up, I'm going to wash." Truly, I stank. I always did after a show. Suspecting Hugo wouldn't care didn't mean I wanted to smell funky. At the very least, Ed would razz me.

By the time I'd soaped and rinsed, Hugo had donned the condom. His cock stood proud.

My insides turned to molten liquid.

He leaned in for another kiss. Then pulled back a fraction of an inch. "Turn around, Axel. Know that I've got you and I'll never let go."

Whether he meant just while he was making love to me or if this was a forever thing, I wasn't certain. What I did know was I planned to never let him go. Nothing would come between us ever again.

The time to make that pledge wasn't this one, though.

I turned my back to him and braced my hands against the cold shower wall.

He trailed his fingers down my spine.

I arched back into the touch.

He kissed my shoulder blade.

I had to blink several times. And not because I had water in my eyes. His tenderness spoke to me. As hard as my cock was—and as much as I wanted this to happen—I appreciated him taking a moment. To savor. To rejoice. To indulge.

Then he slid his finger down my crack to my hole. Slowly, he ran his fingers around my rim.

"Okay—so here's the deal. I got a butt plug and have been using it regularly. So just fuck me already. Right?"

He chuckled. "You never were patient."

"I was fifteen."

"I was talking about ten minutes ago."

"Oh." I wrinkled my nose, even though he couldn't see. "Yeah, that's kind of true."

He kissed my shoulder blade. "And I love that about you."

I wiggled my ass, trying to press back against this finger. "That's not the only thing you love about me."

His motion stilled. "No, it's not. And I'm not going to launch into a poem listing all the things I love about you."

"Oh, thank Christ. Fuck me, Hugo. We're on the clock." I had no notion of how much time had passed. That and my cock wanted relief so badly I thought I was ready to cry.

He sank a finger deep inside me.

I sighed.

He wiggled it.

I grinned.

He added a second.

I held my breath.

After scissoring and pressing deeper in, he hit my prostate.

I'd spent a lot of time getting to know that wonderful bundle of nerves over the past four months. Alone. In my room. Daydreaming of the flesh-and-blood man pressing himself against me.

"You ready?"

"Oh my God, Hugo, fuck yes." I grit my teeth, fighting the teetering orgasm my body chased as he massaged my prostate. I was not going to come like a fucking teenager until the man was inside me.

He removed his hand.

Moments later, his crown pressed against my opening.

I tried to angle myself, but I was clueless. This just wasn't something I'd done standing up before.

"Steady." He gripped my hips as he slowly eased inside me.

The burning pain quickly morphed into relief as he slid across my prostate. "Okay, I'm ready."

He chuckled. "Who says I am?"

I clenched my inner muscles.

He moaned.

Yeah, that's what I thought. I leaned forward and stuck my ass out.

His grip on my hips tightened. Then he moved. His thrusts were slow and steady at first, but eventually—with each grunt—he pushed harder. Soon he was chasing the same orgasm I was. "I need you to jerk yourself, Axel. I can't let go—" His hips snapped and his cock surged.

Needing no further encouragement, I rebalanced with one hand against the shower wall and took myself in hand. Three tugs later and my balls drew up. "Oh shit, Hugo, I'm coming."

"Yes, please." He slammed into me.

I came. Hard. With my cum mixing with the jetting spray.

He thrust in three more times before holding himself steady, shuddering against me.

His fingers were going to leave bruises on my hip and I didn't give a shit. I fought to regain my breath as I absorbed both the warmth of the water and the feeling of rightness that settled over me.

Banging on the door had Hugo pulling out of me.

I yelped.

"Sorry." He sounded genuinely upset. He placed his hand on my back.

"Remember to toss the condom." Ed's disembodied voice carried through the door. "And make sure you put on clean clothes. No one wants to smell your funk."

A long pause ensued, and I was about to straighten.

"Or your spunk."

Hugo groaned at Ed's comment.

I spun around and pressed a kiss to his lips. I eased my finger along his hip, down his crack and then I tapped his hole. "One day."

He nipped my neck. "Yes. That. And more."

I liked the idea of more. I grabbed the body wash and squeezed some into my hand. As I lathered it up, I gazed into his eyes. "I've had a crush on you since I was, like, fifteen."

"Yeah, I got that." He offered a rueful laugh, then gasped as I pressed my hand to his belly and trailed it lower. "I'm forty, Axel, not fourteen."

"I bet I could—"

He pressed a kiss to my lips. When he pulled back, he still had a rueful smile. "Ed."

I wrinkled my nose. "I'm going to pay him back for this." I considered. "Drat."

"What?"

"Well I sort of did this to him last year, so this was payback. I don't want to start a feud."

Hugo grinned. "That's very mature of you." Then he sobered. "You realize you could have any guy or girl out there in the audience, right? Why are you spending time with a washed up forty-two-year-old music teacher from Vancouver, Canada?"

"Maybe because he gives really good blow jobs?"

He scowled.

I laughed. Then grinned. "You inspire me to be a better person and to write these songs. Fuck. Sometimes I wish they would stop coming to me. It was like that back when I was seventeen and eighteen. Songs everywhere. For a while..." I swallowed and looked down at the shower floor. "For a while, the drugs drowned them."

He tucked his index finger under my jaw and tipped it up so our eyes met. "You like the songs now?"

"I like you." I willed him to believe me. "I love you."

"Well, I like listening to your songs. I love watching you compose. I want you to write all the songs all the time."

I snickered

He pulled me into a hug.

Another bang on the door. "For fuck's sake, I want a shower too." Big Mac.

Hugo laughed.

I did as well.

We rinsed off, shut off the water, then dried ourselves in silence in the enclosed space. With the fan running, my bandmates wouldn't be able to hear us unless they were plastered against the door.

Ed might not do that...but I wouldn't put it past either Songbird or Thornton.

The documentarian had sort of become part of us.

Might Hugo as well? Possibly not. Probably not. He loved his kids. His school. His life. And I wasn't going to be the one to ask him to give any of that up.

As long as we talked every day, I'd be okay when I went on the road with the band. Thornton wouldn't always be able to join us, and I doubted Geneva Alvarez could just drop her reporting gig to hang out with Songbird as we did our cross-Canada tour starting in January.

Hugo tried to towel dry his hair.

"We have a hair dryer."

"Frizz."

I smiled.

He kissed me

We hung our towels and headed out of the bathroom and down toward the front of the bus.

Meg whistled.

Super loud and super shrill.

Big Mac covered his ears.

She grinned. "Just practicing for when we have our kids." She set a hand on her stomach.

I stopped in my tracks.

Hugo hit my back and nearly toppled me forward.

"Good goddamn." Ed whispered the words reverentially.

"Three months." Meg continued to grin as she cuddled in against Big Mac. "I was recovering from surgery and, you know..."

"I hear birth control is a thing." Songbird giggled. "Although thinking of the two of you, uh, making a baby—"

"Oy." Thornton's complexion took on a puce quality.

We all broke into howls of laughter.

I snagged Hugo's hand and shoved him onto the bench behind the table, then hustled over the freezer. "You shits better have..." I opened the door.

To be greeted with two wrapped ice cream cones. One chocolate and one vanilla. Hopefully Hugo didn't have a preference because I did not—under any circumstances—share my chocolate.

As I made my way back to him, though, that resolve faltered. Okay, so I'd just delivered the best concert of my career. But who was I to be selfish? "Chocolate or vanilla?"

Ed gasped. He rose and swept his arms out, encompassing everyone. "Everyone make note of the date."

I tried to swat him, but he evaded me.

"Uh, I like vanilla." Hugo cocked his head. "What am I missing?"

Ed pressed his hand over his heart. "Axel never shares his chocolate. Ever. I think there might've been bloodshed if you'd chosen wrong."

"Hey." I tried for hurt.

Everyone, including Hugo, howled.

I handed him the vanilla cone. Then I crawled in beside him.

He put his arm on the back of the seat.

I cuddled up.

He pressed a kiss to my temple.

Meg's explanation of how her birth control pill apparently stopped working and yeah, the pregnancy hadn't been planned, but she figured if she could drum after boob surgery then what was a protrusion from her abdomen?

Songbird tapped Big Mac. "At least he's scrawny. No big kids, I hope."

Meg winced. "All the men in my family are well over six feet. I'm petite."

"Are you having a boy?" I didn't know when someone could tell what they were having.

"Hey, gender is just a construct." Thornton grinned. "And I suspect she wants to keep you in suspense. You're a terrible secret keeper."

"Hey!" I pursed my lips. "I might resemble that comment."

Hugo squeezed my shoulder. "Yeah, you do."

Everyone laughed.

All was right with the world.

But I needed to give more. I snagged Hugo's hand. "Walk with me?"

He cocked his head. "Uh, sure."

We scooted off the bench seat and then headed for the front of the bus.

"Hey, no more hanky-panky." Ed howled that advice as we made our way down the stairs.

"You wish. Go get in your bunk and enjoy yourself. Preferably with your man."

Hoots and hollers followed us. Once we were on the ground, I guided him back toward the food trucks.

He patted his stomach. "Even after the sex, I'm not hungry. That ice cream hit the spot."

"We need to talk." I didn't want to sound ominous, and we could've just stepped behind the bus, but I was feeling sentimental.

"Yeah, sure." He squeezed my hand. "Are you okay? Because that was pretty intense."

I chuckled. "You think? The fucking in the shower part or Ed interrupting us?"

"Perhaps both?"

Still, I guided us. When we arrived at the Greek truck, however, I pulled him around to the back. Where it all started. A year ago.

"I owe you an apology."

He blinked, his pupils wide in the near darkness. "You don't." He hesitated. "Sorry, I can do better. Why do you think you owe me an apology?"

"For going radio silent on you for all those months after the twins were born." I rubbed my chest above my heart. "I was thinking of you all that time. You were my first thought every day, that I needed to get my personal shit together so I'd be worthy of you, so I could come to you with a clear mind. I wanted to talk to you. I composed a thousand texts and deleted them all. Because I knew once we were talking again,

I wouldn't stop. And you deserved the version of me not all up in my head. You deserved the best."

"Axel."

"I'm not quite finished." I drew in a long breath. "I know I can come off as egotistical. Selfish. I get that. Part of it is the attention thing. I forget to ask people how they're doing before I launch into my life. Sometimes I forget important things. But I'm working on all that. I want to be the best that I can be. *You* make me want to be a better person."

"I don't see what you're saying." He winced. "Okay, the radio silence was a shitty thing. Maybe understandable...but shitty. Then you chose Marley, and you sent me the ticket, and I wondered if this was just to be kind. Like you thought you maybe owed me something. Or if this was a desire to truly get back together."

"Then I nearly blew you behind the food truck."

He chuckled. "Well, there was that. Griffin's arrival was well-timed."

"We can watch him perform. Together."

"I'd like that."

I pulled him toward me. "What I'm trying to say is that I love you. I really love you. Like with my whole heart...not just my cock."

"Oh, well that's good to know."

"Be serious."

He grasped my cheeks. "I couldn't be more serious. I always knew you were special. But not until last year did I realize you were someone I could be with. Romantically. And yeah, I love you too. The real you. I don't give a shit about the way you present to other people. Or even the way you are with the audience. I care about you. What's in your heart. What you're thinking. This kind and generous man who picked me."

I leaned in to give him a kiss. Gentle, light, and sweet. When I pulled back, I smiled. "You realize this is a forever thing, right?"

"Oh, I'm counting on it."

"Good. Because I'm a one-man kind of guy. This is it for me."

"Oh thank God. I don't want to be jealous. That's not who I am. But I'm also heavily into monogamy."

Slowly, I drew him into my arms. This time, when our mouths fused, tongues were involved.

Later, as we snuggled in my bunk, I admitted to being the happiest I'd ever been. Just because I opened my heart.

Epilogue

Hugo

Renee nudged me. "Worrywart, knock it off."

"How are you not..." I flailed my arm, encompassing the sight before me.

Two babies, their father, my fiancé, and a massive Samoyed playing on the floor.

Scarlett kept trying to grab the dog's fur.

Matthew had decided the pup's furry belly made a nice pillow.

Copeland was supposedly supervising. In fact, he was scrolling on his phone and periodically showing Axel more baby photos. As if having the two creatures right before him wasn't enough.

And Axel—my dearest— was untangling grubby, grabby fingers.

Midnight, oddly named for a shaggy white-furred dog, licked Scarlett's hand.

The little girl giggled.

Renee snorted. "You were the one who adopted the dog. And I'll mention—again—that she's six and from a family with three children."

And there'd never been an incident with any of said children, but that didn't alleviate my stress. The family would still have their beloved pet except the wife's father died and, after extensive discussions, the family welcomed grandma to their home.

Who happened to be deathly allergic to dogs.

The children had been torn—gain grandma and lose Midnight.

I'd been repeatedly thanked because the family were so happy Midnight had found a loving home. The whole two daddies thing didn't faze any of them. I'd offered to let them visit, but the trainer we'd hired suggested that might confuse the dog.

We sent photos.

Now, seven weeks later, in the thick of Christmas, things were settling.

Midnight loved her new home.

Axel, who had sold his condo, bought half my house, and moved in mere weeks after returning from Black Rock, smiled all the fucking time. He occasionally had moments where he appeared disconcerted. That was understandable, given Ed had been close at hand for all those years. Still, cell phones were a thing, and I was quite certain Axel had sent thousands of photos to Ed and Thornton already. Our house. Our yard during the first snow. Our dog. Our dog during the first snow.

Our couch was *covered* in hair. Keeping up with her leavings was a full-time job. She'd also keep me company during the long time the band would be touring the country this winter.

Renee elbowed me. "We're watching her during March break. Re-member? So you can go meet up with your hottie in Toronto for the big concert?"

Massey Hall. Sold out. Nowhere near Toronto's biggest venues in size—but certainly their most prestigious.

"Yeah." I wrinkled my nose as Scarlett wiped her snotty hand in Midnight's ruff. *Extra brushing tonight.* "You're sure you don't mind?"

"Sheesh, Hugo." She nudged me again. "We can't handle a dog all the time, but we want one. This is perfect. She visits and then she leaves." My best friend grinned. "You don't want kids, but you like spending time with them. You come over to babysit. Seems perfect to me."

The offer for me to babysit stood, but it'd taken Copeland several months before he'd been able to leave the babies entirely alone with me. Not that he didn't trust me...well, sort of. The diaper disaster of November 2024 loomed large every time I offered to change Matthew.

Some people really needed to develop selective amnesia. Or learn to overlook minor catastrophes. No infants were injured. The couch...yeah, that was a different story. A smile stretched my face.

"Am I allowed to be this happy?"

Renee stared. "Of course. You're a good person—although even bad people deserve moments of grace. Look at what you do for your students every day..."

More money had come our way. For all the arts programs in the school. I was peeved it'd taken me dating a celebrity to get us funding, but it was what it was. Axel, interviewed by Geneva's rival—much to her annoyance, but also with her blessing—pointed out all schools needed funding for the arts. That no matter what some politicians thought, arts were incredibly beneficial to children of all ages.

I was so fucking proud of him.

And many of the schools in the region received additional funding.

Blowing out a breath, I tried to find the right words. "I had everything, growing up—"

"Except love." Renee always filled in that bit quickly.

"Well...I had Leonora." I blinked. "My parents weren't cruel."

"Indifference is a form of cruelty."

"They never raised a finger to me."

Axel gently stoked Scarlett's downy hair as she pointed to Midnight, with her faced screwed up in a still-toothless grin as if the dog was the most amazing thing ever.

Frankly, the pooch might just have been.

"You want some eggnog?" Renee nudged me. "I'm spiking mine with rum. I know you won't."

Not a drop of booze in over a year. I wouldn't risk it with Axel. Being able to kiss him without worrying if I had liquor on my breath was way more important than any potential buzz I might enjoy.

"I love eggnog."

"That's disgusting." Axel wrinkled his nose.

"Would you like a cola?" Renee grinned. She knew him well. As much as I was trying to get him to drink less of the stuff, he still mainlined it.

Only a slightly bad habit. Certainly nothing in the grand scheme of things.

"I'll take an eggnog." Cope grinned. He'd put his phone away. After taking about fifteen photos of the twins with Midnight.

Some things would never change.

And that warmed my heart.

Renee and I moved into the kitchen. As I got down the four glasses, she pulled a carton of eggnog and a can of Axel's favorite soda from the fridge. I loved that she kept a stash for Axel. For me. To ensure we knew we'd always be welcome. And since their Victorian was way bigger than our post-war bungalow, we spent a fair amount of time here.

I'd never been happier.

"Are you seeing your parents over Christmas?" Renee poured the three glasses of creamy eggnog goodness.

I took advantage of her preoccupation with preparing the drinks to center myself before answering. "Leonora and the kids are here. Her husband had to stay in Greece...which maybe isn't a bad thing. A slow introduction to the children first, right?" I accepted the glass she handed me. "I think the thawing might be a permanent thing." I glanced toward the living room. "My parents are not exactly happy about my upcoming marriage, but the fact we told them in person meant something."

"Most undramatic proposal ever."

I laughed. "Hey. I gave him a ring the morning after he moved in. I feel like that was very romantic. Homemade French toast, crispy bacon, fresh orange juice, and a ring."

"Did you squeeze the orange juice yourself?" She knew the answer to that question.

"What's your point?"

"That you're going to be incredibly happy. Oh, speaking of happy..." She nabbed a couple of ice cubes and added them to the soda she'd poured. She handed me Axel's drink, then picked up hers and Cope's.

"Incredibly happy...?" God, sometimes she needed to work on her timing.

"Have you heard Razor Made?"

"Weren't they on the radio the other day?" My nose itched, but I'd manage until I gave Axel his drink.

Renee and I moved into the living room.

"Geneva did a profile for them. The lead singer was arrested at an environmental protest last year. He chained himself to the Lion's Gate Bridge."

Axel grinned as I handed him the glass of soda. "Malik, right? That kid's got pipes."

"Kid?" I squinted. "Isn't he twenty-seven?"

"Yeah."

"And aren't you twenty-nine?"

"Yeah."

Renee and Cope both laughed.

"I heard they sent an audition off to the Rocktoberfest organizers." Renee sipped her eggnog.

Axel cocked his head. "How'd you hear that?"

"I'm friends with the drummer's mother. Lovely woman."

"The drummer or the mother?" I'd be googling the band when I got home.

Renee laughed. "The drummer's a nice boy. His mother's a lovely woman."

"Ah."

Axel pointed at me. "We should see if Thornton and his crew want to record them. Do another documentary."

I glanced uneasily between Renee and Cope. "Uh, Thornton's debuting his documentary about homelessness on the West Coast."

"Right...so he needs a new project."

"I'm not certain what his angle would be. Or if they'd want him to find it."

Axel held my gaze, then winced. "Good point."

I doubted the band had a skeleton in their closet. Or a young woman in their past who'd died of a drug overdose. But no one was squeaky clean.

"Well, if Geneva's done a profile, then they're on Pauletta's radar." Axel grinned. "I think we're going back to Rocktoberfest. Although it'll be interesting with Big Mac and Meg having a newborn."

Renee blinked. "Yeah, we love you two, but we never considered taking these babies down to Black Rock. Even if we'd had a camper."

"We'll have to hire a live-in babysitter." Axel grinned. "This might be fun."

I saluted him with my eggnog. "If anyone can make it work, it'd be Grindstone."

He winked. Then his gaze swept the room. His smile brightened. "You know, even without Ed, this is the best Christmas ever."

I'd worried how he'd cope without his best friend. Ed and Thornton were enjoying a visit with Thornton's parents in Portland after the wedding ceremony. Then the newlyweds were headed to Europe so they could spend New Year's Eve by the Eiffel Tower.

Not my cup of tea. No, I had everything I wanted right here.

I wrapped my arm around Renee's shoulder.

She leaned into me.

Cope and Axel clinked drinks.

Truly, the best Christmas ever.

And, I believed, the beginning of a great life filled with love, friends, and true happiness. With the man I loved by my side, I believed I could do anything.

So could he.

Together. Forever.

In Another Life

I was just a boy when I first met
    you everything was a blur
caught in the noise in need of rescue
wishing to be heard
you held out your hands of course I took them
thinking is this meant to be
if only you knew how much I needed you
or what you meant to me
I know you meant, what you said
it's not the time
but in another world or a different life
you are mine

is there something I'm not understanding
about how this all works
if love is a story some are happy
and others left to hurt

you're stuck in my head like a melody
or some kind of catchy tune
alone in my bed I'm humming memories
that always rhyme with you
Frozen in time, you're a raindrop on my soul
our stories entwined I don't want to let go
of this destiny made out of none but flesh and bone
tell me you are mine and ill finally feel at home

I know you meant, what you said
it's not the time
but in another world or a different life
you are mine

Want to know about the rockstar who chained himself to the Lion's Gate Bridge? Check out Malik and Spencer's story in *Voice to Raise*.

Have you read Ed and Thornton's book? Check out Axe to Grind!

Want more Gabbi Grey?

Check out her *Love in Mission City* series, set in beautiful British Columbia.

The first book is

Ginger Snapping All the Way (Love in Mission City Book 1)

Stanley's Christmas Redemption (Love in Mission City Book 2)

The Beauty of the Beast(Love in Mission City Book 2.5)

Sleigh Bells and Second Chances (Love in Mission City Book 3)

A Daddy for Christmas 2: Foster(Love in Mission City Book 3.5)

Rayne's Return (Love in Mission City Book 4)

Gideon's Gratitude (Love in Mission City Book 5)

Quinton's Quest (Love in Mission City Book 6)

Love in Mission City: The Boyfriend Gamble

Love in Mission City: The Four Seasons

Love in Mission City: The Boyfriends Duet

Love in Mission City: The Shorts

Puppy Pride

A Daddy for Christmas 3: Lorcan

Rayne Check

Archer's Awakening

Leo's Lust

Finn's Find

Thought You Were the One

Love Without Reservations

Page Against the Machine

The Lightkeeper's Love Affair

Ace's Place

Marcus's Cadence

Not in it for the Money

Also:

Axe to Grind (Road to Rocktoberfest 2023)

Grindstone's Edge (Road to Rocktoberfest 2024)

Voice to Raise (Road to Rocktoberfest 2025)

Hugh (Single Dads of Gaynor Beach)

Anthony (Single Dads of Gaynor Beach)

Xavier (Single Dads of Gaynor Beach)

Love Furever (Friends of Gaynor Beach Animal Rescue)

Husky Love (Friends of Gaynor Beach Animal Rescue)

Yorkie to My Heart (Friends of Gaynor Beach Animal Rescue)
A Furever Home (co-written with Kaje Harper – Friends of Gaynor
Beach Animal Rescue)
My Past, Your Future
If Only for Today
Catch a Tiger by the Tail
Solstice Surprise
Valentino in Vancouver
You See Me
Sun, Surf, and Surprises
Ginger in the City
Caressa's Homecoming (Bound by LoveBook 1)
Cole's Reckoning (Bound by Love Book 2)
Sizzling Sydney Nights
An Uncommon Gentleman
A Sensible Gentleman
A Wounded Gentleman
Didn't See You Coming
Finding Noah (Foggy Basin Season 2)
Noah's Holiday (A Foggy Basin Short Story)
Hot Rucking Canadian
Big Rucking Disaster
Unlocked and Unlost

Audiobooks
Ginger Snapping All the Way
Stanley's Christmas Redemption
Sleigh Bells and Second Chances
Rayne's Return

Want a free short story? The story is set in Gaynor Beach, California where there are plenty of single dads and puppy rescues! You can sign up for my newsletter so you can keep up with all the great stuff I'm doing as well as pictures of my own pooches, Ally and Finnegan.

Hemingway's Happy Day

Interested in knowing more about Gabbi?

Sign up for her newsletter

Follow her on Bookbub

Follow her on Instagram

USA Today Bestselling author Gabbi Grey lives in beautiful British Columbia where her fur baby chin-poo keeps her safe from the nasty neighborhood squirrels. Working for the government by day, she spends her early mornings writing contemporary, gay, sweet, and dark erotic BDSM romances. While she firmly believes in happy endings, she also believes in making her characters suffer before finding their true love. She also writes m/f romances as Gabbi Black and Gabbi Powell.